House of Childhood

House of Childhood

ANNA MITGUTSCH

translated by
DAVID DOLLENMAYER

OTHER PRESS · NEW YORK

We wish to express our appreciation to the Austrian Culture Ministry for its assistance in the preparation of this translation.

BUNDESKANZLERAMT ▪ KUNST

Copyright © 2000 by Anna Mitgutsch. First published under the title HAUS DER KINDHEIT by Luchterhand Literaturverlag GmbH, München.

Translation copyright © 2006 David Dollenmayer

Production Editor: Robert D. Hack
Text design: Rachel Reiss
This book was set in 11 pt. Apolline Regular by Alpha Graphics in Pittsfield, NH.
ISBN-13: 978-1-59051-188-6

10 9 8 7 6 5 4 3 2 1

Library of Congress Cataloging-in-Publication Data

Mitgutsch, Anna, 1948-
[Haus der Kindheit. English]
House of childhood / by Anna Mitgutsch ; translated by David Dollenmayer.
p. cm.
ISBN 1-59051-188-3 (alk. paper)
I. Dollenmayer, David B. II. Title.
PT2673.I77H3813 2006
833'.914–dc22
2005003880

House of Childhood

Part I

Chapter 1

FOR AS FAR back as Max could remember, the photograph had stood on the dresser. It made every new apartment they moved to one more place of exile. Unlike all the other objects they unpacked after every move, its significance reached deep into the past, and like a pledge it required the keeping of a promise. In the midst of their life it pointed toward a presence that was painfully absent.

"That's our house," his mother would say as she reverently picked up the photo. "Perhaps we'll go back there in a few years."

From his mother, Max had learned that memories were the one thing you couldn't lose. You just had to be careful not to let them go, like the ships the spellbound children watched slip over the distant edge of the Atlantic and disappear. In the first years after their emigration they often went to the shore, where their mother Mira pointed at that gray and sometimes invisible line that divided sky and water. "Europe's over there."

The border was a straight line in the distance that never came closer. If he had had to find an emblem of his mother's sadness, it would have been the invisible house that had vanished beyond the horizon.

But over there, in a small town in Austria, the house stood waiting. And its image, shrunk to the size of a black-and-white snapshot, waited on Mira's dresser on Delancey Street, later in Brooklyn, and after she had to sell the dresser, on the kitchen counter in Crotona Park. Then it disappeared and for a long time lay framed but face down in the bottom of the linen closet. Not until after her death did Max set it up next to the color photo he had taken years later during a visit to H. But the new picture couldn't compare with the sepia melancholy of the old one. It seemed naked, almost offensive, as arbitrary as a vacation snapshot. He took it away.

The house he wanted to inhabit at some future date wasn't the dilapidated building from the twenties whose owner he now considered himself to be. It was rather a childhood dream nourished by his mother's lifelong yearning to someday finally go home again.

Max had decided to return in her stead. Not right away, not even in the foreseeable future, but when his life in the present had slowed down, perhaps even come to a stop—in a future that with the passage of the years somehow never came closer.

Later, when he was retired, he said, "It won't run away on me." For the past that had accompanied him his whole life long was always there. It would appear whenever he called it.

"I'm a nomad," he would say if someone were too inquisitive about his plans. "It's how I like to live. You're only responsible for your own mistakes and you're free to leave any time you want."

In the eyes of others this gave Max the appearance of living lightly, of an irony that abjured any claim to permanence, of having succeeded in fending off the burden of multiple responsibilities.

The images were distant and fragmentary, surrounded by the impenetrable darkness of oblivion, like objects a wave momentarily lifts flashing into the sunlight, only to bury them again in the eternity of the Atlantic. How could he know if they were the stories of his mother's longing, the after-images of his dreams or hers, or precious artifacts that his fifty-year-old consciousness had preserved forever in memory? A white house loomed like a castle above a river. Cool, black iron bars. Were they part of a fence, a garden gate? Stone steps flanked by loose, dark earth, hard to climb. The crunch of a gravel path and a vague feeling of joyful expectation. A dim memory of people whose appearance remained in his memory like a smell, like the taste of something sweet or bitter. The finality of a house door being shut. A pool of colored light gleaming at the foot of the stairs and the rainbow spectrum of the ground glass window on the landing. A large bright room with white double doors, colorful beasts with tails and horns on a carpet that retained its warmth long after the sun had left the room. A dark marble table on whose edge he had gashed open his chin; the scar remained visible for a long time—into puberty, until he had begun to shave. He remembered a table lamp with long moss-green fringe and the sofa with lion's feet. It must have been winter; in his memory, light-colored blankets were draped over its back. His Aunt Sophie would wrap them around her cold legs. A Venetian lion with mouth agape sat on the balustrade of the terrace. When Max was three or four, he would stick his hand into that mouth after a rain shower and it would come out wet. He couldn't imagine himself as a four-year-old, although there were photographs of him. Grown-ups appeared and disappeared, disembodied, faceless, but still clearly recognizable. They wore the faces given them by the few photos from back then. They wore them like masks they would later exchange for faces he could clearly remember, or they would retain them forever, their only face in the changeless youth of an early death.

There was one photograph of the whole family gathered on the broad steps leading to the front door, five adults and three small children, three generations. It must have been in the early twenties because the women, Sophie and Mira, wore hats like up-ended flower pots and loose summer dresses gathered at their hips. Their faces were blurred and half lost in deep, mysterious shadows, the men very straight-backed and stiff in their dark suits and serious expressions. Only Mira wore the triumphant smile that Max knew from other photos of her youth. Her face shone as if it had gathered all the light of the picture into itself. By comparison the thin face of her older sister seemed a delicate shadow. In her wedding picture, the stage clouds of the photo studio massing in the background, Mira stood in the midst of her family in the same proud self-confidence. She was the center of attention—the long white train gathered at her feet and her beaming smile, strong teeth, wide mouth, and full lips. Saul, her groom, kept sheepishly in the background as if he were only a shy guest at his own wedding. And in the picture in front of the house, too, Saul turned his face to the side as if eager to leave, an impatient stranger with a different goal. Max always thought the long bearded face of his grandfather Hermann looked like his own, probably because Mira had told him how much he was like her father. But Max had no memories at all of the third man, Sophie's husband, and there were no other pictures of him. He was a phantom who moved inconspicuously through his short life and left almost no traces.

There were other photographs in a marbled cardboard box Max acquired later, after Mira's death, along with yellowed, faded letters and greeting cards: his two brothers Victor and Ben as children on a sled in front of the house in H. and Mira, in high spirits and a broad fox-fur collar, with a snowball in her hand; Mira in a light-colored swimming suit on the terrace while the children, naked and indistinguishable, played around an outdoor pool. But Max always considered the picture of the family gathered on the steps a document, less fortuitous and private than the others, as if marking a pause for proud stocktaking in the history of these three generations.

At the time of this photograph, the house was brand-new, with a contemporary simplicity in the clear, plain lines of its facade. His grandfather had had it built for his two daughters and their husbands on a large piece of land, a meadow that dropped off so steeply toward the river that the farmer who owned the surrounding fields had sold it off cheaply as a building lot. In his memory, this meadow was a humming wilderness glistening with light and with a smell he sometimes unexpectedly thought he recalled but could never identify. It was probably this meadow that gave him the impression of having lived in the country as a young child until, as a five-year-old, he was overwhelmed by Manhattan, the archetypal city. Compared to it, the few impressions of the town from his early years were of a rural market center with bright streets, three-story houses, broad empty squares, and a wooden bridge that to his childhood eye seemed to curve into the sky like a rope ladder without rungs. There on the bridge or on the terrace of the house on days when a warm wind blew, space filled up with infinity and he could comprehend his parents' distant goal: America. The glistening river curving broadly through the middle of town and the colorless sky fused into a transparent gleam. This image lodged in Max's memory as the characteristic feeling of his early childhood that he strove his whole life to recover: brightness, space, the holiday stillness of a never-ending summer afternoon.

The most important people in his early years were his mother and his grandfather. Mira was older than one might have gathered from the photographs. She had studied biology for a few years and then gotten married. Max was her youngest child, a third son instead of the longed-for daughter. For as long as they lived in H., Mira remained what she had been since her mother's early death: her father's favorite daughter. He encouraged and supported her every talent, however slight, convinced of her uniqueness. When she fell in love with the penniless Polish medical student Saul Berman, Hermann financed his education as well and later bought him a medical practice in H. in order to keep his children close by.

His mother's birthplace, Tabor in Bohemia, lay for Max in biblical remoteness. There his great-grandfather had owned a weaving mill. After the First World War, Hermann opted for Austria and moved to H. but remained loyal to the textile business. In Mira's stories he was larger than life, generous and just, with a natural air of authority that even his adversaries had to respect. In her eyes, no man could compare to him, not even Saul. For Max's whole childhood his grandfather, whom he resembled, was the model he was expected to prove himself worthy of. "Your grandfather would never have put on a shirt with dirty cuffs," Mira said. "Your grandfather had narrow hands like you, but they were always clean and well-groomed." Or she would remember with a dreamy smile, "My father had a weakness for nice shoes." She must have had absolute trust in him, for she submitted to his political sixth sense and emigrated with Saul and the children even though she had everything she wanted in H. and must have had the premonition that she was leaving behind both her father and the security in which she had lived until then. She had always brought even her slightest problem straight to him.

On Sabbath evenings and holy days, Hermann sat at the head of the white-clothed table and sang the kiddush, blessing the wine. He was the head of the family behind whose back Saul made rebellious jokes. But he was also the grandfather who, on evenings such as these, would put the children to bed and patiently teach them the prayers, word for word. He was not pious, but clung fast to tradition. On the square in front of the synagogue after services, people approached him with the respect due to a member of the synagogue board, and from Hermann's brilliance a glimmer of warm good-will fell upon his grandchildren.

Many years later, while looking through the local press of the time, Max found his grandfather's name among the founding members of a charitable association for brides lacking dowries as well as of a fund for Eastern European refugees after the First World War. But the political connections of Mira's father protected him only from the first wave of deportations that followed the *Anschluss*. He stayed on only a few months longer than the other members of the congregation, alone and impoverished, in the city that Jews were officially no longer allowed to inhabit. He had no desire to emigrate. He was eighty-four years old when he starved to death in a Polish ghetto.

The image of Max's father from those distant years before their emigration was strangely blurred, reduced to a few photographs, as if Saul himself had not been present or had entered and left the house as a stranger, as Mira's lover, as a guest, restlessly, with the hunted look of someone uprooted from his native soil. He had never spoken of where he came from; missing were the stories that could have made him more comprehensible. There were no grand-parents, no relatives on his side. It was as if Saul had appeared from nowhere, someone who had designed his life entirely on his own with no need for a past, for an ancestry that would explain him. Perhaps wife and children, medical practice and house had repre-sented a new beginning which, after a short time, he rejected. No sooner had they landed in New York than he proved to be no more sentimentally attached to Europe than he had been to his child-hood in Przemyśl, which he had left at seventeen. But Max's image of his father was distorted by the bitterness of his mother, whose later abandonment he shared as if it were his own.

Had there been farewells, a mood of departure, rooms that were emptied, last visits, tears and pledges to return? Max had no memory of them. Only the empty word "America" was familiar to him, and each of them had filled it with different expectations.

For the four-year-old, America was the birthday present wrapped in shiny paper, the big surprise. They embarked in Bremerhaven on June 10, 1928. A week later, Max spent his fifth birthday seasick in his berth with no Promised Land in sight.

Nothing from the first weeks and months after their arrival did Max remember so vividly as his mother's despair. It was impossible to go to her, to seek her protection from all that was new and potentially dangerous. Her mood went from grief to angry accusations against Saul to self-recrimination. She had known it from the beginning, from the moment the North German coast slipped out of sight: happiness and youth were now gone for good; they lay behind her in the security of the small town, with her father, in the rooms of the house for which she had developed an obsessive yearning. In loss it gradually became transfigured into something unrecognizable, a stately villa whose high rooms with plaster embellishments she could vividly conjure up, on whose terrace she stood leaning on the marble balustrade, surveying the valley below. In her dreams it was always summer, a cool summer morning, and she was without care and knew herself loved. The morning sun lay shimmering on the floors and furniture like the reflection of a river, the lace curtains billowed in the wind, promising a beautiful day lasting all her life, a life that had come to an abrupt end. And in time, the few blurry pictures in Max's own memory merged with Mira's fantasies, and when she sat on his bed at night, the two of them stacked everything together like blocks: wishes and dreams and transfigured memories. Together they marveled and built of them a magnificent palace with a marble colonnade above a wide, curving river valley in a faraway hilly, hazy landscape where a peaceful town lay in an eternal fairy-tale sleep.

As Max grew up and his life was filled with his new surroundings, his mother remained alone with her longing and grief, and there was no one left to help her keep alive the dream of her house.

But not until the news came that her immediate family and all her relatives were dead did Mira stop talking about it and doggedly hoping for it. There was nothing left to preserve for later. She was cast onto the stony shores of the present, thankful only that her father's political vigilance and Saul's restless urge for change had at least saved the lives of her children.

But before that, in the almost unbearable humidity of their first summer in New York, for which she was totally unprepared, the sly cruelty with which disaster afflicted her must have seemed to Mira like the conspiracy of some higher power that spared no effort to torture her. When they got to New York, no one knew what had become of the crates in which they had sent ahead their personal belongings, the few indispensable objects from home. They waited several months but still they couldn't be found. They had disappeared for good. And that was only the beginning of a chain of misfortunes and obstacles placed in her path by this ever-changing, violent, ruthless city. Much later, when Max had long since made the connection between the irritable bitterness and unconditional affection that bound everyone who had grown up in New York to the city, he realized that Mira, unlike his father, had never been able to appreciate New York because she'd never been willing to let herself be carried away by the American dream. She remained a European all her life: class-conscious, devoted to the past, loyal to a cultured and somewhat smug way of life compared to which American manners must have seemed crude and insulting. She had trouble learning English, although she knew French and later, in Brooklyn, learned to speak Yiddish with her friends. The lively, educated Mira of the winning smile and self-confident charm reacted to the foreign city with panic and agitation, convinced that New York's rude inconsiderateness, its blindness to the welfare of the individual, was a malicious plot against her alone. The people hurrying past in the street, jostling, pushing her aside in stores, seemed to say: Who the hell do you think you are? What do you want, anyway? Mira felt alone—ignored and at the same time attacked. She was overlooked or snapped at, and the ways she had learned to defend herself belonged to another world.

A few weeks after their arrival at Ellis Island, the family moved into their first apartment on Delancey Street, an acceptable transition from their roomy house in town back home. The apartment's high-ceilinged rooms faced the street on the third floor of a brick building from the turn of the century, the era in which the Williamsburgh Bridge was built and Delancey Street was widened to a boulevard. Without his being aware of it, all the rooms of Max's childhood had probably contributed to his unerring sense of proportion, light, and shadow: the tall windows with their little cast-iron balconies hanging like baskets above the sidewalk, the view of the piers and steel cables of the great suspension bridge, the broad boulevard, the dark paneled walls of the gentlemen's tailor on the ground floor of the building, its somber elegance behind shadowy awnings. Their big apartment on the third floor, however, was bright and empty, open to all possibilities. The large living room could be used for his father's practice, as soon as he had passed the tests for which he was studying, and required absolute quiet. But in reality, his father radiated a vibrating agitation. New York seemed to electrify Saul, filling him with plans and energy that brought tension and conflict into the home. Even Max could sense the nervous restlessness that had overcome his father, the pull of the city that challenged, enticed, and beguiled him, even though he didn't yet fully comprehend that it was tearing down his defenses, throwing into question all the prohibitions and rules he had lived by until then. New York's promise of limitless freedom went to Saul's head. Unbeknownst to his family he was meeting with immigrant Jews from Russia and Poland who were full of crazy ideas that, after staying up all night, seemed completely reasonable and logical. At home Saul sat in the empty living room that would one day be his examining room and stared blankly into the textbooks that kept his wife and children at bay, while from below, from the crowded boulevard, the importunate noises and colors of New York found their way up to him, until at last he laid aside his books and, dizzy with the newly awakened joy of life, let Manhattan's hot breath blow in his face.

In an optimistic or perhaps just desperate attempt to include his family in his great adventure, Saul took them on many excursions that first summer, the summer Max remembered as one long, jolly outing. Usually they took the subway to Central Park, rented a boat, and rowed under bright willow branches and across the lake, with the many-storied buildings pale blue in the background, like far-off Alps in a warm spring wind. They walked through Central Park with a stamina they never would have expended on the country around H., south from the Belvedere Castle past the rhododendrons and wild cherry trees, through the sweet, heady smell of sassafras in the man-made ravines where streams of weekend strollers slowed and backed up. The zoo had only recently opened and there were otters and a lethargic pair of bears named Jake and Priscilla. Before they left the park the children got a big bag of hot buttered popcorn—for them a completely novel delicacy—from one of the numerous lemonade stands. On days like this, after the long subway ride back downtown, they all emerged amicably into the steamy Lower East Side, sated with their experiences and weary from the heat, and neither Saul's nervous restlessness nor Mira's suppressed anger could cloud their harmoniousness.

This festive mood continued into a mild late fall with a department store shopping spree and Sunday outings to Luna Park in Coney Island or to the air-conditioned foyer of the Roxy Cinema with its multicolored illuminated fountain, while new ice skates for the entire family promised another high point in wintry Central Park. But the fun was already beginning to lose its luster in the icy cold of winter.

Conflict was in the air. Doors were slammed with a hard, irreconcilable bang, and Mira sat crying in the kitchen at midnight. In the morning, their father had still not come home and their mother couldn't control her agitation. In the night, Max could hear his parents fighting again.

Everything happened in this one fall: Max started school, and during the endless tedium of the mornings he felt for the first time abandoned and fearful of his classmates' ridicule. He didn't know their games, and in his panic and confusion he spoke German. By the end of October it became clear to his parents that their money had run out and even the savings Grandfather Hermann sent to support them were not enough to rescue them from imminent poverty. In Max's memory the stock market crash and his parents' separation merged into a single catastrophe that put an end to his carefree childhood and forever shook his confidence in savings and possessions. Even thirty years later, when he had become affluent, it seemed stupid to hoard money and squander any chance of happiness.

The economic crisis finally touched off in Saul the revolutionary spark that he had so far suppressed for the sake of his family—his fury at everything bourgeois, everything Mira embodied, his visions of a freer, better world. He became a Zionist. He had finally found the calling he had sought without knowing it. He would prepare for the founding of a Jewish state in Palestine. Max would later remember bitterly that, at a time when Mira and the children had to do without all the things they were used to having, Saul was treating patients without even asking if they could pay. He'd accept a symbolic dollar per visit, and Max never forgave him for it.

In the winter of 1930 they left the sunny apartment in Delancey Street because they could no longer pay the rent. Saul helped with the move, but before the furniture had even been arranged in the two bleak rooms in Brooklyn, he picked up the suitcase waiting by the door and returned to Manhattan. He left his family and moved into a furnished room he had found in a run-down tenement house on the Lower East Side.

In Brooklyn, Mira could no longer protect the children from the harsh surroundings that responded to her repugnant fear of contact with indifferent, almost playful brutality. Max, left to his own devices, grew into a different world than he had known up to then, and he liked it: sooty sandstone buildings crowded together; dark, dank alleyways in which you never quite knew where the stench came from; rusty fire escapes imposing their shabby geometry on the facades; and little grocery stores, dim basement holes whose only daylight fell through doors that never closed. It was, however, still a familiar world with Jewish shops and mostly East European Jewish immigrants—a world that represented for Mira a precipitous decline in social status, a regression back several generations, but also a certain refuge and reconnection to old, abandoned traditions. She began to attend synagogue again every Friday evening, as she had when she was still her father's obedient daughter, less from some reawakened piety than for the sake of the warmth of familiar rituals that comforted her in her loneliness. In the next two years, she forged friendships here that would last to the end of her life, an ersatz family of immigrant women with whom she would grow old, for whose sake she learned Yiddish in order to be closer to them, and who stood by her, even if their help was not always effective.

Max, the youngest and therefore closer to his mother than his brothers were, was taken along when she visited her friends. There they sat in tiny, stuffy rooms filled to bursting with gaudy East

European kitsch, family snapshots, and wedding photos. Publicly they made a show of their contempt for the Old Country that had denied them the right to live, but in these living rooms and kitchens they seemed to replace it with nostalgic longing. Max was petted and fed sweets and sat silently listening when his mother cried while her friends advised her to refuse a divorce, or when she told them he was living with this other woman and letting her and her children starve while he treated his patients for free. Somebody had always heard a new rumor that Saul had been seen at this or that Socialist or Zionist meeting, and what the other woman looked like or what she had said, and that she was always there at his side as if she were already his wife, and supposedly she even rewrote his articles and corrected his English. It was here, among these women, that Max witnessed his mother's furious incomprehension that the man to whom her father had entrusted his beloved daughter—to say nothing of her dowry—had abandoned her. His childish capacity for love absorbed this shock to her existence—he wanted to compensate and avenge her. Sitting on the fire escape above the kitchen window, where he went to do his homework undisturbed and watch the street life below, he dreamed of the day when he would see her return home. He would be a grown-up and would send money to her in Europe. She would live in the house with the high-ceilinged sunlit rooms, sit in a wicker chair on the white terrace and eat breakfast, look out over the river and into the distance, and think of him to whom she owed it all.

Gradually her life settled into the silent calm of defeat. The divorce was made final and Mira became more quiet and composed. Max saw his father on Sundays, occasionally on Saturday afternoons, when he would pick up his sons in order to bestow on them what he considered important: fresh air and culture. Max was attracted to his father, but the hostility he thought he had to maintain for his mother's sake prevented him from showing his affection, and so his father turned to Victor, who made no bones about his enthusiasm for Saul's political ideas. The four of them often rowed across Conservatory Lake. The fresh breeze rippled the water and set the sparkling light dancing; in the clearings on the shore young families picnicked in the spring green, and Max felt like a miserable traitor. When he returned home he couldn't look his mother in the face. "Was it nice?" she asked, but he ran past her to his refuge on the fire escape.

All the same, the afternoons Saul spent taking his sons to museums and art galleries—with the puritanical dedication of the European bourgeois he didn't even aspire to be—had a more profound effect on Max than on his brothers. Even when the boys had become bored adolescents shambling past the exhibits but looking more at the other visitors, Saul didn't give up. He dragged them grimly along to every new exhibit: to the Metropolitan, the Cloisters, but above all to the new and scandalously avant-garde and defiantly anti-European Whitney Museum. Max wasn't any more interested than his brothers in the pictures on the walls and the objects in the glass cases. What he did notice was the prevailing ambience of these large spaces; he saw how the light falling through the windows could make objects grow dim, or disappear, or stand out, as if they were floating in space. In these galleries he learned to pay attention to how in the course of a day the light would steal across the floors and surfaces and transform them, how it picked out and obscured details, awakened images and just as suddenly extinguished them. He observed how an eeriness unexpectedly crept into the corners and nestled there, felt how mirrors could conceal an almost inescapable loneliness. He delighted in how the ornamental plaster work on the ceilings led an independent, extravagant existence unnoticed by the visitors below. Even then Max could sense the intimacy of large open spaces and his own urge to lend them a unique atmosphere. Although he didn't realize it yet, he had discovered his talent, but he did know that a room was much more than just a place to live: it was a certain way of orienting oneself in the world, the expression of an attitude toward life.

Home life was dominated by poverty and deprivation. The apartments they lived in after Delancey Street all had something provisional about them. The cardboard boxes stacked in the corners made them seem more like emergency shelters. The boxes and suitcases always stood ready for the next move that was never long in coming. Mira despised cheap department-store furniture, but their old furniture had to be liquidated piece by piece in pawnshops and auction houses. His mother's stubborn insistence on the provisional nature of her present life was a refusal to accept a lot she could not believe was meant for her. It had to be a mistake of fate that she wouldn't acknowledge.

Max first tried his hand at interior design at the age of eleven. It upset him that he could never bring his classmates home because there was only the crowded kitchen and the two bedrooms. With money he had saved as well as some stolen from the housekeeping money, he bought a used couch of blue velveteen and a spread of the same color for the second bed, put a brass tray onto a newspaper stand he hammered together himself, and made a living room for the space of an afternoon. His mother had the couch carted away and restored the old order, but no one could take away his dreams of generously proportioned rooms, light, space, and objects of restrained elegance.

His attempt to decorate their two-room apartment in Brooklyn caused the only conflict between him and his mother that Max could remember. He was *der Kleine*, her favorite child and the one who least resisted her need for love. With his narrow face, reddish-brown and slightly wavy hair, round forehead, and thoughtful gray-brown eyes, he resembled her more than his two brothers did. Their closeness needed no words. It was grounded in his dreamy adoration of what was, in his eyes, her peerless beauty, in their shared dreams and stories from a past that had held nothing but happy days, and in the son's vivid desire to restore that happiness to her. But it was probably also the harmony so easily attained by kindred spirits, their sense of well-being in each other's presence.

For the first time in the summer after Saul left her, Mira took the children by herself to the Fourth of July celebration at Battery Park to see the fireworks. They were standing right by the break-water among the expectant crowd when a stranger handed Max a red rose. "Give that to the beautiful lady in the hat," he said, point-ing to Mira who was in the midst of conversation with her new friend Faye. Then Max saw his mother for the first time through the eyes of a strange man: her handsome, no longer slim but very feminine figure, narrow-waisted in a wide skirt, her dark hair parted in the middle and pulled into a Spanish knot in back, the somewhat silly, saucy little hat that had slipped over one ear, the red lipstick on her full lips, and her almond-shaped, slightly slanted eyes. Max was very proud of his beautiful mother, and it was he whom she bent down to kiss when he gave her the rose, with only a fleeting noncommittal glance at the stranger. Since Saul had left her, her beauty seemed to Max more fragile and vulnerable. He was the knight she could count on. Late in the night and half asleep, he heard the noise of her sewing machine. To keep them afloat, she took on badly paid piecework assembling bathing suits. He had a burning desire to grow up quickly. He wanted to be rich for her sake and give her everything she had to deny herself now.

Max's oldest brother Victor was as much of a stranger to him as if he weren't part of the family but rather a distant relative who lived with them, a loner who said little and went his own way— bossy, obsessive about little things, and with an intimidating age

gap of six years that made him seem grown up. Victor's role model
was Saul. He coolly deflected his mother's attempts to win him
over, and during the crises and emotional outbursts of the divorce, Victor defiantly took his father's side and courted his
favor as far as his reserved nature allowed. A mediocre student despite ambition and a dogged work ethic, he said he wanted to go
into politics after college, like his father. Victor went off to college
before he was eighteen. If his mother wanted to know how he was
doing she had to call Saul. From then on, Victor's rare visits home
were dutiful but grudging.

Benjamin, two years older than Max, was the childhood play-
mate whom he followed everywhere and shared every secret with.
It was natural to look up to Ben. He was the family genius. Every
year he skipped another grade and his swiftness of mind made
them all proud. Intelligence, Max was convinced, was a matter of
how fast you could think. For his own part, Max was the brooding
type and his thoughts never reached a conclusion. They wandered
into approximations that branched out into possibilities that en-
gendered still more possibilities until he gave up. Ben, however,
had the kind of elegant intellect that spreads out over the world
like transparent wings and puts it in order. He also had the gift of
imagination, was a juggler of dreams he shared with Max. Yet never
did Ben become ensnared in the web of his fantasies; he let his
dreams float off like bright balloons, knowing that they would
never be realized. But for hours, often for whole afternoons, their
dreams allowed the two brothers to forget their narrow, impoverished surroundings.

None of the apartments that were the way stations of their decline was left voluntarily. Every time they moved out because the
rent was raised and they fell behind in their payments. Landlords
called up at all hours of the day and night threatening eviction, or
turned off the heat in the winter so that the family had to sleep in

their overcoats. The cold of a winter's night was a formative experience of Max's youth, a condition that came to seem normal to him. The landlords lived in their big houses on Long Island unaffected by the cold. Early in the morning, about five, the radiators awoke, hissing, knocking, and gurgling. Then they could take off their coats and still catch two hours of warm and pleasant sleep. At eight or eight-thirty, just when they left the house, the heat would reach its tropical zenith. But when they returned home from school in the early afternoon, only a bit of lukewarm heat remained, and by nine o'clock in the evening, they dressed as if for an expedition into the biting cold of the nocturnal city.

In all these years, Mira never managed to find people powerful enough to help her effectively. She tried to defend herself, but in her angry, heavily accented stammering—when she got excited she lost her bearings in the foreign language, couldn't think of the right words, bollixed up her syntax—she could only appeal to fairness and humane compassion, exactly what she was being denied. Sometimes her friends' husbands intervened on her behalf, sometimes she found a sympathetic official, a creditor who could be cajoled, but most of the time she lost these battles and, in time, came to expect nothing better, convinced that the catastrophe had begun long ago and now must run its course. Saul was of little help to her, for he too was living in poverty during the first years after their divorce, and the deeper he was drawn into politics the more annoying he found the troubles of his first family. He earned the permanent enmity of his two younger sons when he allowed an angry teacher provoked by fourteen-year-old Ben's sarcasms to spank the boy.

Mira moved with the children from Brooklyn to the East Bronx, to an apartment on Crotona Park, which lay below street level at the back of the building. Only dimly if at all did the two younger brothers realize that with this move they had fallen from the lowest rung of the social ladder onto the hard ground of urban destitution, but for Mira it was painfully, hopelessly clear. Max was twelve at the time and getting into fights with gangs of Irish Catholics; he joined a gang of Italian immigrant kids. For many years, long after he had left the Bronx, Max liked to boast about how he'd managed to survive all those fights without ever getting his nose broken. Two blocks away the black ghetto began. The only way to survive was to be able to defend yourself on the street.

"My mother raised us on soybeans, seaweed, and grains," he'd say, "long before it was fashionable to eat that stuff. It was supposed to make us into big, bad city wolves, Bronx guerrillas."

The knowledge she had acquired as a biology student but never been able to earn a living with was applied to feeding her children, but there were so many things she couldn't give them.

Max had to do battle for two, for Ben was no fighter. Ben was a thinker, an intellectual, fearful of physical conflict. He even avoided the friendly contact common among boys. His timidity attracted derision and teasing, and his tart rejoinders would inevitably invite physical attacks. He was the loser in every fight.

Max's happiest memories of Ben were tied to the foul ditch behind their six-story wooden tenement. Their windows faced this smelly back yard. Pale weeds grew luxuriantly beneath the rotting wooden steps, stinging nettles and skinny saplings that would never become trees. Scattered among the weeds were rubbish, tin cans, glass shards, broken appliances, and sometimes things they could use: rusty bicycle parts, dismembered radios, and objects whose value revealed itself only to Ben's imagination. It was their first outdoor playground since emigration, and the wealth of Ben's inventiveness made it magical. The next building crowded up so close against this back yard that their playground was only a narrow canyon lying in shadow for all but a few hours in the middle of the day. The buildings on either side of them towered like fortresses; even during the day, lights were left on in the apartments, where the mysterious life of a proletariat that Mira wanted nothing to do with was acted out without shame or guilt.

Every Friday afternoon they set off on the long trip to Brooklyn, slept overnight in sleeping bags on the floor of Faye's little kitchen, and rode back to the Bronx on Saturday evening. Max had his bar mitzvah in the synagogue where Mira had sought comfort in the most desolate days after Saul's departure, far from his Jewish classmates in the Bronx. Here he knew no one except for a few old people. There was no one he had to be brilliant for except his mother. As so often in his life, his burning desire was to make her happy. Victor had long since moved out, and just at the time of Max's bar mitzvah Saul had to go to Washington for an important meeting with Chaim Weizmann.

In just a few more years, only a handful of photos would be left to remind Max of the childhood shared with Ben. The last photograph Max had of his brother Benjamin had been taken the day he graduated from City College. In front of the Liberal Arts Building, Ben stood in the sun at a slight angle, as if he were leaning sideways against a stiff breeze, his narrow, gentle face as soft as if the bones had not yet attained their final form. There was no hint that in a year, in the psychiatric wing of a Brooklyn hospital, a diagnosis of schizophrenia would put an end to all expectations of a brilliant career.

Ben's slow slide into irredeemable psychosis occurred over many years. In time, neither shock treatments nor psychotherapy brought any relief, and the antipsychotic drugs gradually compromised his health. There were times when a restricted but almost normal life seemed possible, times full of frenzied plans and short-lived progress, an apprenticeship with a newspaper in Manhattan. But after a few months Ben returned to the apartment in the middle of the day: he couldn't stand the pressure of the deadlines, couldn't meet the demands for production. It took all his strength to keep his fear in check, his agitation, the tumult of voices in his head. He let himself go, neglected his appearance, was beaten up by vagrants, got picked up by the police, sooner or later always ended up back in the locked ward.

Even when he could live at home, he lived liked a stranger under the same roof as his family, irritable and secretive. Nothing was left of the brother Max had played with in the ditch behind the house. It was hardest to see him suffer and find no words that could reach him. The drugs changed his appearance: they bloated him, caused white secretions at the corners of his mouth and eyes, slowed his movements. His silent suffering was an accusation. He reproached Max for the life he would have in the future—Max, not Ben, the more intelligent, the genius.

"By rights I ought to hate you," he said, "except you're my kid brother."

Mira and Max hid their sorrow from each other.

For a while Ben spent time with one of his former teachers who would pick him up from the hospital and take him to his house outside the city, in Mount Kisco, where there were pine forests and little lakes in the nearby Hudson Valley. There Ben made paintings on pieces of white cardboard the size of book covers and became convinced that his calling was to be an artist. He made hundreds of these works on cardboard using all possible media: charcoal, watercolors, colored pencils. In his manic phases he ran through New York, forcing his cardboard works on friends and acquaintances, ringing doorbells and frightening strangers with these unwanted gifts. When he sensed their fear he became panicky, begged, pleaded, and didn't give up until he had gotten rid of all his signed pictures. Back in their apartment he gave free reign to his frustration and panic. In the end it was Max who, helpless and guilty, had to reach for the telephone, because he could no longer stand to watch the self-destruction of his beloved brother.

They dropped Ben off at Bellevue Hospital on a November evening, and after dinner they sat across from each other at the kitchen table. Mira pretended to be reading the *Forward* while Max filled out a welfare application for his brother. Glancing up, he found himself looking directly into her dark, grieving eyes. She must have been watching him for a while, and though she said nothing, he knew what she was thinking and could sense the tenderness of her grief. As clearly as if he had slipped into her consciousness, he saw himself and his brothers as small children playing on the summer lawn before the terrace in H., himself and Ben as adolescents at this table, where now only he and his mother sat. Her gaze glided over his hands, then she smiled and looked back down at her newspaper. Max too looked at his hands lying on the application form as if they were something he had never noticed before: long, powerful fingers with a fuzz of reddish hair shimmering in the light of the table lamp. Only she could remember how small these hands had once been. He smiled back and his eyes filled with tears. Now she had only him, now only he could compensate for all she had suffered.

In the following year, America entered the war. Mira and Saul made a second attempt to send Sophie and Albert an affidavit and tickets for a boat to New York. Victor and Max both got drafted.

Chapter 2

THE FIRST TIME Max returned to H. since their emigration, he was twenty-two and wearing the uniform of a corporal in the U.S. Army. In the fall of 1945, H. had been destroyed by bombings, like many other towns he had seen. The wounds the war had inflicted, the poverty, and the hostile defiance of the vanquished populace depressed him. There were almost no civilian cars on the streets, only military vehicles and emaciated figures riding bicycles or pushing handcarts. He regarded their gray, weary faces with curiosity and repugnance. The bridge was not the same one as in his early childhood, but it still marked a boundary: the boundary between the American and Russian zones. He stayed in a hotel in the center of town that had been requisitioned by the American military government. The house next door was half collapsed; he could see the pattern of its tattered wallpaper. The pavement was broken, and even the houses and streets that had escaped destruction exuded the same gray weariness as the faces of the passersby.

It was a hazy autumn day when Max climbed the hill with his parents' address in his uniform pocket. The row of houses at the bottom of the slope, near the entrance to the air-raid shelter, seemed to be uninhabited, their windows shattered by explosions, their roofs burned down, and only charred frames still standing on the foundations. The wreckage had already been cleared from the street.

The houses at the top of the hill had survived undamaged. The rustle of brown autumn leaves on the cobblestones only emphasized the stillness of the upper-class neighborhood. Everything seemed as peaceful and untouched as if there had been no war.

He recognized the house immediately: the low, ivy-covered retaining wall along the street, the high stone steps, the bay window, the massive front door. The trees growing around the house had been planted before he was born, while it was still under construction. They had grown tall and now cast a melancholy darkness around the house, spreading dank shadows across the mossy flagstones. Their tangled limbs and branches battled each other for sunlight. The maple leaves and the delicate needles of the larches glowed in their fall colors.

Planting the saplings so long ago must have been an act of hope for the young couple. There was a photo: Mira and Saul, a little older than Max was now, maybe in their mid-twenties, both wearing light sports clothes, holding a thin sapling over a shallow hole, as if to demonstrate how its root ball would be placed into the hole and buried. The little tree had only one fork and a stem thinner than Mira's wrist. Now it had become a tree over thirty feet tall, and neither of them had seen it grow. Only strangers took pleasure in its autumn foliage.

In front of the house was a scooter—a board painted red, with a steering bar and two rubber wheels—and a bright blue wooden wagon with the same kind of wheels as the scooter. A plump young woman was beating a rag rug hanging from a bar that blocked access to the terrace.

Max asked if she lived here and realized that it was an utterly superfluous question.

She regarded him with silent hostility. He was in uniform, an American soldier, and his fluent German failed to elicit even the slightest trace of surprise or cordiality.

In the spring of 1938, Sophie had written to her sister in New York, "Albert has been arrested. If we have to go away, I'll leave an extra key with the neighbors."

"The Kalisches used to live here," said Max, and searched her face.

She stopped beating the rug, gave him an offended look, and dashed past him, hunched over as if she were being pursued. He heard her double-lock the door. He knocked, waited a long time, and imagined her standing on the other side, her breath shallow and cautious, separated from him only by the heavy wooden front door. Invisible to each other, they stood this way for long minutes, in a proximity guaranteed to breed hostility.

Then Max walked around the house. In the garden, overgrown and autumnal, tall pink and purple weeds obscured the edge of the slope. The sun poked through tattered clouds flying across the sky and pulled from the river in the valley below a joyless, leaden light.

He tried to peek through a window into the ground-floor rooms. If his memory was right, the kitchen had to be here. But a tightly drawn lace curtain blocked his view.

He stayed a while longer, skulked around the house like a burglar, took pleasure in imagining the fear of the young woman inside, thought about how he could gain entry, then let it go. He knew that he had to leave again in one or two days. He was counting on being discharged soon. He planned to return to New York and resume the life the war had interrupted. The house would have to wait. He was certain of his rights, but he wanted to talk to Mira first and verify the legal situation. He was young. He had time.

But when he returned home and told his mother about the house—the tall trees and overgrown garden—she showed no trace of joy or enthusiasm. He sensed only her silent resistance. Three times she had sent her sister an affidavit, the first one to Vienna in the summer of 1938, the other two to Prague. But Sophie had lost her nerve and fled to the house of relatives in Budapest, where the war caught up with her. No affidavit could help her there. Since the day when a family acquaintance who had survived the Holocaust told Mira of Sophie's deportation, she had a foreboding that all the others—her brother-in-law Albert, her father—were dead, that none of her relatives was still alive. The painful realization that the catastrophe could have been avoided only added to her grief and self-recrimination. Had Sophie feared being a burden to her? Had she so little trust in her? Hadn't she received any of the affidavits? Had she, Mira, tried everything possible? She would never know, would never be able to imagine Sophie's last months of life. Max spared her feelings and didn't talk about it. When he spoke of regaining ownership of the house, she wasn't interested. What for? Never would she set foot in H. again, she declared. When someone who had met her father in the Lódz ghetto wanted to visit, she refused to speak with him. "He's dead," she said, "what else do I need to know? Isn't that enough?"

Max never heard her mention the house in H. again or talk about old times. No memory could ever console her now—everything that had once given her hope and consolation was transformed into sorrow. She stopped speaking German from one day to the next. And even though she would have been perfectly capable of saying everything in English, Mira lived from then on in an inaccessible silence, a disoriented emptiness, despite the one or two old friendships she still maintained.

She had moved back to Brooklyn, into an apartment close to her synagogue and her friend Faye. Saul had found it for her. In old age they had drawn closer again, bound in cautious friendship. He called her regularly, asked if she needed anything and how she was doing. "Don't worry about me," she said, "I've got everything I need. I'm doing fine." But it seemed to Max that it was too late in her life to make amends; the emotional damage could not be repaired. He was the only one who spent every Sabbath with her and took her to synagogue on the holidays. He spoke the blessing over the wine and challah and dutifully ate her Shabbos dinner, the invariable sequence of traditional dishes: chicken soup with matzo balls, fish, and strudel. She liked it when he stayed the night. The bed in his tiny room was always freshly made. He knew that she lay awake in her bed, happy to hear his sounds in the otherwise silent apartment: the late evening news, the back of the easy chair he always bumped into on his way to the kitchen to look for a snack in the refrigerator, the water splashing in the shower, and the hum of his razor. Then he would stop a moment by her door. "Good night, Mom," he whispered, and it always sounded unnatural to him when she answered through the closed door, "Night, night. Sleep well." He longed to hear what she used to say in the old days, in his childhood, *Schlaf gut, mein Schatz.*

Now only in her accent could he catch the echoes of lost intimacy, the language that had belonged to them alone. This familiar sound was probably what he found both attractive and disconcerting about Eva. When he was seventeen, before the war, he often spent time in the émigré cafés listening to the refugees' soft, melodious German and basking in the illusion that he was one of them. In the Eclair on Broadway Max would drink a *melange* and imagine himself transported to the Vienna of his mother's stories. With the coffeehouse as a backdrop he saw himself as an elegant dandy, a flaneur.

It was in the Eclair that he became acquainted with Eva. She was sitting at a table alone, smoking, with her eyes glued to the door. A mane of dark hair fell to her shoulders, and from time to time she shook it back with an impatient toss of her head. Their eyes met and it seemed to him completely natural to go over to her. He could have sworn she was waiting for *him*. He spoke to her in German. She gave an amused smile and answered in the inflections of his mother that turned every sentence into a mildly provocative question, "I'm waiting for somebody, but go ahead and have a seat."

They met every day. As soon as school was out he ran straight to her, to whatever place she told him to meet her. It seemed to Max that anything that didn't pertain to her had ceased to exist. He was so overwhelmed by the love that had struck him like a bolt of lightning that he was convinced everyone he encountered must notice his transformation. For her sake he went to his father, hat in hand, and asked him to arrange an affidavit for her parents and younger sister.

Eva was two years older than Max and had the advantage of seeming more grown up. With stubborn determination she ignored anything that didn't serve her purpose. She was impossible to impress, and she accepted his devotion with the hauteur of a princess, but his enthusiastic admiration of her Viennese origins was incomprehensible to her. "You haven't got a clue," she rebuked him. "You never had to live there."

She wanted to become an American as quickly as possible, learn the language, conquer the city and her fear of it. There was a desperate audacity to the escapades she got him into. "We're going to the Café Luxembourg today," she would decide, ignoring his objections that it was too expensive, only rich people went there—film stars, millionaires. Reluctantly he followed her, stared at the floor in embarrassment, expected the staff to be scandalized and throw them out. But Eva sat right down at the bar, looked around defiantly, checked out the patrons and waiters with what seemed to him brazen directness, wrinkled her nose, and declared in her guttural accent, "It's too vulgar. Let's go."

Once outside, she giggled with relief and Max confessed, "I was ready to die in there! I'd never dare go in there alone."

"Me neither," Eva said, "but I'm not going to let anybody intimidate me. That's the only way to make it, you know? You've got to stay in training."

He took Eva home with him only once, and it was a mistake. He realized that as soon as he followed her gaze as it glided over the furniture, paused on the cast-iron radiators, and came to rest on the window. Not twenty yards distant in the apartment across the way a fat woman in a pink top with shoulder straps slapped the face of a little boy.

"Have you lived here long?" Max winced at the tone in which she asked Mira this question—as if interrogating her.

He could sense his mother's suppressed indignation as she replied, "Why do you ask?"

"It's a pretty depressing neighborhood," Eva asserted.

"New York is depressing," Mira answered, as if she were fighting a duel rather than having a conversation.

"I think New York's exciting," declared Eva with a dogmatic self-assurance he hadn't noticed before and considered unnecessarily aggressive.

They ate in silence. Mira had gone out of her way to cook a good meal, but Max could see Eva didn't like it. "I didn't come to New York to eat Wiener schnitzel," she said as he walked her to the subway.

"She's cheeky," Mira declared angrily, "She doesn't respect you. She still needs to be taken down a peg or two."

"She's had it hard," he objected, "She's all alone. You've got to admit that she's gutsy."

"She'll use you and throw you away," Mira predicted.

In the end she was both right and wrong, for Eva was neither calculating nor egotistical, only vastly ambitious. Max was the first boyfriend she had tried to make into a man she could be proud of. In this last vacation, the summer after he graduated from high school, he worked for a construction company. Every apartment he entered with a can of grout or a bucket of paint in hand he would redesign in his imagination. Eva insisted that he apply for a scholarship to study architecture. She wouldn't even consider marrying a man without a college degree, she declared.

She invested her own ambition in his education, gave him assignments. He had to draw Manhattan's new buildings: the McGraw-Hill Building, Rockefeller Center. Then they would stand there and compare his sketches with the real thing. As always, her powers of observation were sharp and objective. She saw that his talent was not for construction design; rather it was the interior spaces that inspired him, the overwhelming dimensions of Grand Central Station, the light that streamed in broad bands through its high arched windows onto the marble floors. They strolled from the twilight of the ticket counters into the pools of light where he stopped, bedazzled.

"Don't you get the feeling you're being sucked up into shafts of sunlight till you just float out the windows?" he asked.

She nodded, "It's like we're standing in a magic place."

"It's like a cathedral."

"No it isn't," she contradicted, "That's something you don't know anything about."

Despite his awe-inspired attempts to be like her and become worthy of her, the passion of this first love affair soon cooled. Max was not caught completely off guard when Eva confessed that she had fallen in love with someone else. Her wedding announcement appeared on the same day Ben was first admitted to the psychiatric ward. In the dazed numbness of the days that followed, her wedding caused Max no pain. He heard later that she was expecting a child. After the war he got a call from her. "My husband moved out," she said matter-of-factly. "It's the best thing that could have happened to me." They remained friends, saw each other from time to time, went out for dinner. Though the spark of their love was extinguished for good, Eva never married anyone else. She brought up her child by herself and from then on, her whole energy and ambition were concentrated on her daughter and her own career. She went back to college and made a name for herself as a journalist.

After a few semesters Max abandoned the study of architecture. His desire was to design interiors and restore facades, not build buildings. He was an *Augenmensch*, someone for whom sight was the primary sense, an aesthete. He loved beautiful things, and his sense of well-being depended on what he could see. For two years he worked with a sculptor in Vermont and lived alone in a cabin in the woods. In Montreal he learned how to work with plaster and wood, and after his first commission, which fell into his lap by chance, he decided that his apprenticeship was over. This commission took him back to Manhattan, where a gallery owner wanted him to restore the art-nouveau facade of a narrow building on Fifth Avenue. He remained more fond of this project than of all his later ones. Years later Max still considered this facade, completed when he was twenty-eight, to be his masterpiece. With one stroke, his life was transformed. He earned more money on this job than he had previously made in a year. Now there was no desire he couldn't satisfy for himself or his mother. Except for one: to extinguish the past and restore to her the house of her youth.

Suddenly he was dealing with people whose way of life had once intimidated him. He looked over the shoulders of his clients as they wrote out checks for the sums he needed for materials, fixtures, and workmen, and it was a long time before he stopped having nightmares that the money had disappeared and he had to answer for it. There were months when he turned out plaster models like a man possessed, without sleeping, almost without pausing for breath. He drew and discarded dozens of sketches, rode herd on his subcontractors, pitched in himself, and deep into the night—alone on a ladder in the middle of an empty room, absorbed in the play of light and shadow from lamps of various wattage—he studied the effects of his stucco ornamentation. At times like these, he couldn't remember when he'd last eaten. It made no difference to him where he slept—sometimes right on the job, in the apartment he was restoring, on the floor, wrapped in a blanket among the plaster buckets. But then when he led the owners through the finished rooms, basking in their astonished excitement, he felt like a patron himself, bestowing these princely interiors on them as a gift, not without a touch of regret, not without a bit of envy.

For himself he restored an apartment near Central Park. From the roof of the building he could look out over treetops and lawns, a green and hilly landscape at his own front door. He showered Mira with presents and elegant clothes she never wore. "When am I supposed to wear them," she asked, "when I go dancing?"

He got to know women. He was an eligible bachelor—cultivated, generous, at the beginning of his career. Women felt he understood them; they confided in him. His inquiring, sympathetic gaze drew from them secrets whose intimacy surprised even them. He moved through these years as through a dream that—even while dreaming—he knew he would awaken from. What he earned he spent generously. It looked as if wealth didn't matter to him, almost as if he was in a hurry to get rid of it. When friends advised Max to be more frugal or gave him stock market tips, he would just laugh derisively, "My father lost more in the Crash of 1929 than I'll ever earn back." He said it meant more to him to see the joy and surprise in the face of a woman when he gave her a gift.

Back then he believed that this intoxicating obsession with his work would last his whole life. "I'm a candle burning at both ends," he told his friends, "my brain's just bursting with ideas." He agreed to daunting projects that would take years to complete, and among his clients were heads of state and ministers from former colonies who were setting up the New York consulates of their new republics. There was no architectural style of the 19th and early 20th century that he couldn't understand and integrate into his designs. But his true love was reserved for the light brown, meticulously trimmed sandstone familiar to his touch from his childhood years in Brooklyn. And he continued to be attracted to the ornate balustrades, whimsical bay windows, and elegant stairways that made him dream of Europe. He had little affection for the glass towers of the postwar era.

Although Max never gave up the idea of some day retrieving the house in H. and living there in intermittent retirement, it receded into some distant future far from the hectic present. He loved the New York life hurtling through his days and nights like a racing pulse. He was a match for it. But sometimes, especially during the long, oppressive summers when the desperation and shrill fury of poverty and the brutally literal survival of the fittest were most apparent, there were hours when he longed for that distant place of serenity. It was as if Mira's yearning had crept into his imagination, a gentle, insistent yearning that could be numbed but never fully silenced. There were times when Max had enough money to be able to spend six months or a whole year in Europe, but before he could make up his mind to do it, there were new, intriguing jobs, or a woman, or his brother Ben was having a crisis and he couldn't leave his mother alone with the responsibility.

Somebody had introduced Max to Ed Pears. The big trucks with his name on them that delivered fruit and vegetables were a familiar sight to everyone in New York. Mr. Pears told Max he wanted him to design the kind of apartment over whose threshold one could carry a new bride. Max was sure the Boston millionaire was setting up a love-nest in Manhattan for a mistress, so he was taken aback when he saw Pears's daughter Elizabeth—an awkward, skinny young woman—strolling through the empty rooms of the penthouse apartment on Central Park beside her tall, regal-looking mother. She gazed up at the stucco ceilings and then turned her small, timid face toward him and asked which room he'd recommend for her studio. It wasn't love at first sight; Max couldn't even say for sure if the nearness he felt had anything to do with love. It was more like the intimacy of some shared knowledge they didn't speak about because they didn't have to. It seemed to him that they had already leaped over the first breathless steps of infatuation the moment she turned her keen, almost terrified gaze on him. It was as if he reminded her of someone, as if she recognized him. "Do we know each other from somewhere?" he asked in confusion. She shook her head with a sad smile. "Some people remind you of something," she said, "but you just don't know what it is."

Elizabeth was a painter, talented, headstrong, endowed with a kind of sixth sense that made her seem extremely astute and insightful. She took her family's wealth for granted; she wasn't ashamed of it but took no credit for it either. She introduced Max into artistic circles previously closed to him. He thought of himself not as an artist but an artisan, a lover of beautiful things and spaces. What his talent had accomplished seemed to him the natural result of his need to assess and shape every space he entered. Elizabeth introduced him to the Russian painter Peter Blume. In her apartment he first met two men who would become his lifelong friends: Paul Friedberg, at that time still dreaming of child-friendly playgrounds in the slums of the Lower East Side, and the concept artist Sol Lewitt, whose sculptures Max visited in the museums just to give them furtive kicks. Elizabeth entertained them all in the art déco apartment that Max had restored according to contract, as if it belonged to a woman waiting for the arrival of her lover. She never showed her own paintings except on the walls of her apartment. They had an expressiveness that seemed out of date and aroused more curiosity about her than about her art. Max hung a self-portrait she had given him in his apartment, an unsettling painting in dark oils with deep shadows and her bright eyes wide with terror, the portrait of an emaciated woman face to face with death.

After a few months his desire for Elizabeth was so thoroughly extinguished that every hopeful glance from her, every caress elicited only panic from him. He didn't want to hurt her feelings, so he told her that he had read an essay by Sigmund Freud that seemed to fit him to a tee, just as if Freud had anticipated his problem. He explained to her that it was physically impossible for him to love a woman of his own age or even older. It must be some sort of incest taboo. She even wore her hair like his mother, with combs in it. No, no, even if she changed her hair style, the damage was already done. It was early spring and they were walking through the park. In the trees only a haze of green caressed the branches. It was still unusual to see people walking coatless in the afternoon sun. Max turned his head to look at a young woman whose loose blonde hair gleamed in the sun. Elizabeth followed his gaze. "I was never that young," she said.

They remained friends, once the bitterness of their breakup was over, and their friendship deepened to an attraction that was free of expectation and so more capacious than a mere love affair. They still went together to the Stieglitzs' in Mamaroneck and to Mark Rothko's studio. Max kept his love affairs secret from her.

After her mother died, Elizabeth moved to London. They carried on long conversations on the telephone, and she told him how much he meant to her. In her letters she wrote what she would never have said to him in person, that he was the only man she'd ever loved. Such declarations made Max self-conscious and confronted him with his own inadequacy compared to her unwavering devotion. She gave up her apartment on Central Park and, when she visited New York, he picked her up at the airport and brought her to his apartment. For as long as Elizabeth stayed with him, he kept his woman friend of the moment out of his apartment; he would meet her elsewhere. Elizabeth slept in Max's bed and he set up a cot in the study. She lay beneath the blanket with her nightdress buttoned up to her chin, as chaste and silent as if she didn't even want him to hear her breathing.

After a few days, the initial tension would relax. They would visit old friends, return home long after midnight, then talk until dawn. Only occasionally, when they bid each other farewell again, could he sense her longing.

During the ride to the airport they would make vague plans for trips together that both knew would never be realized.

The last time they saw each other, Elizabeth was more gaunt than usual and very pale, an exhausted, prematurely aged woman. The eyes burning in her emaciated face frightened him, and when he embraced her he could feel her skinny shoulderblades like clipped wings beneath the cloth of her jacket.

"Are you sick?" he asked.

She just smiled and shook her head.

And all he could think of when they parted was to make her promise to eat more and regain her strength. By this time she had already made him the heir of her enormously profitable import–export business. She was only fifty-two when, a few months later, she died in London of the cancer she had kept secret from him. Only when he read the letter she had left for him did he fully comprehend how lonely she had been. "Don't blame yourself," she wrote. "The full extent of your humanity only emerged once you lost interest in me. It's easy to be magnanimous when you're in love, but you remained so after love was over."

———

Max was forty-seven. Although his hair was already showing the first signs of gray, up to then he had felt ageless and invulnerable. But within six months he lost both Elizabeth to an early death, and then the only woman with whom he could have imagined living together. He lost her to his own fears, fears that were so intense that for a long time afterward he couldn't even name them.

He had met Dana in the Russian Tea Room on a night when Artur Rubinstein was dining at the next table. Dana was a student at Columbia who earned her tuition working nights as a waitress in the Russian Tea Room. The way she moved among the tables with economical gestures and a warm smile, it seemed as if this were her house and her party. The European elegance of the candelabra, Oriental carpets, and velvet-lined booths made this the rendezvous of choice after premières at Carnegie Hall next door. Dana's black high-necked dress and pinned-up hair lent her an old-fashioned charm. But what astonished Max even more than her appearance was her intellect. She seemed to draw from the same abundant source of imagination and breathtaking speed of intelligence as Ben before he fell ill. Her witty responses were as light and swift as rapier strokes, and she moved from table to table with a dancer's agility, the focus of admiring glances. She drew Max into her spell while keeping him at a distance. He had never been so proud of a conquest as when she finally agreed to meet him for lunch.

"I can't believe I've managed to win over a woman like you," he said.

She laughed, "You haven't yet."

He picked her up after closing time. He didn't go into the Russian Tea Room anymore. He admitted he couldn't stand it when Dana treated other men just the same as him. Everything about this affair was like a fairy tale, unreal, and for the first time he feared that it could end some day. Not his love, but hers could vanish as inexplicably as it had appeared and leave him behind in a life he couldn't bear to live without her. "Our love must never end," he implored her one night, and was himself surprised at the vehemence of this new longing for permanence. He was used to panicking any time a woman suggested a lasting commitment. With Dana he talked about their future together. He took her home to meet his mother and was as pleased and proud as a husband that the two women liked each other.

"She reminds me of Ben," he said to Mira. "Don't you think so?"

"Not really," she answered. "Maybe she looks a bit like him— her eyes, her narrow nose."

She cast him a quick, inquiring glance. "Don't worry," she said, "nothing will happen to her. She's got both feet on the ground."

Then Dana got pregnant. Even though she was still a student, she wanted to have the child. But Max was seized by a fear he didn't completely understand himself. He wanted Dana, that hadn't changed. He absolutely did not want to lose her, but he absolutely didn't want the child either, absolutely not.

"Why not?" she wanted to know. "We're going to stay together, didn't you say so?"

"I can't explain it to you."

"You don't love me. You're in the market for someone new, that's it."

He didn't want children, he screamed at her in panic. He'd never want children. He didn't want to bring children into a world where they'd have to suffer so much.

"Like who?" she asked.

"Like my brother Ben."

Finally she gave in, agreed to an abortion. He paid for it, still believing their love would survive this. Dana dumped all the presents he had given her on his front doorstep—glass smashed, jewels among the shards. She sent him word that as far as she was concerned, he was dead. She stopped waitressing at the Russian Tea Room. At the sound of his voice she hung up the phone. She sent his letters back unopened. A few years later he saw her by chance in Central Park. She was sitting in the shade of a sycamore tree whose roots ran across the gravel path like crossties. She was laughing and gazing enraptured into the face of the squirming infant she held under the arms and lifted up over her head. He walked by without greeting her. What could he have said?

Fatherhood, he said that evening to a woman he was already getting tired of, fatherhood was a form of immortality he'd never aspired to. She gave him a puzzled look, but he no longer cared whether he was making a good impression.

After Dana vanished from his life, it seemed to Max that all his imagination and strength deserted him. For the first time he turned down jobs. He felt empty, as though he had reached some end point, and had an overwhelming desire to get out of New York. He had the inheritance from Elizabeth, he was free of financial worries, but this knowledge only increased his despair. He found a place for Ben in a supervised group home and arranged a generous pension for his mother. But Mira was by this time living in a bewildered world of her own. He hadn't noticed the change in her right away. He thought it was only her body that had taken another step toward death. He felt the coolness of her cheek when he kissed her. It seemed to him that life and warmth were steadily escaping from her body, and her back and fingers were ever more stiff and twisted.

Mira had ceased to take an interest in his life the way she used to. She had withdrawn into mistrustful silence and perceived things that seemed to him fantastical and bizarre. She reported that the same car always parked below her window. It stood there from early evening until just before midnight, and every time the man got out of it, he would glance up at her. He always noticed her; she could tell by the way he grinned. Then he would light a cigarette and go into the house across the street. "I'm sure he's observing me from there," she said, her eyes wide with fear. She also heard a rustling in the telephone. "Your voice sounds like it's coming from another planet," she would whisper. "I can't talk now. Someone's listening in."

"Who do you think is so interested in what you're doing that they're spying on you?" Max would ask impatiently.

"You're naive," she said with a mysterious expression. "You only see the surface of things, but I know better."

On her birthday he took her out to a restaurant in Manhattan, but she hardly touched her food.

"Eat," he urged her. "Don't you like it?"

She sat cowering on her chair, close to tears. "Don't you see them staring at me?" she asked and cast frightened glances at a waiter leaning in the doorway. "He's watching me the whole time," she whispered. "We should leave before he gets reinforcements."

"Get ahold of yourself, Mother." Max was annoyed. He was too busy with his own problems to be seriously concerned with Mira's delusions.

Once he found a bouquet of white roses wilting in the trash can. "Why don't you put them into a vase?" he asked in astonishment. "Who gave them to you?"

"Saul did," she said. "He wants me to die. He sent me white roses, that's a curse."

Mira wasn't simply going crazy, for between her bouts of persecution anxiety she went out, visited her friends, chatted with the check-out girl in the supermarket, visited Ben, and always gave an accurate account of his condition when she telephoned Saul or Max. Friends came to her for advice. She could perceive their subliminal moods and with her acute sense for the invisible she interpreted reality in ways that made sense only to her. The neighbors thought her an eccentric old woman. Her friends smiled indulgently when she went overboard with her interpretations; they said she could hear the grass grow. She was certainly still sharp-witted, but suddenly and without warning she would start floundering in a net of occult messages and apocalyptic threats she could no longer distinguish from what was happening in the world around her. In the moments when panic threatened to destroy her, the homeless man she would sometimes give a ten-dollar bill to could become transformed into the angel of death.

Max had assumed that Mira's memory of the house of her youth had faded in the course of all the years in which she had never mentioned it. Late in her life, shortly before her slow death in a nursing home, she found a new source of solace. She had gotten into the habit of taking excursions on suburban buses that she usually rode to the last stop, then strolled through the streets. One time, in one of the little vacation communities built on pilings with decks jutting out over the dunes on the coast just east of Bridgeport, she had discovered a little path between two garden fences that led to a hidden cove. It was a quiet little inlet, protected by an overhanging rock that cast a soft blue shadow onto the late afternoon beach.

Once she took Max to see this cove, but he didn't realize how important the place was to her. He felt only irritation that they were obviously on a private beach. He'd seen the No Trespassing sign up on the garden fence. They might get chased off. It was a cool, windy September day and the choppy water didn't invite swimming. And it annoyed him that she walked into the water in her white sneakers and impatiently ordered him to roll up his pantlegs and wade out with her, as if he were a child. The spit of land was rocky and ran far out into the shallow water whose restless whitecaps washed over the line of seaweed and broken shells. There was no one to be seen and no boat far and wide, only the rhythmic lap of the waves on the rocks of the shore.

Max was peevish, still unwilling to acknowledge the signs of change in her character.

"I shouldn't have showed you my cove," she said. "Take me home."

It was their last outing together, the last time he drove her back to Brooklyn into the blinding light of the setting sun, in the opposite direction from the commuter traffic heading out of the city. Soon thereafter Mira suffered a mild stroke, and when she had recovered physically, Max moved her to an exclusive retirement home in New Rochelle.

Now, in her increasing confusion, she began to speak German again, and Max, the only visitor she still recognized, discovered that her youth and the house in H. were still fresh and unfaded in her memory.

Then Mira took off without telling anyone. She must have caught the commuter train to Stamford and then transferred to an Amtrak train to Boston. Prudent despite her confusion, she took along a small bag with everything she needed: money, a towel, toilet articles, a nightdress. They picked her up at a turnpike entrance in East Haven, at the end of her strength. She told the policemen she wanted to go to her beach.

She went into a nursing home and was confined to a wheelchair after a second stroke. But usually when Max visited her, she lay in bed as motionless as the objects around her. Her mouth didn't smile when he came in. Her eyes were fixed expectantly on the paper bag in his hand, which held the same present every time he came: the ice-cream sundae she loved so dearly but had always resisted so as not to gain weight. Then he sat on her bed and watched as she struggled to get the ice cream and chocolate sauce to her mouth with the little plastic spoon without dripping any on herself. In the end she always gave up and let him feed her.

"How's my father Hermann?" she asked.

"Fine," said Max. "He sends you his best."

"Say a nice hello to him from me. Why doesn't Sophie come see me?"

He was silent and fought back his tears.

He lifted her into the wheelchair and pushed her down the hallways, past the nurses' station, where he'd ask casually how she was doing. "She's as stubborn as a baby," said the nurse reproachfully. After an hour he kissed her on a cheek that felt like wrinkled tissue paper, and when he walked out through the revolving door into the sunlight, he had to use all his willpower to keep from screaming.

Mira lived on a few more years, swinging between moments of sharp clarity and long periods of twilight. In one lucid moment she made her will and asked to be cremated after her death, a violation of Jewish law. She wanted her ashes scattered in the wind and sea at the cove near Bridgeport. Victor and Saul were against the idea. They thought it was just a symptom of her clouded mind, but Max could understand why she didn't want to be buried in this country where she'd never really been happy. Her life, after all, had finally found peace in this place, if only for the space of a few afternoons. On this tiny beach no bigger than a garden sheltered from the wind, she had been able to escape for a few hours from a world that had broken her spirit, and surely, when she looked out over the endless gray surface of the Atlantic, she saw before her mind's eye the house of her happiest years.

Part II

Chapter 3

ON AN AUGUST day in 1974, bleary-eyed after a long flight, Max boarded an express train for Vienna in the Zurich *Hauptbahnhof*. The clear blue sky and cool wind put him in an expectant mood. During the taxi ride into the city, reading all the signs and directions in the language so familiar to him from early childhood—but more to his ear than his eye—he had been seized by deep affection for this unknown town and its people, indeed for the entire continent, the Old World. Everything was so small and close together, so clean after the sticky summer heat of New York. He was prepared to love Europe. In such elation he left the city he had just barely arrived in, eager to finally get to H.

At first he was alone in the compartment. He watched single-family houses with their fenced-in gardens slide by and wondered how he would feel in this other, more cramped but obviously satisfying, life.

In Sargans two ageless women joined him in the compartment. They sat down with weighty deliberation, as if they never intended to rise again, their legs planted side by side like posts, their skirts pulled tight over their knees. Max listened to them talking about their grown-up children, the wedding of one's youngest daughter, the grandchildren of the other, their health problems, the illnesses they had recovered from. The husband of one was at a spa convalescing from an operation, so she wouldn't have to cook for a few weeks. . . . After a while Max stopped listening. He didn't understand everything they said, and it was a strain to eavesdrop. They spoke in a broad, gutteral accent he had never heard before, not in the familiar, questioning cadences of his mother or Eva. Still, the sounds of the language of his childhood gave him a twinge of wistful sadness.

Mira had had no talent for mimicking the sound of other languages. Her English sounded like her German, a bit nasal, the vowels turned into diphthongs, the consonants soft and drawn out. When he played with other children, Max always felt ashamed when his mother showed up with her ludicrous, incomprehensible English. *Bohunk* was what they called people like her with Eastern European accents, *just off the boat*, a taint that immigrant children were at pains to cover up. In the early years they'd spoken nothing but German at home and Mira would send her two oldest sons out shopping to conceal her own uncertainty in the foreign language. When Max started school he could only speak German and just a few words of English—some expressions he'd picked up on their outings because he liked the way they sounded.

When he couldn't find his cap he cried out plaintively, "*mein Kapperl!*" and the other children had mocked him.

Later, as adolescents, he and his brothers would speak English with each other and German with their mother. His brothers' German became more and more proper, free of the Austrian accent that colored his own. Once the war broke out, you had to be careful about speaking German in public and from then on, for the rest of her life, Mira used the foreign language even though she never really mastered its nuances.

Max had nodded off in his corner, waking only when the woman with the lacquered permanent sitting opposite him heaved a deep sigh and then a snort of laughter. "*Ja*, those were the days," she said. She uttered the words in a wistful voice and it was clear she was talking about her youth. "You remember how we used to go hiking in the mountains every Saturday?" she asked her friend. "We had so much energy in those days, dead tired from a week at work but up and on the go by four a.m. anyway." "The *Mädelführerin* . . ." interjected the other one, "what was her name now? You know, the one with the braids pinned up on her head—we loved her so much. You remember the song?" She hummed a few bars, the other one hummed along, sang single words, interrupted herself. "How did it go? I'm getting so forgetful!" They laughed. "It was so long ago. Remember how we stood in front of the cabin and watched the sun rise, and the campfires at night?" They recalled the men who were teenagers back then. One of them had already known the man she would later marry, the other had her sights on a boy who was later killed in the war. "That was '38," she said. "My God, and it's as though it was yesterday."

Max looked out the window at the landscape, the narrow valleys, the conifers close to the tracks, the gorges with streams hurtling down into the valleys. Here and there a village appeared, undeniably picturesque with its church spire, balconies adorned with geraniums—a picture-postcard landscape.

Here's where they'd been young, and here's where they were growing old. Max recalled an afternoon at the shore two months ago. In the rays of the setting sun the choppy waves had gleamed like the scales of a giant fish. He couldn't bring himself to open the urn. He'd rolled up his pants and waded out into the water as Mira had done on their last outing together, then carefully let it slide into the water.

Max felt a mute fury rising within him. He went out into the corridor and let the wind blow his hair.

———

When he finally stepped off the train in H., Max was too tired to look for a good hotel where he could settle in for an extended stay. Right beside the station he found a guest house with a sign at the door reading *Zimmer frei*. That'll have to do for tonight, he said to himself: a bed, a washstand, a door that keeps the outside world at bay. In the lobby and the hallway it smelled of rotting kitchen refuse and the toilet, and the landlord was grumpy. He rested his elbows on the reception counter and watched in curiosity as Max, panting, dragged his suitcase up the narrow stairway.

From the window of his room Max looked down onto the square in front of the station, the park ringed by parked cars, the trees covered with the gray dust of a long summer, and a couple of dreary figures on the park benches. Without having to open the window he knew it was quiet down there, as if the post office clock next to the station wasn't the only thing that had stopped running.

Later, a voice announcing train information woke him from restless sleep. He dreamed of white fences, white wooden houses, snow-covered roofs, a harshly lit albino landscape that made his eyes smart. How could you turn off the light in your head so it stayed dark even when you opened your eyes? He pressed his fingers against his throbbing temples, but it didn't help. He awoke with a headache, vaguely remembered the dream, and told himself it must have been a dream about death.

"Are you visiting relatives here?" asked the landlord as Max took a seat in the breakfast room.

"No," Max answered, "I don't know a soul here."

"But you were born here. It says so in your passport," the landlord persisted.

Max was silent.

"Have you been away from home for long?" the owner wanted to know. He'd set out the breakfast dishes of heavy white porcelain and the coffee pot for Max and made no move to withdraw.

"This isn't my home," said Max.

"You're an American," the man said, "but you were born here." He had a stubborn persistence and wouldn't be put off until he got an explanation.

"Tell me," said Max, "is there a Jewish congregation here?"

"Why do you ask?" The landlord was taken aback. He looked searchingly at Max for what seemed like several minutes. Then a lightbulb seemed to go on and a sly, furtive grin flitted across his face. Max had the impression that his gaze had suddenly become cautious and secretive. Assiduously, the landlord fetched the telephone book, wrote the address on the back of a cash register receipt, said, "But of course" when Max thanked him. "A pleasure, no problem."

Something had changed, but Max couldn't put his finger on it and the landlord asked no more questions.

———

Spitzer was waiting for Max in his office, and if it's true that the first moment of an acquaintance determines the character of the relationship, then the prospects for this one were favorable. He sat at his massive desk, slightly stooped, slender-boned, his glasses slipped far down his nose, with alert, solicitous eyes. Perhaps it was just the gigantic proportions of the desk and the height of the ceiling that made him seem so fragile. Spitzer's brown eyes shone with an almost joyful warmth that Max felt to be spontaneous sympathy.

No, no, he protested, he hadn't come to the office just because Max had called up. He was always here, every day, except for holidays and Sundays.

Spitzer was the secretary of the congregation, sort of its chairman, *Schammes* if you like, also cantor if need be.

"I'm a compulsive fusser," he told Max, "that's why I spend more time here than anyone would expect of me."

Max told him about his encounters so far: the women in the train, the nosy landlord, and that he felt he was being watched ever since the innkeeper had looked at him in that sly, furtive way.

"Don't take that too seriously," said Spitzer. "We're a small town here, not New York. Most people here don't know any Jews. It's probably more curiosity than ill will. I live here, too," he said with a laugh.

"What's that supposed to mean?" asked Max, "Why don't they know any Jews?"

"Only a few have come back," Spitzer explained, "and everyone here claims not to remember. Nobody talks about it. They don't and we don't either, at least not in public."

"How can you live here?" Max asked. He didn't mean it as a reproach, but Spitzer took it that way.

"Everyone's got to decide for himself," he said, and although he hadn't moved, it was as if he had pulled back, as if his eyes took on a defensive look.

"Of course one can live here," he asserted and glanced out the window at a fire wall. "It's no different than anywhere else."

Just look at this room, Max thought to himself. Then he asked, "Do you ever get any direct sun in here?"

Outside it was cool, almost autumn already. A light rain had been falling all morning.

"No," Spitzer said amicably, "that's north. But it's not depression I suffer from, just rheumatism."

He knew all about lawsuits to recover stolen property, Spitzer assured him. He'd had to take a hand in quite a number of them, not the least in his own case. "These suits can take a long time," he said. "Sometimes they go on for years." He seemed to be in his element, giving Max the name of an experienced lawyer whom he ought to get in touch with right away.

"I don't need a lawyer," Max insisted. "The case is as plain as day."

Spitzer laughed. "That's what everybody thinks: they took something away from me, now they've got to give it back. What's right is right. But the people on the other side have their little tricks. You'll need a lawyer."

Max shook his head, "Not me."

Spitzer gave him an amused wink.

The next day they climbed the hill together. It was a quiet neighborhood of big houses, just like when Max first visited it after the war. Back then he hadn't noticed the cemetery wall halfway up the hill, overhung by birches and weeping willows. If you turned around at this point, the city lay spread out below with its green onion domes and gray and red roofs. Up here, the houses stood back from the street behind high cast-iron fences or clipped hedges. The cars parked in front hadn't been here right after the war. His house was one of the few separated from the street only by the old, low retaining wall, already damaged in several places. Max was annoyed by the signs of domesticity around the house: the child's swing hanging from the bar where the woman had been beating her rug back then, the rubber boots by the door. He saw in them an arrogant self-assurance that overrode past injustice as if it were the most natural thing in the world, as if the crime had never been committed. Max spotted a woman of his own age standing in the neighboring yard. She looked directly at him and Spitzer over the fence without expression, her hands on her hips.

Had Sophie left anything with the neighbors for safekeeping before she was driven out of her home? Books, furniture, paintings, the beautiful Delft porcelain for *Pesach* that Max could still remember? Should he go over and speak to the woman? He decided to talk it over with Spitzer first. Spitzer was familiar with the people here. At some future point he would surely ask the older neighbors, but not now.

They walked around the house. The suspicious neighbor rounded the corner of her own house to keep an eye on them. Begonias were growing in flower boxes on the balustrade of the terrace. Max had found a photo of this terrace in his mother's marbled cardboard box. He'd had it framed a few weeks ago: Mira, nearer and in better focus than in most of the other pictures—it was almost a portrait—stood in a long light-colored dress, her head thrust slightly forward with a surprised, inquiring smile on her face, leaning her arm on the white pillar. At her elbow the little stone lion reared up on its hind paws.

"The lion's not here," Max said in astonishment.

Spitzer laughed. "That's not the only thing that will be different."

The house was covered in coarse gray stucco. Spitzer pointed to a damaged place in the wall, then to terrace flagstones that had sunk deep into the damp earth and a loose gutter in the front of the house.

"A bit neglected," Spitzer noted. He had already done some research: the house belonged to the municipality.

"Look over there," he said. Max followed his pointing finger and saw a curtain move.

"What are you doing there?" the neighbor woman called over the fence.

"Do you remember the Kalisches and the Bermans?" Max called back.

"Never heard of them," said the neighbor. "It must be a long time since they lived here."

"Yes," said Max, "it's been a long time."

She retreated into her house, shaking her head.

"I want them to know I'm here," said Max, and Spitzer gave an indulgent smile.

In the offices of municipal departments and judicial officials Max soon ran into barriers he hadn't reckoned with. His knowledge of the language wasn't sufficient to understand the officialese with which, he was convinced, they were trying to intimidate and discourage him.

"What does that mean?" he had to ask all too often. "I don't understand that."

They met his irritable impatience with obstinacy. An official would stolidly repeat the incomprehensible phrases until Max left in a huff. Again and again he was infuriated by the same sentences: *Everything seems to be in order.* That was the officials' working assumption. He was informed that no errors were to be found in the title register. *As a purely legal matter* his claims were unverifiable.

"What do you mean *as a purely legal matter?*" he wanted to know. "What law are we talking about here? Which regime are you working for, anyway?" Max asked.

They cautioned him sharply to keep a civil tongue in his head.

"They have no sense of injustice," he complained to Spitzer, "not the slightest feeling of guilt."

As a purely legal matter, insisted the court official whose narrow, uncommunicative face Max had come to know well in the course of several weeks, as a purely legal matter there were several serious problems with his claim to ownership.

"Is that so?" Max asked. "And what might they be?"

He thought he saw a brief flash of amusement in the otherwise cold and indifferent eyes of the official as he replied, "You haven't even established that you are who you claim to be."

"You've seen my passport," Max objected.

"No offense, but it might be a forgery."

The official's face was once more correct and impenetrable.

For a while, Max and this official left each other alone while Max waited for corroborating documents from New York. The Manhattan police sent a letter to the effect that there were no records of charges against him, not a single previous conviction, not even a traffic violation, neither a parking nor a speeding ticket.

He needed a confirmation of residence, Max explained over the telephone to the sergeant at his local station. He relaxed as soon as he heard the officer's casual colloquialisms.

"What's up, buddy?" he asked.

Max could just picture the man he was talking to: a stocky fifty-year-old Irish-American amused by the unheard-of request that he send to Europe official confirmation that a Mr. Max Berman owned an apartment on the Upper West Side.

"Confirmation of residence," he said to someone in the background, "have you ever heard of a confirmation of residence? You should probably call your building supervisor," the officer suggested.

Finally a lawyer who had often helped out when Ben got into trouble was able to obtain the necessary document and advised him to engage an Austrian lawyer to pursue his suit.

"Enjoy yourself in Europe," he said, "and let somebody else who's qualified do the work for you."

But Max clung stubbornly to the idea that he had to regain his inheritance on his own. It was like a game with rigid rules and no shortcuts allowed.

A congenial, slightly perplexed official at the Registration Office regretted that Max had not come to them sooner. If he had come sooner, the Commission for the Restoration of Property would have taken up his case and would have known exactly what to do. He, too, thought that Max needed professional help.

Another official, this one suspicious and monosyllabic, regarded Max over the top of his glasses as if he were a con man trying to swindle him. Every time Max entered his office, he was sitting with a notepad in front of him, chewing morosely on a pencil. But once he got warmed up, he cheerfully placed obstacles in Max's way. He held long abstract discourses on the laws of inheritance, on testamentary and non-testamentary shares in an estate. It seemed to make him happy to display his knowledge to an attentive listener. When Max brought the discussion back to his own case, the official, with great zest for action, started drawing up a *strategic plan*. That's how he put it, "It's imperative for you to have a strategic plan. The first thing we have to do is secure the death certificates of the deceased owners."

"But three of them were murdered. How am I supposed to get death certificates?"

He was not qualified to answer that question, the official explained impassively. "How do you know they were killed, anyway, if you can't prove it?" he asked.

Max kept control of himself, "My uncle was deported to Dachau in the spring of 1938. My aunt was taken straight from the loading ramp to the gas chamber in 1944. My grandfather starved to death in Lódz."

The man leafed through his documents in embarrassment. This turn in the conversation had made him uncomfortable, but only briefly, for he'd just discovered something in his papers that seemed to give him relief.

"Just a moment here," he cried happily, "this changes everything. Look, the house was legally expropriated because of tax fraud. In that case you have no chance at all of getting it back, since it was duly and properly seized. As a purely legal matter," he added with an engaging smile as he looked up into Max's face.

Without a word Max strode from the room and went straight to Spitzer's office.

"I can't take this anymore," he said and sank onto the cracked leather of the visitor's chair in front of the desk.

Spitzer laid his hand on the telephone receiver. "Should I call the lawyer now?"

"Do I have a choice?" asked Max resignedly.

The lawyer, Dr. Leitner, an unimposing fellow whose sandy-colored exterior was reminiscent of the camouflage of certain wild animals, was optimistic. There was nothing unusual, he said, in a verdict of millions of marks owed to the Tax Office of the *Reichsgau* against a dismissed official and small shareholder whom this *Reichsgau* was about to relieve of his property and his life. He mentioned similar cases that hadn't taken more than six years to be settled and sought to calm his client with reassuring gestures of his manicured, almost graceful hands. Those cases were from the early fifties. Everything was much more difficult back then, he explained. Back then the country was still contesting its legal succession from the *Reichsgau*, bolstering its argument with a decision of the Constitutional Court. And besides, he said with almost inaudible irony, back then one still had to deal with government officials who had been economic advisors to the *Reichsgau* as early as 1938 or '39. "The majority of them have retired in the meantime." Dr. Leitner gave a subtly cryptic smile.

In an astonishingly short time Dr. Leitner was able to unearth brownish crumbling documents bearing the Imperial Eagle and the swastika: the entire correspondence among the Tax Office, the Property Administration Office, and the Gestapo. Received, processed, transferred to the local District Administrator over the signature of a *Staffelführer* and the salutation *Heil Hitler!*, appraised in reichsmarks and later, when it was all up for sale, discounted, everything inventoried—the furniture, a Biedermeier console table. Suddenly all these objects stood clearly before Max's eyes again: the little oil painting by Pissarro of an avenue of autumnal trees, a picture that had always filled him with inexplicable despondency; lace curtains and various Oriental carpets (including the one with the mysterious beasts), Meissen porcelain figures (a shepherd boy was missing one of his delicate little hands), a two-armed and a nine-armed silver candelabrum (Sabbath and Chanukah), a complete service of Meissen (with gold edges and an onion pattern; it was reserved for the holiday table), pearl cufflinks (while their owner wore prison stripes in Dachau), two wristwatches, a double strand of pearls, a pair of emerald earrings that Max could not imagine without the ears of their owner—without the arms, hands, the human beings who had worn all of these things. These he saw all the more clearly before his mind's eye: slim, slightly anemic Aunt Sophie with her great frightened eyes, withdrawn and inconspicuous next to her high-spirited sister, Albert's round bald head in the photo on the terrace.

From this correspondence Dr. Leitner deduced the following chain of events: a *Sturmbannführer* in the SA had expressed interest in the villa—suddenly they were calling it a villa. In his application he made reference to his persecution under the Austrian Republic, demanded reparation for the damage he had incurred, actually demanded the house as compensation for his sufferings under the Dollfuss regime. The Tax Office requested permission to *interrogate Albert Israel Kalisch, in protective custody in the Dachau Concentration Camp since March 15th of the year 1938. Request denied* by the Security Service. Instead, Sophie was summoned to appear. There was no record of her interrogation. After that, in the early summer of 1938, she must have been removed to Vienna. That's where Mira sent the first affidavit, Max remembered, but he couldn't recall the address. Why hadn't Sophie tried to get out? With the affidavit she could have bought Alfred's release.

Among the official correspondence with letterheads sporting the Imperial Eagle was a handwritten letter from Sophie to the Tax Office in H. "My husband," she wrote, "who was put in the Dachau Concentration Camp for tax evasion, possesses neither the means nor the character for such fraud." The letter was dated 30 June 1938. Did she still believe in the official lies at that point in time, or that the whole thing would prove to have been a mistake? Was she waiting for Albert to be exonerated? She had no funds, she wrote, but an affidavit for herself and her husband was on its way. Hadn't Saul and Mira already sent the affidavit in May? Hadn't it arrived? Had she changed addresses? Was Max mistaken about the dates? Could it have been that she was afraid to go to the office where she would have to stand in line to apply for a *Steuerunbedenklichkeitsbescheinigung*—a tax clearance certificate? By that time Sophie was no longer young. She must have been over fifty. Had she gotten sick? Would she have kept it secret from Mira if she had been bedridden? What had she witnessed or experienced in the streets of Vienna in the months before the pogrom that made her flee—on the spur of the moment and before Albert could be released from Dachau—first to Prague and then Budapest? There she had relatives on her mother's side, the mother who had died as a young woman.

Max contemplated Sophie's handwriting, familiar to him from her letters to his mother: a nervous, erratic hand in which individual letters seemed to head off in all directions. Maybe she'd been left-handed like Benjamin, maybe just beside herself with fear. In Mira's reminiscences she was a dreamy, timid girl, childish, unworldly, and secretive. She'd taken so long to show interest in boys that their father was starting to worry. She married late—much later than Mira, although she was five years older. She had married a dependable, quiet man whom nobody could remember very well. Sophie didn't look very much like her younger sister, and she possessed none of Mira's lust for life, her carefree self-confidence. But also nothing of Mira's rebelliousness, quick temper, and fits of despair. Instead of rebelling, Sophie would run away. That's just what she did when she fled to her relatives in Hungary, although she hadn't seen them since childhood. She couldn't stand it anymore in the room they'd assigned her to, she reported to her sister. She had to share the room with a family of five. What did she do during those months in Vienna? Did she wander around the city? Did she sit shyly on her bed all day in that room, unable to assert her own rights against the demands of the others? She'd been Saul's receptionist and later spent a few years working in a lawyer's office. She read a lot. The open books lying upside-down on chair arms, tables, even on the edge of the bathtub, were always Aunt Sophie's books. In those days, after she'd been evicted, had she taken some books along? Did she have enough privacy to flee into the protective world of a book?

There were moments when Max saw Sophie with unbearable clarity: timid, desperate, alone. Albert, who was a good deal older than she, had been her only protection in life, because life—even her serene peacetime life—quickly became too demanding for her. Inconceivable that she had simply left Albert in the lurch.

For all the thoroughness with which the correspondence of the *Reichsgau* documented the confiscation and redistribution of their property, the dispossessed themselves were barely visible. It wasn't about them, after all. They'd been removed. They no longer stood in the way as the skirmishing got under way among the Tax Office, the Security Service, and the Provincial Administration, for each institution of the new government asserted its claim to most of the booty. An official of the Provincial Administration puzzled over whether Albert Israel had now *changed his place of residence to*

Dachau, since Dachau was located within the territory of the Reich, or was it a case of emigration? At issue was the payment of the *Reichsfluchtsteuer*, the penalty fee for fleeing the Reich, which had to be discharged from the *proceeds of the sale of real estate* since Albert and Sophie were now destitute and thus of no more interest to the local authorities. The correspondence between the Main Revenue Administration and the Provincial Administration dragged on for many months. Finally, in December 1939, the Tax Office, which for two years had been the acting owner of the confiscated booty, received official notification that it was *released from the obligation to pay the Reichsfluchtsteuer*, since it had been positively established that— as the notice put it—*Albert Israel Kalisch has merely changed his place of residence within the territory of the Reich*.

The history of the house was far from over at the murder of its owners, a fact Dr. Leitner had to remind Max of, for he seemed to be losing interest in the face of so many documents and the subtlety with which the authorities had haggled over their prey.

"She was unworldly," Max said in discouragement. "My mother always said so. 'If only Sophie hadn't been so unworldly.'"

"In those days you couldn't afford to be unworldly," Dr. Leitner remarked dryly.

The SA *Sturmbannführer* who apparently took credit for Albert's arrest continued to insist on his right to acquire the property at a favorable price. His application, however, was turned down, for the son-in-law of the Provincial Director had become interested in the villa. The Provincial Director issued him an *Unbedenklich-keitszeugnis*—a Certificate of Nonobjection—and emphasized that his *Aryan family tree had been growing in German soil from the beginning and without interruption*. The son-in-law purchased the house and land for a fraction of the amount that Albert had been accused of evading in taxes. In addition to the villa, he acquired a rum and liqueur distillery whose previous owner had been Jewish, and in which Albert had held some stock. The son-in-law had been a member of the NSDAP since 1928 and on the application for purchase listed his occupation as "businessman." He was obviously proud of a 1934 indictment for civil disorder that had forced him to flee to the Reich. He returned to Austria in March 1938 to organize the plebiscite in his electoral district. He declared his total net worth to be 60,000 reichsmarks, but in answer to the question, "What amount do you intend to invest?" he wrote "RM 5,000." This party member and *Obergruppenführer* got the house for nine thousand reichsmarks, of which he paid eight hundred in cash.

He lived in the house for five years with his wife and three children. Max found one of them, the son, in the telephone book. He was tortured by the thought of the Provincial Director's daughter in Sophie's kosher kitchen.

In 1943 the *Obergruppenführer* went bankrupt along with his liqueur distillery. The house was taken over by the subletters, a party member from the National Socialist Social Welfare Organization and the wife he had married that same year. At the end of the year, ownership of the house was transferred to the Provincial Administration. The party member, not drafted because his work was critical to the war effort, remained in the house even after 1945. Although dismissed from his job by the U.S. Military Government, he was hired back by the city in 1947, being a *person of minimal culpability*. So now Max knew the name of the woman who had refused to answer him or let him into the house on his first visit at the end of the war. She would be about fifty now, his own age. Her children were probably at university or already had their own families. When they talked about "home" they meant his house. Their memories of childhood were of the rooms from which people like their parents had driven Sophie and Albert to their deaths. Here they had celebrated holidays and birthdays, here the party member and his wife had spent their twenty-seven years of marriage. They had practically become *indigenous*, and if you asked the neighbors how long the couple had lived here they would say, "Forever. For as long as we can remember." Sure, they weren't the owners, but what difference did that make? They had a life-long right to live there and paid a laughably small rent to the municipality of H.

Max no longer felt like asking the neighbors any questions. He thought he knew enough. He walked up the hill once more to take pictures of the house beneath the tall trees, the neglected terrace, the windows with their net drapes tightly drawn—a fortress that refused to reveal its interior because it belonged to other people and would still belong to them even if the municipal administration had restored to him what was his. How could he expect people who were almost exactly his age to freely surrender the place they called home? The house would be his in the foreseeable future, his lawyer promised, but Max had no wish to see their rooms or come into contact with their petit-bourgeois domesticity. He would preserve inviolate the images that Mira's recollections had left in his memory.

On one occasion Max was sitting across a desk from a young judicial official who had the same last name as the party member. It was a common name in this city, as one could see from the long list in the telephone book. This official paged apprehensively through the title register. He admitted that it was the first time he had ever had to deal with a problem of this sort. He spoke very quietly, in a pained voice, as if looking for the right words of comfort in the room of someone gravely ill. His newly healed acne scars were glowing from shame or embarrassment. Max felt sympathy for this young man but also wondered suspiciously whether his guilt-ridden naiveté were credible. Had this fellow really never wondered what had happened in addition to the war, which he was perhaps just barely old enough to remember? Max was unsure of himself, just as he'd been at the time that Mira's illness was just beginning to be noticeable, when she sensed persecution in every unfriendly gesture, every random remark. Was she catching wind of something he simply lacked the antennae for, he'd asked himself, or was she simply being tortured by the casual thoughtlessness of everyday life? He'd fended off his mother's suspicions with forced optimism because he couldn't stand to see how she was being consumed by fear. In general, Max liked people. He was easily moved by their sorrows and hardships, sometimes even to tears. Whence the distrust he so readily felt since coming to this town, he wondered?

When Max strolled through the streets of H. on days like this and looked into people's faces, he asked himself every time, would they have hidden me or reported me? He ended up sensing the same unease that had hounded his mother through life. On some days, the faces of the people he encountered filled him with an indefinable fear. He didn't trust them, any of them. In the inn next to the train station, where he was still staying, they'd gotten used to him. The landlord continued to treat Max with a certain cautious watchfulness and on some days with ironic obsequiousness. But the aged chambermaid, who groaned every time she bent over, so that Max gave her a hand whenever he happened to be in the room while she was straightening it up, as well as the landlord's wife, both seemed overjoyed every time they caught sight of him.

"How do you explain it?" he asked Spitzer. "On the one hand they claim to know nothing, on the other they treat you with this mixture of subservience and arrogance. And when you talk to them, they act insulted and look away."

"That's just the way they are," Spitzer said imperturbably, "small-town folks. They're insecure, afraid."

"And what about that young judicial official who was so ignorant?"

"They didn't talk to their children about it," Spitzer said.

Max shrugged his shoulders. "After all, I didn't come here to like this town or even to understand it."

He'd set himself a task, and when it was completed he would return home. For it had become clear to him during these weeks how much New York meant to him. There would never be a shadow of a doubt that that's where he belonged, between Alphabet City and Crotona Park.

But it wouldn't take long after his return for the old yearning for Europe to reassert itself. It wouldn't happen right away, but it would gradually take root and begin to influence his choice of the furniture and objects that he ordered for his customers, the projects he got interested in, as well as the women whose company he sought out. Even here in H. there were certain times and places when Max felt a fleeting sense of well-being, almost familiarity, that touched him lightly, like a vague recollection, an affinity that couldn't be explained. Were his old dreams reawakening, dreams of a Europe that had already been destroyed before he was born, the utopia of his mother's memories?

Every day he met his lawyer in a coffeehouse that made him almost feel transported back into that time. He liked the dusty light that filtered through its curtains, the impersonal, polite hum of voices, and also the reliable arrival of Dr. Leitner, about whom he knew nothing and who asked no personal questions. Leitner was properly turned out, from the high gloss of his polished shoes to the part in his thinning hair, and he imparted to Max the serene conviction that he would get his due in the end. Leitner's office would write to Yad Vashem, where they kept complete lists of the victims, he explained. His dry, elaborate formality often provoked Max to sarcastic comments that Dr. Leitner didn't understand. They confused him but he never allowed himself anything as emotional as being visibly insulted.

At the coffeehouse door, decorated with arabesques in milk-glass, Dr. Leitner briefly doffed his beige hat, gave Max his hand, and disappeared beyond the arcades, who knows where. Probably to his office, then later home to a supper prepared by an inconspicuous wife and then to bed. That's how Max imagined Dr. Leitner's life.

Max himself walked toward the wide Hauptstrasse, bustling at all hours of the day, past store windows in which he could see his own reflection, astonished that he wasn't more visibly different from other passersby. At a small, inviting bakery whose white curtains were always freshly starched, he turned into the Färbergasse and was immediately engulfed by the gloom of its narrow, crowded houses. Only an arched gateway granted a glimpse into an interior courtyard with an old linden tree.

The well-worn steps leading to the Jewish community center were by now so familiar to Max that he no longer needed to push the light switch next to the door. After a few steps, daylight from the second-floor hallway would illuminate the way. Spitzer was always there. He pretended to be busy, but Max had the impression that he was waiting for him. Like Dr. Leitner, Spitzer was a fixed point on his daily rounds through town, an interlocutor he could count on, and yet he knew hardly anything about him. Max would have thought it indiscreet to ask questions about Spitzer's private life. He was perplexed that such aloofness could coexist with so much friendly sympathy. It seemed to Max that the center of Spitzer's life must be located somewhere inaccessible even to himself, somewhere unimaginable.

"I was just with Leitner in the coffeehouse," Max reported. "I think he's the most decent and emotionless person I've ever met."

"He's extraordinarily passionate about injustice," Spitzer demurred.

Max gave an ironic smile. "He certainly would have hidden us."

"Is that the test," Spitzer asked, "you apply to everyone you meet when in doubt?"

"Does that surprise you?" asked Max. "How would you suggest I divide up the local population? Into humorous jokers who design strategic plans to place as many obstacles as possible in your way until you give up, and, on the other hand, decent, boring people like Leitner?"

"Leitner couldn't have hidden you," said Spitzer. "He was categorized as a second-degree *Mischling* himself."

Max was astonished. "And I thought I knew everything there was to know about him."

"You see," said Spitzer with an impish smile, "we're more complicated than you think."

Max felt offended by that *we*. Was it really possible to feel that one belonged here?

Leitner's history inspired Spitzer to start telling stories. He loved anecdotes, especially when they were macabre and full of black humor, and then at the end of the story, he laughed until tears ran down his cheeks. Spitzer couldn't stop laughing as he told the story of his cousin and got to the place where he was a waiter on a cruise ship off the coast of Florida and while bowing spilled a bowl of soup down the front of a lady's evening dress. The cousin started to cry, weeping so heartrendingly in front of everybody that the lady gave him some money and tried to console him. "But he just kept on weeping," Spitzer said, stifling a laugh. "He kept crying and she kept pulling bills out of her purse, which just made him cry all the harder." Spitzer looked at Max and guffawed. But Max wasn't able to laugh with him because he'd already heard the whole story and knew that the cousin had jumped from a boxcar and made his way through occupied France alone at the age of fourteen, from there to Cuba, then to Florida, later to New York, where he lived in a room with no outside windows except one on a stinking air shaft—and the accident with the soup had happened on the day he learned that, of his entire family, he alone had survived.

The cousin was doing well, Spitzer said, he had married in the meantime, had children, a good job and an apartment in Queens on the twenty-second floor of a highrise with a marvelous view. One of these days Spitzer would have to pay him a visit.

There were others, he said, some right here in the community, who weren't doing half as well as his cousin. Ilja, for example, that was a sad story. They had to look after him regularly. As a child he'd been hidden in a hole in the ground for four years by Polish farmers. Four years in which he wasn't allowed to speak, not even a word. And now, as the only person in his family who'd survived, Ilja was vegetating in a nursing home, silent and feeble-minded. "He never managed to return," said Spitzer.

Spitzer said little about himself. He was born and went to school in H., had his bar mitzvah in the synagogue next door.

They were standing at the window, next to Spitzer's enormous brown desk with a green ebonite inset, and looking down into the courtyard below, one side of which was formed by the eastern wall of the synagogue. A pile of wooden pallets lay in a corner against the firewall of the building opposite.

When they were clearing out a house in the Hofgasse a few years ago, Spitzer recounted, he'd discovered a Torah scroll in a dumpster in front of the building, without its ornamentation, missing its cover, just the parchment, tattered and torn, the upper layer softened by moisture, but rolled up and still legible. He'd recognized what it was by its wooden handles sticking out from under an old water-damaged rug. He hadn't seen it the previous evening, only noticed it in the morning, and it had been raining all night. Somebody must have kept it hidden all those years and then disposed of it secretly, by night and in the rain. Spitzer kept it in his office closet for a while, but it wasn't usable anymore, it was too damaged. They'd considered burying it in the cemetery. Finally his brother had taken the Torah scroll along to Israel.

He removed a photograph from his desk drawer, "Here's how the synagogue looked."

Max looked at the slightly overexposed photo of a classicist temple with broad steps leading up to the portal, Romanesque windows and columns, a round window with six-pointed stone masonry on the front facade. In the open drawer lay a photo of a young woman. Max picked it up.

"That's Flora," said Spitzer. "We were both twenty-one in 1946 and we got married. She died in 1954."

He took the photo from Max and pushed the drawer firmly shut.

"Why did she die so young?" asked Max.

Spitzer gave a slight shrug. "When she was liberated she weighed thirty-eight kilos. She never really recovered. I shouldn't have stayed here with her. We wanted to rebuild the temple," Spitzer continued in a strained voice, obviously eager to change the subject. He pointed over to the east wall of the synagogue. "Inside it was completely burned out. The roof had been burned, too. They finally had to put it out, or the fire would have spread to other buildings. Up to the end of the war it was a burned-out shell, then it was converted into a warehouse. We've been negotiating with the city for years about the restoration, a tough slog. But now the young people are running away on us. They're emigrating; why should they stay here? Sometimes I think, why should we rebuild the synagogue if nobody will be here to use it?"

"Where were you in '38?" asked Max.

"On the run, down the Danube in a freight boat with my older brother, just turned thirteen, a very sheltered child up to then, my pockets full of money and Mother's diamonds sewn into the lining of my jacket."

"And you came back again." It was more a question than a statement.

"My brother too, but no one else."

Max was silent. He didn't want to repeat the same question he had asked at their first meeting and sense Spitzer's withdrawal. But it seemed that Spitzer had anticipated the unexpressed question, for he said irritably, "You've got to have a home somewhere, you can't always choose for yourself. All sorts of people want to know why I subjected myself to this community as the center of my life, people I haven't asked for their opinion, and do you think anyone ever said, 'It's nice that you're back'? Not a chance. Of course the people who knew me before the war were uncomfortable that I'd come back. But somebody's got to take care of what belongs to us: the cemetery, the community center, the synagogue. I grew up here," said Spitzer with a trace of defiance. "I've got memories, including good ones. And anyway," he looked at Max in annoyance, "I shouldn't have to justify myself as if I'd done something bad, something somehow indecent."

"I didn't say anything," Max responded.

Delivery trucks pulled into the courtyard and parked for the night. Workers locked the gates of the warehouse.

"Let's go," Spitzer suggested. "It's six."

"And where were you in '38?" Spitzer took up the thread of their earlier conversation.

"In New York. I was in love with a girl from Vienna. It was the first time I was really in love. She was only a year older than me, but much more mature. I told her that my father had been born in Przemyśl. I'd always imagined Przemyśl as a village, a little romantic Hasidic village. She laughed at me: Przemyśl wasn't a village, to say nothing of Hasidic. I was enormously in awe of her, because I was absolutely unable to impress her in any way. Her name was Eva. After the war she sent me to college and married somebody else. But she nourished my passion for the Old World, she and my mother."

As on every Thursday, Spitzer tried to persuade Max to come to Friday night prayers.

"God's not my thing," Max demurred. "I could never work up much interest in God. I went to synagogue with my mother to make her happy. It was important to her to gather us all around the table and see how much we liked her food. I spent every Friday evening with her as long as she lived in her apartment in Brooklyn. Since then, I haven't been inside a synagogue."

"You don't have to pray," Spitzer said. "Just come once and take a look. Besides, we've had trouble lately getting ten men together."

"Maybe tomorrow," Max promised. But he knew that he'd spend tomorrow, too, in his room on the Bahnhofsplatz, with a bad conscience, thinking about how much longer he could hold out in this town.

Chapter 4

BUT BEFORE SPITZER had a chance to remind Max again of his religious duties, an unexpected funeral forced him to abandon discretion. Spitzer sent Nadja to go fetch Max and say he should come to the cemetery because they had only nine men and they needed ten to say kaddish. "He should come right away," he emphasized, "we're waiting."

Quick and determined, she ran straight across the park, blind to everything around her, with none of the coquettishness of young women self-conscious about their appearance, even when no one is watching them, as if always in front of a mirror.

Max was standing at his window wondering what he would do today. He'd been in town for a month. It was the end of September, beginning to get cool, and the evenings seemed to drag on forever. He watched curiously as a young woman ran across the grass. She wore flat shoes and her legs were a bit too short. A black skirt too tight across her hips revealed sturdy calves but not her knees. The wind blew her dark, straight hair off a high forehead. When she disappeared from view and there was soon a knock on his door, he knew that she was coming to him and that Spitzer had sent her. He had to come right away, she demanded, so peremptorily that Max instinctively resisted.

Couldn't she muster a bit more charm, a little of the art of feminine persuasion?

"Not now," Max said coolly, "I've got things to do."

"They're waiting for us to come back," she explained and continued to face him determinedly, but for some unexplained reason her face suddenly assumed a look of tense, almost joyful anticipation. From close up, Max found it an unusual face, especially in a town like H., which seemed to produce an astonishingly uniform-looking population. She gave the impression of being darker than she really was. He wondered what Tartar ancestor had handed down to her this wide face and pointed chin, these narrow, slanted, almost Asiatic eyes, this generous mouth now pouting reproachfully—her whole stubborn persistence. But she was looking at him with an expression of delighted recognition, so that he asked, "Have we met before?"

"No, no," she replied quickly, reddening, "I've just seen you on the street."

This flattered his vanity. Young women still noticed him even though he was fifty-one. How old was she, maybe around twenty? Immediately Max was ready to view her in a completely different light, no longer uncouth and lacking charm, but instead with an impetuous wildness he found delightful. At any rate, she'd awakened his interest and he agreed to come along.

"Let's go," he said. "Is it far?"

"No," she said over her shoulder, "ten minutes at the most." And she went down the steps ahead of him, as if leading him off.

As he walked along beside her he kept looking at her out of the corner of his eye and wondered if this could be the start of something that would be worth all the time and trouble involved in wooing a woman. Although he'd never been alone for very long, it had been a long time since he'd felt how intoxicatingly easy it was to fall in love. In time, his love affairs had come to resemble each other more and more, in a predictable pattern and—because Max was soon bored—of shorter and shorter duration. He considered himself knowledgeable about women and thought he understood them to the extent that any man could. He liked women, and certainly needed them for his sense of well-being. But sometimes, when he had to explain to yet another woman why he'd lost interest in her so quickly, Max would compare himself to a connoisseur whose palate over the years has grown more and more refined, more difficult to stimulate. He'd been overfed on love, so to speak. It wasn't exactly a complimentary thing to say, but it spared him endless arguments and crises, because there was only one cure for overeating—namely abstinence.

Then too, the losses he'd experienced in recent years, the deaths of Elizabeth and his mother, as well as of his teacher, the old sculptor in the woods of Vermont, had dampened Max's *joie de vivre* and enterprise.

"It's high time you got married," said a friend whose advice he'd always valued, "especially now when you're depressed and feeling alone, you could use the stability of a marriage."

But Max, already skittish about the effort necessary just for an affair, feared that marriage would mean a loss of freedom. Women were exhausting, he argued. If you wanted to make them happy— and that was the whole point of a relationship, wasn't it?—you had to be attuned to them, constantly show how much you loved them. You had to give them presents, and not just objects, but little attentions and surprises, otherwise the whole business lacked fun and excitement. Love required maximum effort, nothing held back. It was an attempt to discover what was unique about another person. And so Max was always disappointed but never surprised when he got so little from women who meant so little to him.

"What's your name?" he asked now, and looked at her profile. From the side she had something of the rapt clarity of Japanese ink drawings.

"Nadja," she answered and turned toward him a face with a generous, stubborn mouth and inquisitive eyes below thick eyebrows that almost grew together above the bridge of her nose. Keep talking, her glance seemed to urge him, ask me something. But she just said her name, and Max was silent.

"We've got to hurry," she said impatiently. "They can't begin without us and there's only nine men at the cemetery."

She's too bossy, he thought, too direct. He liked playfulness, the unexpected ambiguities of a flirtation.

It was hard to keep up with her. Nadja led with such determination that he began to get irritated again as they hurried along. She might look interesting, but she wasn't the least bit seductive. It was an unexpectedly long way to the cemetery and they were almost running the whole time, across busy streets without stoplights or crosswalks, past utilitarian commercial buildings and old gray apartment blocks. An express train slowed on an embankment high above them. At last they reached the wall of the cemetery. Tall trees with luxuriant foliage rose up behind it.

A small, forlorn flock of elderly people stood chatting around a fresh grave. There were no children, only a widow and friends. The widow approached Max and thanked him for coming. Spitzer, relieved that he had arrived, pressed a yarmulke into his hand. "So, now we can begin," he said. The coffin was already resting on wooden slats beside the dug-up pile of dirt. The sun was high in the sky by this time. Max had broken into a sweat running over here. Now, feeling the wind, he shivered. It was so quiet it seemed like the city on the other side of the wall and the morning traffic they had just made their way through had ceased to exist, leaving only the birds in the branches and the prayers he couldn't follow.

The name of the deceased was Mordechai ben Yitzhak, but his neighbors had probably known him by a completely different name. For a giddy fraction of a second, Max felt transported into the distant past. Then the men were grasping the spades. He did it, too, as if he'd come to the cemetery expressly to help bury someone he didn't know. Cool perspiration ran down his back. He felt quite young and strong among these frail old men. A warm sense of belonging pulsed through him as he turned to the others and read the thankful appreciation in their eyes. After all, what was the point of continuing to insist that he had nothing to do with them, that it was purely by chance that his parents were Jews, that he owed them nothing? Clearly, he was needed here. These people accepted him without question and without suspicion.

More than ever before and more strongly than in any other city he'd lived in, Max felt continually reminded here in H. that he was a foreigner. The feeling was reinforced by the swift, intense glances people directed at him. Every time he started to speak he noticed how people stopped to listen and wonder where he was from.

"Don't forget, this isn't New York," Spitzer would remind him from time to time. "It isn't even really a city."

But Max wasn't just any old tourist who attracted attention because he came from far away. It was as a Jew that he sat before the desks of the officials processing his suit to recover stolen property, as a Jew that he went in and out of his hotel. And if he himself had attached no significance to this fact, they wouldn't have let him forget it. You could read it in their faces, in their cautious, inquisitive glances. It showed in their eyes as reserve, self-consciousness, or uneasiness. Max caught them out in their startled, over-zealous friendliness when they found out who he was, as if they had been babbling too freely without self-censure, as if they'd been letting themselves get out of control. At home in New York, Max had hardly ever had to think about what it might mean to others that he was Jewish.

With an amused wink, Spitzer signaled his satisfaction on the Friday evening that Max appeared in the door of the sanctuary, one floor down from where they usually met, directly beneath Spitzer's big, gloomy office. He greeted him like an eagerly awaited guest and supplied him with a yarmulke and a prayer book. Contrary to what he'd feared, Max felt neither intrusive nor hypocritical just standing there and taking a look around, without intending to pray or expecting to feel gripped by sudden piety.

The sanctuary was severely plain and brightly lit. There were a few old benches, probably salvaged from the burned-out synagogue, and behind them rows of chairs as in a lecture hall. At the front was the high, flat *bimah* and behind it an unostentatious dark blue curtain covering the ark. There was something moving about this improvised simplicity, something provisional and transient that made one want to protect it, an impulse Max could seldom resist. And the congregation too—only a few family groups, many solitary individuals, more elderly than young—made a quiet, subdued impression that he had not expected.

With his mother Max had attended a little synagogue in which, unlike the big temples in Manhattan, the men still sat separated from the women and only men were called up to read the Torah. But even it held over a hundred people, and little kids had run noisily up and down the broad aisles and squealed with delight when their mothers caught them. As a bachelor Max had always felt a little out of place there, sensed an unspoken reproach that it was high time for him to get married and have children.

Nadja sat across the central aisle next to an alert-looking little old lady with cropped white hair that she briskly pushed out of her face from time to time. Every Friday evening these two sat contentedly together in the same seats, like mother and daughter, and whenever the old lady pulled Nadja's sleeve to whisper something in her ear, the girl leaned toward her attentively.

Max remarked to Spitzer that there didn't seem to be too many young people in the congregation.

"And why would there be?" Spitzer replied. "Nowadays, life's more exciting elsewhere. Israel attracts a lot of them. They're sent there to visit relatives or attend university, to learn Hebrew, and then they don't come back."

"Who's the old lady Nadja's whispering to?" asked Max, "A relative? Her mother?"

"That's our *rebbetzin*, the widow of Rabbi Vaysburg."

"Is that why Nadja treats her so respectfully?"

"Nadja's our foundling, our cuckoo's egg." Spitzer smiled affectionately at her.

At the age of thirteen, Nadja had shown up in Spitzer's office one day toward the end of the school year and asked if she could participate in religious instruction. The Catholic religion teacher in her school had kicked her out because she disrupted the class.

"And you won't disrupt our class?" Spitzer had asked.

"I don't think so," she said. The problem with the Catholic religion class was that she was Jewish.

Her tale about her mother's Jewish ancestry sounded pretty convoluted, and she couldn't produce any evidence for it. It often happened that way, Spitzer explained. Young adolescents expected to be taken into the community on the basis of some story of obscure Jewish extraction, either to show off or because they wanted to be something special, or often just because they were lonely and didn't want to be part of their own families anymore.

"We turn most of them away," Spitzer said. "Some come a few times and then stop coming on their own. But it was different with Nadja. Nobody could bring themselves to send her away, but nobody encouraged her, either." She was stiff-necked, however. From the start she wanted to be near Frau Vaysburg and would read along with her out of the *siddur*. Spitzer's niece Ofra taught her more about Judaism, but then later moved to Tel Aviv with her parents. Nadja also came to the bar mitzvah class and sat in the last row, the only girl. "That must have been seven or eight years ago," Spitzer calculated.

Sometimes he asked himself, Spitzer went on, if he should suggest that Nadja formally convert to Judaism, but he always decided against it. "One shouldn't proselytize, especially not in such a tiny community." The obscure Jewish grandmothers and great-grandmothers could be the pure invention of adolescents just trying to legitimize themselves. Spitzer didn't put much stock in such stories. But for Nadja he felt a kind of paternal tenderness. He never asked her directly about her parents, except in sentences like, "What does your father think about you coming to the Jews?"

"He doesn't care," Nadja had answered.

It appeared that her adolescent crush on Ofra, who was a few years older, had been transferred into a strong attachment to Ofra's uncle after his niece had emigrated. She sometimes walked home with him as far as his front door, frequently came to his office, asked him to take her along when he went to call on sick members of the community, and offered to be helpful in ways both welcome and unnecessary.

"Sometimes she's like a young animal looking for warmth," Spitzer said.

Nadja had also tried to ask Spitzer about how his parents died, what life was like before he had to flee, about his childhood in the thirties. But he'd brusquely rebuffed her curiosity. "Why don't you go ask your parents what it was like back then?" he'd said. He couldn't talk about those times, she ought to understand that—he didn't want to. He'd gotten quite emotional about it; she was abashed and had apologized. Later he regretted getting so upset. He took her along to visit poor Ilja because she asked to come. He himself didn't really think it right to let her see the misery of this soul that had become unhinged in the darkness and silence of a hole in the ground.

No, it hadn't been a good idea. She hadn't said a word the whole way back.

But to answer her question in his own way, Spitzer took her along to places he perhaps only sought out on her account, places as yet unmarked by signposts and commemorative plaques saying that on this spot had been an auxiliary branch of a concentration camp. He stood before houses that had been built in the fifties on the foundations of camp barracks and on top of buried corpses, until someone came out and asked sharply what he wanted there, or just shooed him away without saying anything.

"Don't you mind living here?" he would ask people. "Here, on this exact spot where your house is standing, Jews were murdered. Doesn't it bother you to live so cheerfully on top of a cemetery full of strangers?"

Nadja got to know a defiant, angry side of Spitzer, a side which only a few people ever got to see. Later she would realize that this was the way he had undertaken to educate her politically: without preaching at her and without revealing his own pain.

Once or twice she stuck her head into Spitzer's office when Max was sitting there. Every time she quickly said, "Sorry! I was just . . . " and withdrew, except for one time when the two men were just on the point of leaving. It was a radiant, almost summerlike fall day, but the office was still clammy and cool.

"Come along with us," said Spitzer when Nadja appeared. "We're going to the coffeehouse."

They sat outdoors in the garden of the coffeehouse next to the river. A breath of chilly air drifted up from the water despite the sun and the midges dancing among the brown-veined leaves of the chestnut trees. The opposite bank of the river sloped up, moist and darkly shaded, toward the cloudless autumn sky. "What a beautiful day!" Spitzer and Nadja agreed happily. Max imagined it was a river valley in a faraway land. He wouldn't allow himself any effusive feelings for this city. He wanted to keep it at a comfortable arm's length. Fleetingly, he wondered what it would be like to be in love in this town, and his eyes fell on Nadja's face. She was silent, lost in thought, and at this moment her face seemed small and sad. Her full mouth, with no lipstick, reminded him of the immediate postwar years when all the women, including his mother, made their lips up into just this curved heart shape.

Then Nadja and Spitzer started talking about Ofra. She wanted to be a singer. She'd been engaged. She couldn't find the right guy. What a beautiful woman! And how Nadja admired her. She doted on her so unselfconsciously, with such longing and vulnerability: Ofra hadn't written her even once. She never wrote anybody, Spitzer answered. What exquisite taste she had, Nadja gushed, the turquoise earrings, the Indian dress with little stitched-in mirrors!

Max asked if they could talk about something else.

"Sure," said Spitzer and put his arm around her shoulder. "Did you know that Nadja's a painter?"

She looked past Max in embarrassment, toward the sparkling river.

"Really?" asked Max with interest. "Have you had any shows? Do you earn a living at it?"

No, she admitted with embarrassment, she'd attended the art school in town and now worked in a printing shop. But she had a portfolio, she added proudly, and for the first time, there was a hint of feminine flirtatiousness in her eyes.

"What do you do in the printing shop?" Max asked.

"Nothing special," she said dismissively, "commercial graphics, poster designs, whatever the customers want." She shrugged. "It's a job."

"There are too many painters these days," Max said matter-of-factly.

She said nothing. Her chin and mouth tightened in tenacious determination. Let her dream: painter, Jew. Let her live in her dreamworld, Max told himself, if that's how she puts up with the cramped paralysis of this town. That will change as she gets older. But it made him indignant and depressed to know how soon all her hopes would be dashed. She was born in the wrong place, he thought. There's no chance for her here, only dreams that will fly away.

He'd like to take a look at her portfolio, said Max with emphatic cordiality, he knew a bit about painting.

Spitzer told her how famous Max was, he'd even restored a house on Fifth Avenue, the symbol of American opulence.

From Spitzer's cryptic smile and the ironic twinkle in his eye, Max gathered that he'd noticed and approved of his incipient interest in Nadja.

***

That evening, Max spent a long time looking at himself in the mirror. He liked what he saw. No doubt about it, his appearance was pleasing, engaging. His dark brown hair with reddish highlights was as thick as ever, just a little gray at the temples. It had grown a little long, but that looked good, made him younger. It was his concession to the times and the tastes of the young. A few gray or, more precisely, colorless hairs in his close-cropped beard were of no consequence at all. He was pleased with these subtle hints that he'd already acquired a good bit of life experience: the laugh wrinkles in the corners of his eyes, the bluish shadows that some days showed beneath them. Many years ago, as a young man, he'd acquired through practice a clouded-over glance, until some woman—it was probably Eva—told him it was too theatrical. But it had already become habitual and appeared on its own as soon as he approached a woman. Spitzer was one or two years younger than he. Even so, he gave the impression of being older, somehow more worn out, with stooped shoulders and thin gray hair. Max had never seen him with a woman.

How did twenty-one-year-old Nadja see them, him and Spitzer? As old men in whom she could confide, in whom she could have a childlike trust? She seemed to him very innocent and inexperienced.

Yes, Max had already asked himself why it was that, up to now, he had not felt the need to try to meet any women in H. Perhaps it was because he didn't trust the people here, not even those born since the war. He would want to ask any young woman he was attracted to what her father had done during the war, and even if he could have refrained from asking, the question would linger between them as a suspicion. It could turn out that the fathers of one or two of these lovely young women had been directly involved in the death of his relatives. It was a small town, with none of the anonymity of a big city. In Nadja's case, he sensed that she was unhappy, that she found this town insufferable and was seeking to escape it, with the angry determination that made her so unapproachable. He thought he understood how she felt and he even admired her, but he was hesitant to approach her only on the strength of this sympathy unless he also felt attracted to her. Let's just see how things develop, Max told his reflection. As far as women were concerned, he always relied on instinct.

Max spent many days in the library studying the official bulletins of the town government for the years 1938 to 1945. He wrote down names, compared them to those mentioned for particular commendation in the *Völkischer Beobachter*, then looked them up later in the telephone book. He found them there, with the same official titles, but now multiplied and supplemented by the names of their children and grandchildren. Triumphant, Max showed the list to Dr. Leitner, who shrugged and displayed not the slightest surprise: but of course, where would they have gone, anyway?

"If they haven't died, you'll find them in the telephone book," he said dryly.

"Everything's going like clockwork with the house," he reported. "Everything's under control." Dr. Leitner was a walking repository of stock phrases that cleverly concealed what he was thinking. But he must have had some sort of feeling when he said, "We've had your grandfather declared dead." He pushed the notarized copies of the death certificate across the desk to him. It had to mean more to him than just removing a few impediments in order to obtain the return of a house for a client.

I don't want the house any more, Max wanted to say. But he knew that he only wanted to say it so that he could, just once, shock Dr. Leitner.

Instead he asked, "When can I move in?"

Dr. Leitner's sandy eyebrows rose toward the hairline above his forehead. Now he did seem troubled. Actually, the situation was as follows: provisionally he was free to use the attic. Two rooms, but with no bathroom or kitchen. The trouble was, it was unlawful to evict people from rent-controlled domiciles.

"You mean I'm supposed to sublet rooms in my own house?"

"That way you could look after everything on your property better," Dr. Leitner suggested. "The house needs repairs. I'd recommend that you oversee the work yourself, otherwise it could get expensive."

"You mean, this is just the beginning of my expenses, and for my trouble I'm allowed to live in two attic rooms?"

This fellow had to be an idiot, Max thought, if this was his advice. Just a plain idiot behind all his decency, his emotionless obsession for detail, feebleminded in thought and feeling. He rose and coolly took his leave.

"I can wait," said Max, "even if it takes thirty years for the last one to leave."

He went straight to see Spitzer.

"Yes," said Spitzer, "I know what that's like. Flora and I lived in one room in my parents' house for eight long years, and the other tenants wouldn't even say hello to us."

"I'll wait till it's empty," Max insisted.

He felt weary and defeated as he walked toward the train station through streets of dour middle-class houses with repellent gray facades. For two months he'd been returning to the station every day like a commuter, like a homeless person. He had vaguely imagined that he would finally move into his house as its owner, if only for a short time—a month, a week, perhaps just one night—in order to savor the triumphant return that should have been Mira's.

———

The following Friday evening, Max called Nadja and was gratified by her unconcealed joy at his invitation for coffee. He decided she had a pretty smile. Why should he leave without at least having a little flirt?

When Max reached his favorite café at the appointed time, Nadja was already sitting at one of the round marble tables, her face turned expectantly toward the door, and when he entered a smile flitted across it. On this morning dense fog hung at the windows and even seemed present in the room itself, a translucent veil that obscured the chandeliers and dimmed the sconces. After their greeting, he had barely sat down when Nadja silently shoved her portfolio toward him. No idle chatter for her. Max took a napkin and painstakingly polished his narrow gold-rimmed glasses—a small, symbolic protest against her peremptoriness. In the murky, subaqueous light he took a look at her drawings. He could see this much: she lacked Elizabeth's light touch as well as her bold imagination. But still, did she have something? A trace of the talent needed to be a painter? *Bridge Club*, she'd written on the lower margin of a pen-and-ink sketch. Too detailed for a caricature, he noted. Still, he knew these types. He'd bumped into them everywhere in H., and he had to admit that he'd never seen them before in such a pitiless, hard light as the one they sat in here, malevolent, quarrelsome, and blasé. Or a pencil drawing with the title *Sunday Afternoon*: yes, they strolled up and down the avenue just so, wearing Tyrolean outfits, hats on their heads, handbags dangling from cocked arms, with sly, sidelong glances, jutting chins, and stolid faces.

He stole a quick look at Nadja. How she must hate living here, how unhappy she must be. She was eagerly watching his hands as they turned over her drawings. He pushed the sheets a little farther away and suddenly saw them more clearly, saw the amateur draftsmanship, the clumsy hand. She won't make it, thought Max, she'll perish here but she'll never be a painter, not even a caricaturist.

Their eyes met, and he read in hers the conviction that he had the power to make her dreams come true. Her credulous gaze was like blackmail, a pressure in his guts—her graceful hands grasping the coffee cup, the lace collar of an embarrassingly theatrical blouse, worn specially for this occasion when, perhaps for the very first time, she was revealing to someone else her angry, tortured soul.

Was it possible to simply tell her, You haven't got the talent?

The rays of sunshine that were beginning to disperse the fog struck her dark eyes and left cheek. Quite possible that she had Jewish ancestors as she claimed, thought Max, as if something too indeterminate to name was revealed in her face—as just a moment ago in her drawings—that he hadn't noticed before.

"Do you have a good camera?" he asked. She looked at him in surprise.

"Because you have the eye," he explained, "but not the hand."

She shut her portfolio and looked at her hands. She shoved out her lower lip like a naughty child. He hoped she wouldn't start crying.

"Try photography," he suggested.

She shook her head and looked straight ahead.

He was relieved. She wouldn't cry. She looked angry, hurt, disappointed, and stubborn. Even if she had more talent, it wouldn't help her. Nadja needed to get out of here. She's still in rebellion with these drawings, thought Max, with this furious view of her surroundings and also this claim to be Jewish that probably turns her whole family against her. But if she stays here, she'll give up sooner or later, marry a local guy. And she can't be too choosy, either, because she's not the type they're used to here. Her family will insist on a church wedding and baptizing the children. At forty her youthful dreams—painting, Judaism—will be far behind her, with just enough left for a bit of nostalgia when she thinks back. Why should she be different from everyone else, stronger than her origins?

Max, silent, waited patiently for her to recover. To distract her from her disappointment he finally asked her about youth culture here in town. Had she been aware of '68 or maybe even participated?

"You mean Israel?" she asked.

"Israel? How come?" Max inquired in perplexity.

"Because everybody emigrated five, six years ago. Almost everybody."

No, he explained with amusement, he meant the counterculture, hippies, Vietnam, flower power, all that stuff. He didn't think much of it, himself; that wasn't what being political meant, in his opinion. He found the aimless energy of these young people tiresome and their slogans naive. And as for the girls, their uninhibited frankness was totally lacking in subtlety.

"Oh, you mean the students," she said indifferently. Her glance became vacant and wandered about the room. She was silent. She didn't seem to get the idea that it was her turn to ask him about something.

In his desperate search for a new topic that could interest her, it finally occurred to Max to ask who her favorite painter was. Instantly her eyes lit up. "Lionel Feininger," she said, "Joseph Stella. You know them?" He nodded, told her about shows he had seen, how as a child he'd regularly gone to the newly opened Whitney Museum. She leaned forward with eager excitement. "And Edward Hopper, have you seen his pictures?"

"You've got to come to New York," he exclaimed. Her excitement was infectious. "I'll take you to all the museums and to the galleries in the Village." He was getting carried away, told her about gallery owners he knew, talked about painters who were friends of his, and under the influence of her delight and his own homesickness for New York he forgot that he was making her all sorts of promises he had no intention of keeping.

It was almost noon when they got up to leave. Their conversation about painting had led to his stories of New York, and once he got started he didn't know where to stop.

"The first time I saw you," Nadja told him, "you'd just bought a *Kipferl* in the bakery and you were eating it as you walked along. I figured you must be an American, maybe from New York."

They crossed the Stadtplatz and walked along the river beneath an allée of chestnut trees. He let her choose the route. Prickly gray-green chestnuts lay on the path, some without their husks and glossy brown. Max bent down and picked up two of them. He offered her the larger one. "Until we meet again in New York," he said.

Mist was rising from the river like steam from a hot bath, rippling gold in the sunlight. Max drew Nadja to him and kissed her. Yes, he knew that this was another irresponsible promise, but he'd worry about that later. What mattered now was to follow his instincts and do what the moment required. She was completely inexperienced, as he had guessed. Her fear of what was happening to her seemed as great as her desire for it. Her whole body was trembling. He put his arm around her waist, and they strolled on. Her solemn silence made him uncomfortable. It's not as important as you think, he wanted to tell her, it's just an attack of romance. But he said nothing. Anyone encountering them would have taken them for two lovers. It's possible that she thought so, too.

Nadja led him to a part of town that Max had never been to before, two-story houses strung along the road almost like a rural village, with rear windows looking down past retaining walls and terraced gardens to a landing along the river.

"This is my place," she declared, "in the rear wing. You can't see it from the street."

They stood facing each other at an embarrassed distance.

"I'll give you my address," she said in the resolute tone he had become familiar with. She fumbled in her portfolio, tore a corner off a piece of paper, divided it in two and handed him one half. They exchanged addresses as if it were a business transaction.

"I'd love to come visit you," she repeated with a sad smile. Then she held out her hand. How slim and cool it was, like a piece of glass. Now he understood what her smile was all about. It betrayed a vulnerability she otherwise kept hidden.

———

Not long afterward, Max left town. He hadn't seen Nadja again, nor had he paid another visit to his house. Whenever he went away, left either a place or a woman, it seemed to him that he had already become estranged from what he was leaving. Soon the house that Mira had spent her whole life yearning after would belong to him. But it was a foreign house in a foreign city, a city that seemed to him like a living being, overgrowing the past in stubborn proliferation, a dull, sometimes malicious, sometimes abused creature with an unmistakable scent he had learned to recognize.

Spitzer and Dr. Leitner accompanied Max to the station. He was glad to be leaving, he said, but he would write, he would call. Spitzer should visit him in New York; they'd see each other again, maybe soon.

The roofs were black with soot and moisture and the streets shone with rain as the train pulled out of the town. The landscape was drowning in the sodden twilight of a sunless day. Tomorrow morning he would be in Rome. He was relieved and at the same time a little depressed, as if he had forgotten or misplaced something important.

Chapter 5

BY THE TIME Max finally got back to an already wintry New York from his trip through Italy and Switzerland, he had long since forgotten Nadja. Indifferently, he put her address into one of the many boxes piled in a closet that contained all sorts of souvenirs.

His address, on the other hand—scribbled onto a piece of paper torn from her sketch pad—lay on Nadja's desk. A framed photo of her mother, who had died as a young woman, stood on the desk, too, above a set of little compartments and drawers. The slip of paper with Max's almost calligraphic handwriting greeted her when she came home at night, like a ticket to freedom.

Nadja's world was a cold place. She couldn't afford to be choosy about where she found a fire to warm her hands for a moment. If she was to have any chance for liberation, it would have to come from outside, for she wanted nothing to do with the people life had stuck her with.

Since moving to this town as a ten-year-old with her father, she had refused to be a part of his life, to use the words *my family* when talking about him, her stepmother, and her half brother. But what choice did a ten-year-old have—without relatives, without advocates—but to accept things as they were? No one treated her cruelly, no one excluded her. They gave her time to mourn her

mother, didn't force her to call the new wife *Mother*, were understanding that she didn't want to go to her father's wedding, never
gave anyone a birthday card, not even once. It was a gratuitous
provocation when she cut their wedding picture in two, threw half
into the trash, and put the other half with her father's picture into
a frame that was too big for it. She caused trouble, became insufferable, starved herself during the day and cleaned out the refrigerator at night. She tried to drown herself in the public swimming
pool, tried to catch her death of cold. Finally they banished her to
a little attic room in the rear wing of the house, next to the garden. By absenting herself and ignoring them, Nadja tried to ne-
gate the existence of her new family—if possible, to extinguish
them—and the sight of this rebellious, angry child infuriated not
just her stepmother but all her relatives and visitors to the house.

Nadja's father was a taciturn man. She'd never been able to find
out if he loved her; in any case, he ignored her. If she wanted to
be with him, she had to chase him down, catch him alone, working in the garden on weekday evenings or on Saturdays. "I've got
to talk to you," she'd say, blocking his path as he dragged the garden hose through the vegetable beds to water the roses he'd propa-
gated himself and was so proud of. Then at some point she'd start
to cry, so every one of her attempts to approach him ended in a
despair that couldn't reach him because he hated emotional outbursts; he'd had all he needed of them in his first marriage. She
could read his disapproval from his tightened lips and flaring nos-
trils, at which point it made no sense to run after him and throw
herself at him.

Nadja's father had no friends, just the acquaintances introduced
to him by his gregarious wife and one chess partner who showed
up punctually every Sunday evening. When his chess partner died,
Nadja's father attended the funeral, sat emotionless through the
dinner that followed, then put the chessmen and board away in a

drawer that was seldom opened again. He'd gotten through the death of his first wife, Nadja's mother, in the same way.

The woman who became his second wife was a font of received opinion. She divided the world into the pernicious and the useful. Earthworms in the garden were useful, cabbage white butterflies were pests, and she swatted at them furiously with a tennis racquet. Nadja was turning out to be a pest. She had to be removed from the house and stuck in a room above a shed in the back wing that could only be reached by climbing up a steep ladder. She couldn't leave this room without making noise because the ladder creaked and the shed door squealed, so they were always alerted to her arrival in the main house.

Those years of silence and emotional poverty had probably atrophied Nadja's need to communicate and her instinct for what others expected, but perhaps she'd already been that way: uncommunicative, rude, blunt. Any friendly approach would upset her balance; a cordial smile or a hand placed absentmindedly on her arm would bring tears to her eyes. As a child she'd had partial facial paralysis. The irregularity of her features—one eyelid somewhat drooping, a slight laxity in her left cheek—had almost completely disappeared, but she had lived with these blemishes for so long and worked so hard to get rid of them that she felt they had marked her for life and she considered herself ugly. Moreover, she had darkish down on her upper lip and chin that she plucked out with tweezers.

Nevertheless, Nadja yearned and loved and suffered just like all the other girls who had an easier time of it and some expectation that their feelings would be reciprocated. At sixteen she briefly managed to attract the attention of an eighteen-year-old. The happiness and excitement were almost too much for her to bear. She was determined to display all her stored-up treasures—everything she loved—to him as quickly as possible, before he had time to turn away. Her hair shampooed and shiny, forced against its will into curlers the night before, in a hopelessly unfashionable dress with red polka dots, she walked in breathless anticipation through the spring landscape beside this blasé high school boy. Intoxicated by the shimmering light, the first blossoms on the cider apple trees, the liverwort in the clearings, she recited poems that made her feel elevated and joyful. In boredom, he kicked pebbles along the path. In one last try, she insisted he climb the steep ladder up to her attic room and there she spread out her drawings for him: the prisoner whose knotty hands grasped the iron bars of his cell, the girl gazing at a distant landscape, the leafless tree at sundown. But he was more interested in the old calendar photos she had thumb-tacked to the wall: a landscape of dunes, a desert whose finely rippled sand looked like a yellow lake in a light breeze, dry earth baked and fractured by the sun, withered stalks in craters singed black.

"You like this stuff?" he asked.

"I like skeletons," she said and laughed.

"This is you, no doubt about it," the eighteen-year-old prodigy declared, "sterile, crippled emotionally and intellectually." He took great pride in his perceptive analysis. He said he wanted to be a psychologist.

Afterward she sat in her room that would never again be the same as it was. It had been devastated, was just as he had described it: sterile and dead.

The afternoon that Nadja went straight from her Catholic religion class to Spitzer's office, it was not on a sudden whim but rather a decision she had been weighing for a while although she couldn't adequately explain it.

Her mother's maiden name had been Siegel, a Jewish name, people said; her family came from the eastern provinces of the old Hapsburg monarchy and her mother was said to look Jewish.

That's why Nadja had brought along a photo of her mother, as a kind of proof. Spitzer was not impressed. Did she have any memories of Jewish relations, Jewish holidays, traditions, a bit of Jewish lore passed on from previous generations?

Nothing. Nadja shook her head. Just an uncle of whom it was said that he always wore a hat and acted Jewish. Clandestinely she used to observe him closely. When her father moved with her to H., they'd lost track of him.

"How do people act Jewish?" she'd asked at home and then realized immediately that this was a bad question, an embarrassing question. So she had immediately corrected herself, oh yeah, she knew what that meant. And so the grown-ups didn't have to answer.

"According to *Halakha* you're not a Jew," Spitzer declared.

"What's *Halakha*?"

"Jewish law."

This law wasn't satisfied with guesses and intuitions, to say nothing of unsettling experiences she didn't even understand herself and so wisely refrained from mentioning, both then and later. Going home from school, she usually took a shortcut through the Municipal Park where the trees formed a green tunnel over the path, just for a few steps, but long enough for her to feel transported to somewhere far away. On an early afternoon in June the leaves had been shining in the midday light like moist blossoms. Nadja was still smarting and enraged at an injustice she had suffered at school. Nobody had come to her defense or helped her, and she wouldn't even be able to talk about it at home. And then, beneath the bright green canopy, she suddenly felt an inexplicable certainty familiar only from dreams, a consolation that made her forget her fury and outrage, an answer she would remember forever after, even if she didn't know quite what to make of it now. Don't let it bother you, she thought, what's important is that you know you're Jewish. A free-floating thought, a rock-solid conviction that lasted but a moment, then fled and was gone by the time she reached home. Yet it stuck with her stubbornly and finally led her to Spitzer's office.

When Nadja attended services, she was relieved that Spitzer accepted her presence without much to-do, and no one else asked questions either. The first few times it took all her courage to sneak out on Friday evening before dinner, enter the building in the Färbergasse, go up to the second floor, and step into the room where astonished faces turned toward her and seemed to ask, What does this girl want from us? Frau Vaysburg always nodded to her in a friendly way. Nadja took it as an invitation to sit down next to her.

Where did she summon up this courage? Was it from the flash of intuition that everything that initially struck her as strange and even forbidden had some connection to her, and that some day she would understand as long as she didn't lose her direction? At first it was like walking a tightrope, each step taking her further from everything she knew. Even though she felt rejected by that world, still it represented solid ground. It made her dizzy to learn the new alphabet, spell words with it, to gradually grasp a system and its correspondences, until finally the scraps of knowledge she was cobbling together started to become familiar and make sense. She acquired knowledge furtively, as though no one was supposed to find out what an ignorant fourteen-year-old she was. She was embarrassed to be among the other pupils who kept her at a skeptical arm's length. She saw herself way up in thin air, on the high wire, dizzy but pleased with her daring. But again and again she would get tired and wish this exertion could be over. At such times she would become fearful. For now she was equidistant from both sides and would not survive a fall. It would be a plunge into the abyss. She would never be able to admit to herself that she had failed and all her exertions had been for naught. It was just that sometimes the shore she was journeying toward seemed unattainable. What if this tightrope walk away from all that was familiar was all that she would ever achieve, and the struggle for balance would last her whole life?

"Maybe you should convert to Judaism," Frau Vaysburg suggested. "Otherwise you're neither fish nor fowl."

"But I don't believe in God," Nadja explained.

Yes, that would make things difficult.

Nadja possessed neither the powers of persuasion nor the cunning to pretend she was pious. She had only her stubborn will power and the conviction that all the knowledge she was acquiring was of vital importance to her.

For a short time—maybe a year and a half all told, if she counted the cautious, shy beginnings of the friendship—Ofra, Spitzer's niece, transformed the city into a livable place for her. Those were the best years of her youth. With Ofra as her tutor she learned to read and write Hebrew, proud of her progress and eager for Ofra's unexpected praise. She was three years older and in Nadja's eyes singularly beautiful, with large animated eyes and exotic earrings beneath shoulder-length hair. She felt more real in Ofra's presence, singled out for something important. The first time Nadja sat on a café terrace with Ofra, it seemed to her that she had the entire population of the city at her feet in reverence and awe. Ofra penetrated her loneliness with circumspect questions, waited patiently while Nadja struggled to say what she meant. There were so many things that she had never articulated, that lay hidden in her drawings and sketches but were so hard to put into words.

When Nadja found the courage to speak she had to talk fast, for she feared that her friend would turn away in boredom before she was finished. At night in bed the dialogue went on in her head.

Her days were a never-ending monologue that flamed up into conversation and died down into happy exhaustion because it would
never be possible to say everything. But Ofra—Nadja was convinced—Ofra already guessed it all and understood.

She was in love with Ofra. That's why the city was suddenly so
transformed for her. Even on rainy days it glowed in a strange light.
Someone would have had to tell Nadja she was in love, and it was
only much later that she understood.

But her hunger had not yet been stilled when Ofra departed.
Ofra was eighteen, had graduated from school, and was going to
live in Israel. She was the first young person from the congregation to leave for Israel. The word *aliyah* was heard with increasing
frequency in conversation after the service, as if it signified an
aspiration to higher honors, a reward one could count on, a cure-
all for bad grades in school. It was a prospect closed to Nadja. The
boys Nadja had attended bar mitzvah class with grew up and disappeared. "You have to let go," said their parents. "You can't stand
in your children's way." When they came back from Israel for a
visit on the High Holy Days or for Passover they were tanned a
deep brown, had something radiant, almost heroic about them,
and they served in the Israeli Army. More and more often, even
among these Jews, the happiness of others caused her only pain.
They celebrated a bar mitzvah or a wedding and the family members that had survived the killing reassembled, unknown faces
from countries as far away as America or even New Zealand, and
filled the prayer room with the family celebrations Nadja had never
known. She was invited to the parties but she was reluctant to take
part in an intimacy that for her was fleeting. This was how one
could enjoy oneself, celebrate, dance the hora, if one had a family.
Spitzer was aware of her pain, gave her a quick hug, told her that
she had a Jewish soul, and whatever he meant by that, to her it
meant: you belong.

In the services, Nadja could count on Frau Vaysburg to sit next to her. During the long hours of the High Holy Days, while the holiday liturgy ebbed and flowed, the hard seats made her bottom sore and her toes got cold, while the men lifted out the Torah scroll and took turns reading and chanting the blessings, Frau Vaysburg told her stories in a quavering girlish voice about growing up on the Rumanian-Bulgarian frontier, about the land and the peasants who had helped them during times of persecution. She could remember the clothes she'd had as a young girl and the first time she'd seen her future husband, but every time she got to a certain point in her narration, she would abruptly change the subject, or her eyes would seek refuge in the pages of the prayer book and she would fall silent. For Passover she brought gefilte fish for Nadja, "So at least you know how it should taste when you make it for someone later on."

Frau Vaysburg put dreams into her head that could never come true. Where others had family stories, roots, traditions, togetherness, Nadja had nothing, neither roots nor soil, only emptiness. She was cut off from her mother's side of the family. They didn't maintain contact; there was no connection, not even an address. From her childhood she recalled a few visits with much older cousins who had no idea what to do with her and startled her when she was alone in the hall looking for the bathroom. They were only vaguely remembered adults, like the supposedly Jewish-looking uncle.

"You've got to decide," said Ofra on the Friday evening before her departure as they walked along the river through town, up the hill into a suburb, and back down the far side to the riverbank as evening turned into night.

Ofra thought it wasn't fair to have two different families, so to speak, two sets of loyalties, to swing back and forth between two allegiances according to your mood.

Nadja said nothing. What did Ofra think anyway? That she was firmly anchored somewhere else where she could blithely live a different life? That she only came to the prayer house out of sympathy, out of naive enthusiasm for anything Jewish, out of a feeling of guilt?

"They don't like us," said Ofra. "I've never felt like I belonged here. It's easier for you. You can choose how you want to live."

"There is no 'other side' I can choose to leave," Nadja tried to explain, and then fell silent at her own presumption. How could she know how Ofra had felt during all those years in school? The older girl never talked about how it felt when her schoolmates boasted about what their fathers had done in the war. Or when all her teachers reminded their classes of an upcoming Catholic holiday. Or when there were school prayers. The German teacher had once written an aphorism by Weinheber into her notebook, Ofra told her, then laughed about it: *Wer nicht gehorchen will, kann nie befehlen.* Who would command must learn obedience. For twelve long years she had been educated in a national tradition that was blissfully unaware of its own origins, that considered itself blameless but was merely shameless.

Nadja could see no chance to escape from home after she graduated from school. There was no money to finance university study in another town. At home they told her that girls don't go to university anyway, they get married.

Her father's wife told her, "Since you're not pretty, you can't afford to be choosy."

A year later, her stepmother began inviting the sons of her friends to dinner. She thought it was her duty. She meant well. It would be hard to marry off a plain, stubborn girl like Nadja. But

Nadja was not interested and promised herself she would leave at the first opportunity.

In the midst of her impotent rebelliousness Nadja acquired an unfailingly sharp eye for the town and its inhabitants. What she couldn't express in words, she drew in angry caricatures, laughable figures full of cunning malice. They brought her relief, granted a sort of superiority, even a brief liberation. They were her revenge.

She had finished school and had been working a few years in the printing shop. She lived quietly in her back room. Every Friday and Saturday, if she wasn't working, she attended services at the prayer house. She had taken over the job of decorating it for all the holidays from Purim to Chanukah, had become an indispensable part of the life of the community. Her impatience had been channeled into vague dreams: some day she would leave this town and never return, some day she would become a real painter.

The first time Nadja saw Max Berman emerging from the door of the community building in the Färbergasse, she had the fleeting thought that she had met him somewhere before. That's why she followed him instead of going up to Spitzer's office as she had intended. He was a stranger here, she saw that right away, and like everything else that came from outside the town, his appearance filled her with happy anticipation. Max was a bit disheveled. He had a short beard and wore a sport coat that would have fit a larger man. His hands were clasped behind his back and he barely lifted his big feet off the pavement as he ambled across the intersection as if it were a promenade. In front of a bakery he stopped abruptly and, taking off his glasses, pressed his thumb and forefinger to the bridge of his nose as though struck by a sudden idea. He walked on, but after a few steps turned back and entered the shop. Nadja kept going, but as she reached the corner and glanced back, he was just coming out holding a paper bag. He pulled out a *kipferl* and took a bite, then continued to eat as he walked on in his absent-minded, foot-dragging way. She smiled in amusement at his breezy lack of concern and it seemed to her that he smiled back.

Ever since the morning she'd fetched Max for the burial and recognized him, she would catch herself daydreaming about him but then quickly banish such thoughts. She took his appearance for a sign that change was possible in this town and in her life. The freedom she yearned for clung to Max like an exotic scent that would linger when he left. She had fleeting visions of a metropolis and was not the least bit surprised to learn that he lived in New York, because he was exactly how she had imagined a New Yorker to be: so easy-going that he ate from a paper bag on the public streets of H. and wore a jacket that sat much too loosely on him. Sometimes, when she included Max in her daydream conversations, she would talk to him in just that friendly, familiar way she imagined from her first impression of him. In his actual presence, on the other hand, she was uncertain of herself. She was afraid that Max thought her a provincial simpleton, and she was painfully aware of her inexperience with men. But she was sure that her drawings would impress him.

But then it turned out to be the drawings he didn't like, and Nadja was insulted by his suggestion that she should try photography instead. She felt misunderstood, yet everything that happened in her life after his departure was measured against his standard. She tried to acquire his ironic view of her world and hoped that he would write to her. His address lay on her desk like a pledge and after she had written him a long letter for Chanukah her days and weeks were consumed with waiting for a reply from him. In February, Max sent her a flattering Valentine's card signed, "From a distant admirer," and Nadja took it literally.

Chapter 6

WHEN MAX GOT Nadja's second letter in February, an Edward Hopper show happened to be running at the Museum of Modern Art. He sent her a postcard of the painting *Eleven A.M.* A naked girl, her face almost completely covered by her long reddish-blonde hair, sits in a blue hotel-room armchair and gazes at the dull late-morning light of a big city. He wrote that he'd walked through the show and tried to see the paintings through her eyes.

Nadja's letters were awkwardly written. Max sensed that she had sat and polished them for a long time, but their clumsiness was revealing. She never said what she really meant. It seemed that every sentence circled around her yearning to escape from H. and her desperate impatience was louder than what she actually said. He knew that he wouldn't be able to withstand this yearning much longer.

The thing that Max's friends liked most about him was his readiness to be of help. He might disappear from their lives for months or years at a time, ignore their letters, or fend off their telephoned invitations with a vague "Maybe later," but they knew that if they needed him, he would be there for them and nothing else would be more important. "My family history," Max would say, "has made intervention in crises second nature to me."

With women, his helpfulness was augmented by what he called ironically his Pygmalion urge, the pleasure he took in discovering talents that were not immediately apparent and giving them opportunities to develop. That's what inspired him, he said, the emergence of a talent they hadn't even recognized in themselves, a special quality or a new kind of beauty just waiting to emerge. That most of these young women eventually became his lovers Max ascribed to his charm. He abominated the idea of a woman being dependent on him.

Max conducted his affairs as an art in whose service no expense or effort was spared. Every new woman would reawaken in him an almost childlike astonishment: at how a smile could transform a face, how a tiny movement of the head could disarm him, how some women could express an entire spectrum of nuances between assent and vehement rejection with an almost imperceptible gesture or a look, how a fleeting glance from the far end of a room could follow him and not let go until he had found the woman who had lured him with her eyes. He was astonished at how being attracted to a plain-looking woman could make her beautiful, at the delicate balance among character, mood, and their visible manifestations. Max was a connoisseur of small gestures, of ambiguous messages, a fickle democrat of multiplicity, a collector with unbounded admiration for his discoveries and yet with no desire to make them his possessions. He was convinced that everything creative stemmed from desire and everything destructive from the need to possess. To marry a woman, he claimed, meant to destroy by force the exception to the rules known as love.

When Max was wooing a woman, he did it in style. He discreetly flagged down gypsy cabs and paid in advance so she wouldn't have to stand at the curb waiting for a taxi to drive by. He bought presents on the spur of the moment whenever he spied a scarf or piece of jewelry in a shop window that reminded him of the woman he desired. When Max was aflame with love for a woman, he sometimes possessed an almost uncanny ability to predict her wishes, anticipate her moods. He was an enthusiastic and elegant dancer—although one wouldn't have thought so to see him shuffling along the street—and took his current girlfriend dancing whether she wanted to or not. But after a few weeks of feverish courtship he would resume his usual life. As soon as there was nothing left for him to discover, his interest would subside, and although he seldom broke off a relationship without explanation, sooner or later the woman could sense the end approaching, and Max was relieved to let it happen.

In the summer Nadja sent him a photo of herself. It spoke a clearer language than her letters. She was sitting on the sandy bank of the river that flowed through H., clasping her knees with her arms and smiling bravely into the camera. He recalled her drawings, their unerring clarity of observation behind the awkward draftsmanship. He recalled the defiance and determination that didn't show on the snapshot. His curiosity was piqued by all her contradictions.

With the help of a friend on the board of a foundation, Max was able to secure for Nadja a scholarship to a small private college in New Jersey. He knew it was only the beginning of what he would do for her. He would need to be both hard-headed and gentle to steer her toward the discovery of her talent. With the decision to get involved in her life, he took it upon himself to provide her with everything he thought she needed. He had never asked her if that's what she wanted, but he was sure she would have agreed.

———

Two years had passed since Max had last seen Nadja, enough time to create an image of her from her letters and the snapshot that distorted his memory of her. And so he was astonished as she walked toward him in the arrivals hall at J.F.K., well-dressed—perhaps a bit too showy—and self-confident. But as they greeted one another her self-confidence was already giving way to the strange mixture of shyness and defiant brusqueness he well remembered. As they emerged from the airport into the humid mid-summer heat, she fell completely silent. Silently, they drove north on the Van Wyck Expressway in his Lincoln Continental whose bulk and roominess obviously impressed her, through Queens and then westward over the East River and straight across the bleakest sections of the Bronx.

"This is where I grew up," Max broke the long silence.

"How awful," Nadja replied.

"Back then it didn't look as bad around here as it does now," he tried to allay her shock. "It's not that many blocks from here to midtown Manhattan. You can drive it in twenty minutes, but it took me ten years to really get from here to there."

Max drove her directly to her college in New Jersey. He had a pressing deadline on a contract and just recently he'd met a new woman, a capricious beauty who demanded his complete concentration. Soon enough, he was convinced, Nadja would make her own claim on his attention.

"You can get in touch with me any time," he said. "Call me up whenever you need me."

She nodded. He could sense her fear and excitement and he felt a little shabby for dropping her off here without further ado and without having shown her the beauties of New York.

After a two-hour drive through a hilly, late-summer landscape, they both caught sight of the college. It was on the edge of a small town, as if small towns were her inescapable fate.

"It's not what I expected," Nadja said meekly.

On a hill above the town of Fairfield they parked the car beside a Victorian building and lifted out Nadja's bags. On the lawn in front of the building young people were lounging beneath the trees.

"Welcome!" said an energetic blonde who met them at the Student Center. She was to be Nadja's academic advisor. "I like this town," she said when Nadja asked if there was a bigger city anywhere nearby. "I like living here because I'm a small-town girl." She drove them around campus in her station wagon while she explained the dorm rules to Nadja in her tinny, schoolmarmish voice. At the door of the room Nadja would share with another scholarship student she took her leave with a cheery "Good luck!"

Max took his leave from Nadja in a coffee shop with a tiny patio and wobbly metal tables. The coffee in the squat mug before her had an overwhelming flavor of cinnamon.

"Come visit me in New York as soon as you want to," he encouraged her.

She looked at him as if to entreat him to take her back right away. But she was silent and only watched him go with the terrified eyes of a child being left alone in a dark room.

In the twenties, Fairfield had been home to a prosperous iron industry. But since then, first the factories and then the businesses and restaurants had closed, people had left to look for work elsewhere, and the town had become depopulated and impoverished. It lay forlornly in a valley between two rivers. The streets were as still on weekdays as on Sundays, and the few people one saw seemed to have endless amounts of time on their hands: the unemployed sitting at the foot of the war memorial with their plastic bags, the schoolchildren hopping off yellow school buses in the early afternoon. Cars circled once through a rotary around the statue of the Civil War hero for whom the college was named, and after this enforced delay accelerated off toward the highway leading to Allentown.

Despite the dreariness of the many abandoned businesses, their windows taped with newspaper, and the deadly stillness of Fairfield's streets, Nadja spent more time in the town than on the campus. There was a bookstore attached to the down-at-heel coffee shop where Max had said goodbye on that first day. Here, next to novels gathering dust, Nadja discovered old art books and prints, treatises on art history and books about experimental photography. Here she encountered Man Ray for the first time and realized that Max hadn't meant to disparage her when he advised her to take pictures instead of drawing them. Perhaps she could have found all these books in the college library, but that's where she went to study, not when she just wanted to browse. Nadja was often the only person in the bookstore, moving up and down the narrow aisles between the floor-to-ceiling shelves. It gradually became *her* bookstore and she entered it with an almost tender pride of ownership.

"Doesn't anyone else ever come in here?" she asked the girl at the coffee machine.

"People around here don't read," the young woman answered. "Most people here have better things to do."

While Nadja gradually began to feel at home in Fairfield, the college campus with its ivy-covered Victorian dorms, its parklike lawns and paths—as idyllic as a remote sanatorium—remained foreign to her. She was older than most of the students and felt out of place with her twenty-three years, like a castaway among children. At first she had been appalled by their unselfconscious attempts to make her acquaintance and she'd fended them off. They seemed intrusive to her. But then they left her alone, and it was hard for her to strike the right casual, perky tone these young people used in conversation with each other. She shared her spartan room with a girl from France with whom she went to the cafeteria and attended campus events, happy to have someone to go with, but they had little else in common. Many free hours she spent in a remote carrel in the library. That's where she studied and in that stillness Nadja passed hours and days in timeless uniformity.

She was bored by the lectures, anyway. In her opinion, five years after she'd graduated from high school she shouldn't have to repeat subjects she hadn't liked in the first place and had thought to be done with once and for all.

"So far I haven't learned anything useful here," she told the blonde advisor after a few months.

The blonde replied that she'd heard that Europeans were impatient and quick to judge. Why not play sports? On a team Nadja might learn what she seemed to lack, namely team spirit and social skills.

Nadja felt she'd been taken to task. It would require a long apprenticeship before she finally understood where she'd gone wrong.

———————

When Nadja called Max up, she got the feeling that she was bothering him. He answered evasively when she asked when she could meet him in New York. He was really busy at work just now; he was on the go all the time. It was almost two months—the worst of the summer heat was long since past—before he invited her.

She took the Greyhound bus through the hilly countryside where trees were already glowing with fall color. Max was waiting for her by the Port Authority ticket counters. He was thinner than she remembered, looking athletic and in a good mood. The warmth of his greeting gave her the impression he was glad to see her.

They rode a taxi through streets she knew from photographs. Nevertheless, the severe geometry of Manhattan's canyons impressed her. They seemed like tunnels leading straight as an arrow toward a distant point that never got closer. She watched mirrored glass facades whiz past, squares like landscapes of stone next to Gothic cathedrals and classicist palaces. And some of these facades were the work of the man sitting next to her in the taxi and telling her the names of the buildings they were driving past.

They drove north on Tenth Avenue and Nadja was surprised when they took a right turn into a short street that in two blocks ended abruptly at Central Park. So this was the address she had copied onto her airmail envelopes: West 88th Street.

They stood before an elegant, old-fashioned building that reminded her of Europe, with balustrades on the first two floors and front steps of black marble. Max lived on the top floor of the seven-story building. The dark brown wood of the floorboards and the narrow, dark console tables and bookshelves in the foyer looked like the hall of a Renaissance palazzo. Max watched Nadja's face with amusement. "It's more cozy farther on in," he said.

The windows were high and narrow with brown shutters that allowed stripes of light to seep through the blinds.

"Come on," Max laid his arm lightly on her shoulder, "I'll give you a little tour of my museum." He gestured grandly toward the many objects—sculptures, tapestries, paintings, bowls, jewel boxes, and candlesticks along the walls, on shelves, on chests and cornices. None of this, he explained, was here by chance. Only a few things had been acquired by purchase.

"Every one of these things," he emphasized, "has an important connection to my life. Every one has a very special personal meaning."

Max spread his treasured possessions before her with the ardent pride of a schoolboy showing his room to a girl for the first time: "Here's a floor lamp from Micah Lexier, and Paul Siskin designed this footstool for me."

He laughed. "Sometimes my artist friends have weird ideas about what's comfortable. They don't believe in conventional proportions. That's why I had to keep the furniture pretty sparse. All these things that people bring for my house demand a plain background."

He showed her a frosty landscape in oil, "Maxfield Parrish. One of the last things he painted before he died." On the opposite wall hung Elizabeth's somber self-portrait, and on a slim art déco console table beneath it stood a folded-out silhouette cutout of a stage with a tiny ballerina in pink tulle.

Max followed Nadja's gaze. "That may be kitsch," he admitted, "but that's exactly the right place for it." He ran his hand absentmindedly over a wide silver frame that looked like handmade lace and held nothing but a lock of brown hair. But he passed over it in silence, moved on to other things, handed her catalogues of exhibits. Many were personally inscribed to him with well-known names she had heard or read about.

"You've known a lot of famous people," Nadja said appreciatively.

"Yes," he replied, "sometimes I was able to do them favors. But women," he added, "seldom say thank you."

She gave him a puzzled look.

"Take this girl here, for example," Max explained, while handing Nadja a heavy gold frame with a photo that had been heavily touched up: a combed-up permanent from the fifties, dark eyes under drooping lids, the face flat and unshadowed. "She was a talented pianist, but unscrupulous and devious." He gave a brief laugh, bitter and almost contemptuous, put the picture back on the shelf, and fished four photos out of a hand-carved cigar box.

"How many women do you see here?"

He watched Nadja intently. His eyes were suggesting the answer he wanted even though she could see nothing but four snapshots of an aloof blonde woman under various lighting conditions.

"Four," she answered cooperatively.

It was just the answer he had hoped for. "You see, she's a chameleon, a quick-change artist! The most intelligent woman I've ever known. And what did she make of herself? She's got some kids, a husband who cheats on her, and who do you think still sends her money so she doesn't have it quite so hard? Me, of course."

He fell silent as he noticed the disapproval on Nadja's face. She found it unpleasant to have to listen to commentaries about photos of women she didn't know.

Max led her to a big corner room with a magnificent plaster ceiling and moldings, white stucco reliefs from floor to ceiling. It was a sparsely furnished library with modern sculptures on the mantelpiece and a plain black dining table and chairs. A Le Corbusier design, he told her. The table was set for two, without tablecloth, but with white porcelain and heavy silver.

"I don't like tablecloths," said Max categorically, "and I hate curtains, too. But I've loved plaster since I was a child. It's what I've always been best at in my work. I don't like mirrors, either. They're a cheap trick and only obscure the clear contours of things."

The stark white of the walls was relieved by the spines of books in narrow bookcases made of glass and stainless steel as well as a large oil by Georgia O'Keeffe: a flaming red blossom from which coiled black stamens.

The kitchen lay beyond white folding doors that suggested a walk-in closet, as if Max wanted to avoid the slightest hint of domesticity. He wouldn't even let Nadja peek behind them. He made her keep her seat while he brought out one course after another and then cleared them away.

"Let me spoil you," he encouraged her. "It makes me happy."

They sat facing each other. The candles cast soft shadows onto his face and made it look thin. For the first time, Nadja noticed the cleft in his chin. She looked at his powerful hands. They resembled the hands of a workman and were much less tan than his face.

He asked her about college, whether she'd settled in and found some friends.

Nadja's answers were noncommittal. She feared that he would take criticism and dissatisfaction for ingratitude. Oh yes, she answered in monosyllables, it was okay. It wasn't what she was used to, but the people were friendly. No, she couldn't complain.

"And what do you hear from home?" he asked. "Do they miss you?"

She turned red. "I haven't written anybody yet. I haven't gotten around to it."

The truth was, she wanted to erase H. entirely from her memory, to make it cease to exist.

When Max asked if she'd started to like Fairfield a bit more in the meantime, she answered that she was sure that Fairfield wasn't the only kind of town America had to offer. He chose to ignore the hint that she'd like him to show her more of Manhattan, however. It was clear that he was being careful not to make her any promises.

Absentmindedly she toyed with the heavy silver napkin ring, turning it in her hands.

"That's my mother's silver," said Max pensively. "She had to pawn it when our money ran out. Years later I was looking for a silver service for a client and rediscovered it by chance in an antique store. There's no doubt it was hers. It's the right monogram and I remember the dent in one of the rings. But there used to be eight of them, and I only found two."

"Was it hard for your mother to leave Europe?" asked Nadja.

"She was already too old to emigrate and she'd been too happy over there. She couldn't come to terms with living here. I think she never spent a happy day here," Max said, "maybe some happy hours, but they all had to do with us kids—her happiest and her most terrible hours."

"It must be hard to get used to America," Nadja said.

"Maybe it's not too late for you," Max hazarded. "You're still younger than she was. There's a different cut-off point for everybody."

Night had fallen. The high windows had been transformed into black mirrors against which the wind whipped gusts of rain. The candles in the three-armed candelabra flickered slightly in an imperceptible draft.

"I've got to go," said Nadja.

In the vestibule he kissed her. She let it happen, but she was disappointed. He was sending her away without making any arrangements to meet again. As she stepped back from his embrace she felt something hard under her heel. She looked down and saw that she had crushed one of her silver filigree earrings. Max picked it up. "Was it valuable?" he asked with concern.

"It was from my mother." Nadja fought back her tears.

They stepped out of the building into a fall storm that snatched the door out of Max's hand. The cab wasn't there yet. Max was holding a big umbrella over Nadja but the rain soaked them from all sides. Fallen leaves in the gutter were sluicing along in a raging flood. Nadja climbed into the taxi while Max paid the driver for the trip to Port Authority. Then she was in the cab, alone in New York for the first time. She decided to come back the next weekend and explore some more on her own.

———

But it never came to that. Early Saturday morning, even before breakfast, Max was knocking on her door to take her to New York. He was driving home from Philadelphia and Fairfield was right on his way.

On this weekend Nadja fell unconditionally in love with New York, a love she would never again withdraw. But she had no way of knowing that on this October Saturday, nor that she would always remember this day as the most beautiful in her life.

At Balducci's in the West Village they ate Caesar salad and muffins with their coffee. In SoHo Max took her to the galleries he had raved about in H. and introduced her to the owners, hinting that she was a painter too. They strolled past booths in the Greenwich Village flea market and Max bought her a set of outlandish Oriental earrings to replace the silver one she had stepped on while kissing him. Late in the afternoon they drove up Madison Avenue to spend what Max said was the most beautiful time of the day in Central Park.

Such a long, mild autumn was new to Nadja. In Europe fall wasn't like that. The clear, thin air in which the outlines of the towers and skyscrapers lay like cut-outs against an immaculate blue sky made her dizzy. The leaves of the maples and ginkgos were lurid and golden in the evening sun, as if they were on fire. Here and there, a leaf drifted to the ground. Not a breath of breeze stirred and only when the sun had set was there a nip of autumn coolness.

In the twilight they strolled south on Fifth Avenue and Max showed her the first facade he had restored when he was twenty-eight. He put his arm around her and when he drew her to him, she felt his heart beating through their thin clothing. Nadja felt certain that something right and inevitable was beginning, that it had already begun two years ago on that autumn day by the river, or perhaps already on the day she first saw him coming out of the community house in the Färbergasse. His face, now so close to hers, filled her with confidence in the rightness of everything to come. That she wished to go home and spend the night with him didn't need to be said.

She said only, "I've got no experience at all."

"I know," he answered, "and that's fine. That just means that later on you won't make the mistake of confusing quick gratification for love."

He taught her that love was like a conversation without words, with no difference between question and answer, that it was outside of the time ticking away somewhere on a mantelpiece in the darkened apartment. Love was like being washed up on a shore where all feelings flowed together, indistinguishable, yet clearer and more intense than ever before.

"Love is mystical," said Max.

Nadja believed his every word and in return received what she longed for most of all: security. He was the teacher, she the pupil.

"Go look in the mirror and see how beautiful you are," Max commanded.

In the harsh light of the bathroom a strange face stared back at her, a wild brightness in its enlarged eyes. This face inspired her with fear and pride simultaneously, as if she had finally arrived at the destination toward which she had been traveling. She felt freed of all her shortcomings.

In the morning, they went to the Museum of Modern Art. Nadja could feel Max watching her furtively as she moved from painting to painting. It was flattering, yes, but it spoiled her concentration. She resolved to come back alone, later. They ate blintzes beneath the art déco mosaics in the Edison Café. Then they strolled down to Times Square arm in arm.

"It's like discovering the city for the second time!" Max was in high spirits and gave her a long kiss in the middle of the sidewalk on Fifth Avenue.

They were experiencing an hallucinatory New York: more than just a city, a labyrinth of promises, a shining dream emerging from the glowing autumn mist, for them alone.

"If this is a dream," said Nadja, "don't ever wake me up."

The evenings were blue and the setting sun set off fireworks in the curving windows of the buildings on Bryant Park. The gleaming leaves of the ginkgos were most beautiful as they floated down, landed with a dry rustle, and were extinguished. Max and Nadja found themselves immediately engrossed by the movies they saw together, mostly European films that struck in them melancholy chords of things long past. . . . It was all equally unreal, both past and present.

Now they spent every weekend together. For Nadja, it was like living in a happy delirium in which nothing mattered anymore except for the hours she spent with Max. The room she returned to every Monday morning, the paths and buildings of the college, lost their reality in the absence of her beloved. She sat in her carrel in the library, she ate with her French roommate, she even got decent grades on her first tests. But everything that happened in Fairfield was now like a strange foreign play.

One night in New York, as she lay in bed beside Max, the telephone startled her awake. Max's answers were curt and grumpy: "Yes . . . No . . . Not now." Then wide awake and in great annoyance, "Listen, I'm not alone . . . Yes, with a woman . . . Why don't we get together sometime and talk about it?" He held the receiver away from his ear while a woman's loud, agitated voice shouted insults. Then he gently hung up.

Nadja looked at him inquisitively. "Who was that?"

"Someone who can't accept that it's over," said Max indifferently.

"Did I run her off?"

"Not really, it was already over. Remember the Saturday I picked you up? I'd decided the night before to end it. We didn't have enough in common. There were too many misunderstandings."

Dawn was approaching, sallow early light filtering through the louvered shutters of the bedroom.

"You're closer to me," said Max, and bent over her. "I share a town with you that nobody here knows anything about."

Nadja shook her head vehemently, wanted to say something, but he kissed her.

Later he said, "Whether you believe it or not, the city you grew up in put its stamp on you. I've come to know it through you."

It was getting light. The sun cast white stripes onto the wall above the bed. Slowly they migrated over the blanket, over the bright wooden floor, then faded away. And his animated face too was transformed in the course of the day: it was close, tender and solicitous; then distant, turned away, pensive or weary; but always ready to turn back toward her, to be in harmony with her needs and feelings—his face as well as his body.

"So you've really fallen in love with me," she said sometime or other in the course of these morning hours. It was a statement, not a question, so she didn't notice right away that he said nothing in reply.

———

Weeks later, as they were leaving Lincoln Center after seeing a new play by the young English playwright everybody was talking about, Nadja repeated her question. "Tell me the truth," she said flirtatiously, "have you fallen in love with me?"

But again Max ignored the question and pointed instead to the illuminated fountain in the middle of the rectangular plaza in front of the building. "Did I tell you that Wallace Harrison made his first sketch for that fountain in my apartment? We were good friends back then, but then fame went to his head." He talked on, but Nadja had stopped listening to him.

They walked back to the house between Columbus Avenue and Central Park West, a short stroll in the evening air already turning a bit frosty, past locked shops behind folding iron security gates and overflowing garbage cans, and for the first time since their love had begun, Nadja was unhappy.

"Do you love me?" she repeated as they lay in bed next to each other.

"Why do you insist on hearing that one sentence?" he answered in slight irritation. "I'll never fall so hard in love again that I can say, 'Now I'm in love.' I'm too old for that."

Nadja laughed, "At what age do you become too old to fall in love?"

"The last time I really fell in love I was forty-two." She was hurt by the melancholy in his voice and the faraway look in his eyes.

"The woman with four different faces?" It was a wild guess.

He looked at her in surprise, "Exactly."

Fury rose in Nadja. She turned her back to him, but after a while she yielded to his caresses.

"You have no standard of comparison," he said, "but don't think it's so easy to find someone like me." And after a while, he entreated her again, "Why should it make any difference whether or how much I love you? Don't I give you everything you want?"

Nadja fell silent. She suddenly realized how little she knew about him. He'd never given her more than brief hints about himself. Or had she neglected to ask him? But how, and about what? Besides, pupils weren't supposed to ask questions, were they? She was starting to feel rebellious.

Max tried to dissipate her bad mood by explaining to her that love was a matter of fate. Good intentions had nothing to do with it. If that inexplicable certainty wasn't there from the very first moment, then it wasn't love. Maybe it was something similar, something that could develop into affection, but love was so rare that one occurrence of it might have to last you for decades.

"And what if just one person feels that way," she asked, "but not the other?"

"Then it doesn't count."

She wanted to know how often he'd felt that way.

Without hesitation he answered, "Three times."

"Who besides the woman with four faces?"

That was none of her business, he replied bluntly.

Then they fell silent.

"Have I ever given you reason to complain?" It was the cool civility of the question that hurt Nadja, as if Max were asking a dinner companion in a restaurant if her steak was done enough.

"No, I can't complain." she replied quietly.

She left before breakfast, without waiting for him to get up. The time of oblivious happiness was past. She felt defeated, but one day she would astonish him. From now on Nadja fought for his love but also feared that the battle was hopeless from the start. A woman with four different faces? She would show him what metamorphosis was: Desdemona, Lulu, Gretchen, Helen, the shrewish and the tamed Kate in quick succession. She was prepared to show him the whole melancholy palette of female existence. Max was astonished and let her have her way. He watched in bemusement as she fought her grim battle for the love that he had never denied her.

"Listen," he reassured her, "relax. Be yourself. I love you in my own way."

Their quarrels circled around the questions: Did he love her? How much did he love her? Did he love her and no one else?

"Don't forget, I love you," he repeated as she left his apartment early Monday morning after a weekend of exhausting debates like this. Standing at the door in his bathrobe he serenaded her departure with snatches of old hits, waved goodbye, blew her kisses. But when Max was out of earshot she said bitterly, "Yeah, in your own way."

For her twenty-fourth birthday Max gave her a Leicaflex, the most expensive camera he could find, with extra lenses and a tripod. He hadn't forgotten his promise.

"What promise?" she asked.

Back in H. he had promised to take her talent under his wing. That's why she was here.

It was true, she admitted, that she hardly did any drawing anymore. Her life had fragmented into a whirl of strange and alien images: the paths and buildings of the campus—an otherworldly refuge where people recovered from encounters with real life—the lean, down-and-out men hanging around the Greyhound station in Fairfield who now greeted her as a regular; the bus ride through a landscape becoming progressively more bare and cold; the obsession that drove her to Manhattan every Friday. She ran to Max, always in great haste, as if every minute without him were an unendurable loss. Every time she thought she couldn't have waited one more second.

"Now you'll learn how to use a camera," Max explained.

"I've known how for years," Nadja declared. Sometimes he was an annoying know-it-all.

"Sure," he said dismissively, "just like everyone else, but not the way you're going to be able to. It's got something to do with the way you look at things. It's a look that strips the skeletons of their flesh and clothing. I saw it in your drawings, and you're going to learn to take photos the same way."

"I once told somebody that I liked skeletons," she said, surprised at his intuition.

"I sneak into other people's heads." Max laughed. "Nothing can beat it for excitement and satisfaction."

Nadja was amused. "So it was the skeletons in my head that got you interested in me." She was disarmed by the playful self-irony with which he deflected every argument, and she loved his dry, subtle wit.

She promised she would take a photography course in the spring semester. In the meantime, Max declared, they would go motif-hunting in Manhattan, as a team, hunter and tracker on safari. From now on, that's what he called their forays into the city.

It was getting cold. Icy winds sliced through the downtown canyons. The season of strolling arm-in-arm through the park was over. They sat in cafés and people-watched.

"Tell me about them," he encouraged her.

She made up stories to go with the faces, the clothes, how people moved and talked. He found it entertaining. He began to admire her for the first time, and his admiration gradually awakened a desire of which Nadja had no inkling. Now he granted what he had withheld from her: approval, the affirmation that she was something special. But not in the way she had hoped. They became a team, and when they put their heads together and speculated about strangers, the pleasure of their comradeship began to cause an imperceptible change in their relationship.

"And now," he said, "set the shutter speed and the f-stop. But unobtrusively, so they don't look this way. Hold the camera in your lap until you're ready to shoot. How does that bald guy over there look? What image would you use to describe him?" he prompted her.

"Like a brooding vulture," she suggested.

They laughed.

Nadja took the picture.

On the way home they discussed the photos they had shot. Back in the apartment they talked about whether they could install a darkroom in the bathroom. Late at night, lying awake in bed next to each other, Nadja asked, "How come we never talk about us anymore?"

"But we do," Max replied, "we're talking about you all the time . . . Portraits are your strength. Stick with them."

For many years, she would do just that. Her dependence on him had to be both scary and flattering, a responsibility that he needed to escape from time to time.

He didn't say: get out of my hair, I need some room to breathe. He just said, "This weekend I've got other plans" and her voice, a two-hour bus trip away in Fairfield, sounded an alarm.

"You sound like a watchdog barking," he said, trying to make it into a joke, but Nadja was not at all amused.

"What are you going to do?" she wanted to know. "Who with?"

"Maybe I'll go visit my brother, maybe I just need to be alone for a change."

Before he knew it, she was standing at his door, ready to overthrow any rival. But no one was there except him. He was sitting at the dining room table that served as his work table when he was alone, ruminating, working on sketches, thinking up topics that might never become books or even articles. He hadn't left the house all day, was sitting in his bathrobe, lost in thought over a pile of papers scribbled with notes in his minuscule handwriting as Nadja stormed furiously into the room. In relief at her mistake, she threw herself into his arms, pulled him into the bed, and he let her have her way, flattered and frightened.

"Don't ever surprise me like that again," said Max on Sunday evening as he took her to the bus.

"But you were so happy to see me," she said in excuse.

Max said nothing and let his gaze wander around the waiting room.

Spring was late in coming. Even in April, a snowstorm blew horizontally for days, piling up drifts several feet high. Traffic ground to a halt and the telephone rang for hours through Max's empty apartment. Where could he be in this storm?

He'd gone walking in the park, through the untouched snow, white and glittering like on a country road. In a few hours the snowplows and dumptrucks would be out smushing the white mass to watery slush. As Max entered his apartment, the silence and distant muffled sounds of the snowy park still in his ears, the telephone was shrilling. It was still ringing when he hung up his coat, when he stepped out of the tub, and it followed him ruthlessly into the kitchen.

He gave up. It was Nadja—panicky, desperate, furious. He shouted at her. Hours later, he apologized, listened to her sobbing for a while, hung up, called again, suggested she should come to him, right away.

They both had the sense that something was approaching that they could no longer prevent, and neither could say when it had started.

"Max," she was pleading before she even got through the door, "I can't stand it there anymore, in that miserable town and that school. I want to live here with you for a while, a few weeks, maybe until summer."

He'd come toward her with open arms as he always did when she needed his comfort and he would take her in his embrace and hold her tight until she calmed down. He let his arms fall.

"No," he said with a sharpness that she had never heard from him before, "no, you're not moving in with me. No way. I won't let you."

"But I've got no one anywhere except you." She fought back her tears.

"No," Max was adamant. "Nobody moves in with me, least of all you."

Then she lost control and started screaming. She hurled at him every vindictive insult she could think of, reproached him with what she'd been storing up for months without mentioning it. She'd found a postcard from the Catskills in his bedroom, postmarked in November, clearly in a woman's handwriting: "Love and kisses from A." She screamed as she'd never screamed in her life, screamed out at him all the misery of her childhood, as if it was his fault.

Max stood far away from her, at the window. His face lay in shadow but if she could have discerned his expression, its coldness and distance would have appalled her. He left the window and went to the bathroom door.

"There's nothing more I can do for you," he said, but his words were drowned out by her outburst.

"If you could see yourself in the mirror now," he scoffed. "You look truly repulsive."

That she heard. She fell suddenly silent, as if this was what she'd been waiting for, had intended to provoke just this confession, that he didn't love her and found her ugly.

"The hell with your jealousy," he said coldly. With the knob of the bathroom door in his hand he told her to leave. "When I come back out I want you gone."

Nadja stood in the middle of the hall and looked around. Her eyes fell on the cigar box. The woman with four faces. She would rip up the photos and strew the pieces on the floor. Instead, she stuck the pictures in her pocket.

She left the apartment, ran down the steps, furious, hurt, horrified at what she had done but convinced she would be back. He would call her up, he would take her in his arms, they would make up. But not now, not right away. Max should be sorry, he should realize that he needed her.

A warm wind blew down the avenues, tugged at the telephone lines, shook the thin, leafless trees. In just a few hours, the snow had disappeared and little lakes of meltwater were flooding the sidewalks. The wind was at her back and urged her forward, as if to make it impossible to turn around and go back.

Had he thrown her out? Had she left him? Nadja didn't know. She couldn't feel her legs as they carried her southward at a run.

She ran past subway stops. She had no idea what time it was. It had been early afternoon when she was still sitting eagerly in the bus; the farm fields were covered with snow. Now evening was falling and a warm, dark wind was driving her away. What she refused to accept, what she banished entirely from her head like an unbearable image, she nevertheless knew to be true: it was over.

Chapter 7

Nadja stayed on at the college until summer, but skipped her lectures and recitations. She went only to the photography course, learned to develop film, how to use the various lenses and filters, how to achieve special effects. She no longer went to Manhattan. She saved the money she earned in the campus post office. If Max wanted her, he knew where to find her. She was still resisting the urge to call him up. He was the one who had thrown her out, so he had to make the first move. But he didn't call. Nadja spent more time in her room than ever, not daring to stray very far from the telephone on the landing below. She lived in constant anticipation of its ring, but not a single call was for her. On the day she moved out her only fear was that now she was definitively cutting herself off from Max, setting off into a wilderness in which he could find her only if she called him. His silence seemed to be for good.

Quite unexpectedly, through an acquaintance from the bus, she found a room in Manhattan, in the Village. It was a nice room in a large apartment with light green furniture. The rooms were crammed with potted plants growing right up to the ceiling and there were two parrots free to fly around in the treetops. The apartment belonged to a professor who commuted between New

York and Philadelphia and was happy to have someone to look after her parrots.

In the first months Nadja worked in the kitchen of a narrow little deli-restaurant on Fifty-sixth Street, where eccentric old ladies met in mid-morning for brunch and office workers picked up their sandwiches in brown paper bags at noon. Here no one paid her much attention yet she didn't feel alone. But Nadja had to find a job that would earn enough money to realize the dream that Max had put into her head. She intended to become a photographer.

One time a colleague, a waiter from Puerto Rico, brought her home for a drink after work. She slept with him, listened to the obscenities he stammered to work up his courage, submitted herself to his impersonal lust, observed him with cool detachment, and was back in her own bed in the Village before midnight.

"Later, some other time, maybe," she said when he approached her again. "See you around."

But nothing she saw or experienced could drive Max from her thoughts. The idea that he was now out of reach plunged her into a feverish panic. Finally, she couldn't stand it any more and started writing to him. At first she chatted in a tone of forced jollity about her job, the quiet side street in the Village, the nice neighborhood with an oleander in front of the building, and the street lined with ginkgo trees. But this tone soon gave way to agitated urgency.

The apartment was filthy with the sharp stink of parrot droppings and Nadja wasn't allowed to open a window for fear they would fly away. It was a hot, steamy August; the heat and the smell forced her to bed, overwhelmed with anxiety. Why couldn't Max sense the desperation in her letters?

"I miss you." Her pleas had started to abandon all restraint. "I wake up and hear your voice down in the street, but when I look out the window, there's no one there or a stranger is walking by."

Quickly, before she could have second thoughts, Nadja dropped these testimonies of her subjection into the mailbox. Then she waited, full of rage at him and at herself, because she knew very well that her waiting was in vain.

She called Max from telephone booths, dialing the only number she knew by heart. She couldn't tell anymore whether it was yearning or vengefulness that made her do it. She listened to how his voice ran through the whole scale from expectant curiosity to annoyance. Her breath was shallow when he asked, "Who's there? Why don't you say something?"

One time she had said something. He was silent for so long that she finally asked, "Are you still there?"

"I'm sorry," he said coolly, "there's nothing more I can do for you."

Then the dial tone hummed in her ear. After that she said nothing and just listened to his breath. The tentativeness and sometimes even fear in his voice when he asked "Who's there?" filled her with satisfaction, a malicious feeling of triumph.

He must have known that it was she who shattered his sleep, after midnight, when she was unable to pass up even a single telephone booth on her way home, compulsively clinging to this last one-sided connection. Until finally one day a recorded female voice said, "The number you have dialed is no longer in service." Only then did she give up.

But still she waited. Every time the telephone rang, her pulse quickened. On any corner, at any subway stop, she might encounter him. After all, the city wasn't that big.

Late in the fall, Nadja found a job in the photo department of a drugstore. They hired her to work in the darkroom and sent her to New Haven for advanced training. When she stood in the red light of the darkroom, setting the exposure time for an enlargement, inserting filters to adjust the contrast, and aligning the print paper in the enlarging frame, she felt in such harmony with herself and her job that she could forget Max for longer and longer stretches of time. It happened sometimes that she didn't think of him even once from morning until early evening when she emerged onto Lexington Avenue.

She never completely stopped thinking of Max—even many years later, he would appear in her dreams—but in this winter she gave up hoping that he would contact her. One day, when the first spring green was appearing on the scrawny trees in front of her building and life was beginning to stir in the parks, Nadja noticed that she was happy.

When the professor in whose apartment she lived spent a semester teaching at some Midwestern university, Nadja had set up a darkroom in the bathroom, so that she would no longer have to develop her own film in furtive haste during working hours. Sometimes she could hardly believe that she was the person moving around this city, so bold and free. Strangely enough, this was the moment she chose, on one of her evenings off, to take another look at the photos of the woman with four faces. She photographed them at various exposures, with different depth of focus, and felt an inexplicable fascination for this face.

It had to be the eyes that were the key to its almost hypnotic effect.

Hadn't Max said that it was a magic face? She borrowed bodies from photos of other women and put this face onto them. Its eyes still stared at her intently, foreign, with a mocking gleam that came and went on the contact prints. It disappeared entirely on soft paper but in high contrast with no medium tones it sprang fiercely out at her. Nadja loved such painfully high contrast. It exposed what gray tones concealed, stripped away the last veil. Nadja was determined to cause pain, to herself as well as others.

"You don't know enough about me," Max had once said. She should have taken the opportunity to sound him out, but at the time her neediness had been too great for her to have any perspective, and she'd also been too young. Who was this woman with the mad eyes, and why had she meant so much to him?

She enlarged the negative until every pore became a crater. With the help of contrast paper and filters she transformed the face into a desolate, withered landscape of death—white, whiter than a corpse drowned in lime, the hair a dark clotted border, as if scalped, a death mask, the curves of cheek and chin cauterized away by Nadja's lust to kill, lost in the blackness of the eye sockets and the jaw below the cheekbone. But she couldn't kill the eyes. They still stared at her from the enlargements hung up to dry on the clothesline—disembodied, wide open.

This face was her first departure from what she had been taught. They'd taught her that a positive was successful when it had as many gray tones as possible in correct gradation. Now she discovered the possibility of using the camera and the darkroom to change reality, to distort and mutilate it if necessary, without pity, in order to bring out the truth.

She entered competitions, individual works of hers got shown. She won a prize in a portrait contest—not first prize, but it was a start. And every time, Nadja caught herself wishing fleetingly that Max would hear about it.

She entered a photo series she called *The Woman with Four Faces* in a competition for a show of New York women artists. The request for proposals had called for works about the invisibility of women—their invisibility to the masculine eye, their destruction in the process of being contemplated. These photos made Nadja's name. They were the beginning of her career: the grotesquely elongated shadow of a woman standing on a beach at sunset; a fleeting reflection in the wing mirror of a convertible, distorted by the speed of the car and the curve of the mirror; a spot of dried blood on coarse cloth, enlarged so much that one could see the degree of saturation of each individual fiber. And the ravaged, nameless woman in the various stages of her destruction, maimed by the gaze of a jealous rival in a darkroom orgy of annihilation. Only Max could have put her back together again, knew the original features of the anonymous woman with four faces.

"Who were you influenced by?" asked a woman journalist.

"I don't know," Nadja replied, "by a man, I guess."

It wasn't the answer currently in fashion, and the woman turned away abruptly and left her standing there.

Nadja was able to quit her job in the drugstore and move out of the apartment with the parrots. At the age of twenty-six she was able to fulfill the dream of her childhood and live as an artist.

Two years after their breakup, she happened to see Max sitting at noontime on the concrete wall around a bank building on Park Avenue, directly across from the Waldorf Astoria. He was looking across at its facade as though he'd never seen it before. He sat in the frosty April sunlight among office workers in dark suits eating their lunches, and he looked dispirited. His beard seemed to have gotten a bit longer and grayer. She had her Leica with her. As she got Max into her view finder he took off his glasses and pressed his thumb and forefinger to the bridge of his nose in the gesture she knew so well. She pressed the shutter release. Only as Nadja turned away was she struck by the shocking realization that she had seen the man to whom she owed her life and career in New York, now firmly established, and she hadn't felt the slightest need to speak to him. With her solitary, practiced eye she had seen him, registered his appearance, taken his measure, and at precisely the right moment, shot him in his characteristic gesture—very professional. And only then, two blocks farther on, by the viaduct next to Grand Central Station, did her hands start shaking.

When she looked at the negative in her darkroom, Max was a stranger to her. A man in his mid-fifties, introverted and depressed-looking, from whom she had stolen a moment of his life, a moment when he had thought himself unobserved. It was the only picture of him that she had developed herself, and yet it was at best an approximation of the man she had loved.

———

Nadja's first commission took her to the ocean. A travel agency wanted her to take pictures of beaches and vacation towns on the New England coast. They suggested to her that lonely lighthouses would make a nice contrast to the colorful crowds on the beaches. In the dreams of city people the lighthouse was the ultimate refuge . . . But any body of water, any view of the sea, would embody the yearning toward infinity, unboundedness. Her pictures were supposed to satisfy this yearning.

In a used Pontiac that was almost as roomy as Max's Lincoln Continental, Nadja drove along the bays and inlets between New Haven and Cape Cod, then continued north to Maine. She got to know the quiet desperation of small-town America, observed how solitary travelers would climb hesitantly from their cars, lean on the cement sea wall that protected the highway from the surf, stare down irresolutely at the empty beach for a while, and then drive off unconsoled. It was September, shortly after Labor Day, and the beaches were empty. She photographed low-hanging cloud banks over a dull, lead-gray sea. Not what tourists hungry for sunshine wanted to see. But then she also took pictures of mirages on the horizon above glittering water, dunes as high as in the Sahara, beach grass in the saturated golden light of late afternoon, deep blue waves like velvet on a cutting table, a sea motionless as a polished mirror reflecting the sky, shells and footprints in the sand of a deserted shore, a boardwalk wandering off into the reeds, the long, finely ribbed sandbanks of Cape Cod, the loneliness of empty summer houses, ankle-deep sand drifts on roads without a single tire track, the melancholy of sunsets in a landscape devoid of humanity, the miles and miles of marshland between Plymouth and Hull that were full of shy wildlife, waterfowl frightened up out of the moor grass and flapping away on ungainly wings. She was on the road for weeks, her camera always within reach, totally concentrated on seeing things: colors, forms, moods. Far out the lighthouses loomed up over inhospitable spits of land, sturdy conical towers exposed to the elements on naked outcroppings, their beacons barely able to penetrate autumn's dense white fogs.

Nadja sought out the desolate loneliness of the vacation towns along the Atlantic coast as if she wanted to compel them to surrender the secrets they hid during the summer. Storm gusts mixed with rain squalls hurled themselves against the sea walls. The pinball machines stood abandoned in the empty arcades. In the evening she sat by the steamed-up window of a diner and listened to some local tell his life story. Sometimes when he was done, she'd ask if she could take his picture.

One cold, damp evening Nadja was the only customer in a restaurant in Nantasket. She was already on her way back to New York. A couple shivering in thin windbreakers sat down at a nearby table. The woman wore a scarf wrapped clumsily around her head and clasped a bag in her lap with both hands. They were so gentle and affectionate with each other that Nadja couldn't stop looking at them. The woman slowly took off the scarf and beneath it her head was bald. It must have been from some kind of chemotherapy. Where there had once been a full head of hair there were now little transparent tufts. The skin covering her skull was quite pale. Beneath her thin skirt a bandage could be seen. But when the man leaned over and kissed her on the cheek as if he were touching something of infinite value, tears burned in Nadja's eyes, so much did she envy this woman.

She took no picture of these two, nor of the writer manqué in whose trailer she lived for two weeks until winter arrived with the first squalls of heavy wet snow. The couple in Nantasket had driven Nadja into Fred's arms.

Far from the beach, behind the dunes and the beach houses, there was a big trailer park, a vacation spot for people who dreamed of living by the sea but couldn't afford a house. Now, in late fall, the trailers were locked up, the brown grass trampled into the mud, and on stormy days one could hear the distant surf. Only Fred was still there.

He had sat down next to Nadja one evening in a seafood diner and started philosophizing about false consciousness and the meaning of life. In the sixties he'd written songs and recited his poetry at readings, he told her, but since then nobody wanted to hear his poems and aphorisms any more, much less publish them. It was just all over.

"Man, we were great!" he exclaimed. He was rhapsodizing about the student movement in San Francisco.

He smoked and talked into the wee hours. They were drinking wine. She stayed with him that night. Nadja had been alone for many weeks, the whole Atlantic coast up to Bar Harbor and back. She'd listened to music on the car radio, slept in motels when she was tired of driving. The sound of the never-ending traffic driving past had made her feel she was still driving even when she slept. Sometimes she'd chat with fishermen about nets and lobster traps and photograph them at their work. And sometimes she'd thought she couldn't stand the loneliness one more day. Now she listened to Fred; he talked to her even if he barely noticed that she was there.

But ultimately, when he tired of talking, he became a warm body dispensing love, a little nearness, an unconventional domesticity. He didn't want to know anything about her. He wanted to talk and sleep with her. He didn't want to be alone when the rain drummed on the roof of the trailer and the surf crashed on the shore like distant thunder. He didn't seem to know himself why he suddenly bent over her in the narrow bed they shared and pressed the glowing end of his cigarette against her skin. He observed her with a thin, inquisitive grin, attempting neither to justify nor excuse what he'd done, while she gathered up her clothes.

Not until she opened her suitcase early the next morning in her apartment did she discover that the single-lens reflex camera that Max had given her was missing.

By this time she no longer blamed Max for her anger at this rejection, nor was she tortured any more by the longing she had felt when first left alone. But often, at work, when she was shooting or in the darkroom, when she was tired, in a hurry, when she thought 'This is okay,' it seemed to her that he was standing next to her—dissatisfied, inexorable—and telling her anyone could have done that, she couldn't stop there. Whenever a print in the tray of developer began to take on clearer, sharper contours and Nadja was enraptured, intoxicated by a successful piece of work, she'd always have to face his skepticism, rebut his amused, ironic glance.

But it was also due solely to Max that she knew she had talent and could never lose it because it was anchored in her powers of perception. This knowledge gave her confidence, allowing her to overcome failures, setbacks, and the discovery of her limits as an artist. Her imagination was not unlimited and that meant she'd never be one of the truly great photographers. She needed reality to measure herself against.

By the time she met the man she would ultimately marry, she had already learned that every new attempt at love meant disappointment. But she had overcome the deepest disappointment;

she'd put it behind her. And that gave her confidence and a certain hardness. But again and again it would happen that a gesture, a sentence said by another man, would remind her of Max, and every time she felt a little stab of regret.

After six years, Nadja left New York. She felt that the city had lost its shine and she longed more and more for a big sky and the quiet of a country morning. By nine a.m. when the stores opened, the morning freshness had already fled Manhattan entirely, leaving behind only the hectic speed that oppressed the streets and the people in them. She moved to a small town in Pennsylvania, only to leave it again after a short time. Sometimes, on the High Holy Days, she went back to her childhood home but never stayed longer than ten days. If she had remained longer in H., it would have been an admission that she missed it. At the community center she learned that Spitzer had visited Max in New York and that Max intended to settle in H. sometime or other; at least, he'd been talking about it for years. Sometime or other she could expect a reunion. She hoped she couldn't be touched by seeing him again, but she was apprehensive about it.

Part III

Chapter 8

EVERYONE WHO MET Max Berman in those years soon heard about his house in H. The people who'd been living in it for forty years thought of it as their home without the slightest sense of injustice. They were the same age as he, and year by year they moved one step closer to death, just as he did. Nevertheless, their aging filled Max with gratification, for it brought him closer to the day when he would move into his house. He was the last person who could assert a claim to the inheritance. Ben died before reaching sixty, his health ruined by the side effects of antipsychotic drugs.

Max's father Saul lived to be almost ninety. They'd had little contact, and not until Saul lay on his deathbed did Max visit him regularly in the hospital. At the funeral, he had his first reunion in years with his older brother Victor, who had moved to Tel Aviv in the fifties. Max had never been to Israel. His roots were in Europe, he'd say, and when he traveled, it was to the cities he'd first encountered as a soldier: Rome, Florence, Siena, Ravenna, Bergamo, Trieste. He loved them for their beauty alone; no painful memories clung to them. For seventeen years he'd been avoiding a return trip to H.

Victor's full head of white hair made him look like their grandfather. "It's been a long time," he greeted Max in embarrassment. "I should have gotten in touch with you sooner."

It was Victor who said kaddish at their father's grave, but only when they began talking about Ben did their pent-up alienation find release in mourning for his tortured life. They spent two days together, during which Max learned that he had a niece, a left-wing Israeli lawyer who worried her father and hadn't given him any grandchildren yet, though she was thirty-two. Despite the photo that Victor showed him it was difficult for Max to imagine that this young woman was a close relative. Victor said he was going to retire to a kibbutz in the hills near Jerusalem.

"And you, you'll probably spend the rest of your life here in New York," he surmised.

"No," Max said, "some time or other I'm going to Europe to live in our old house in H. Do you still have any memories from childhood?"

It seemed to them that the invisible bridge stretching back into the past was so long that it was an effort to people it with their memories. They had been children together in the same house, loved by the same adults, and between then and now lay a whole life in which they had become strangers. But the brothers were still close enough that in these few hours they spent together their early connection, their first years in common, were able to extinguish all their alienation. There was no one left but them to share the images: Sophie reading a book in her rocking chair, their grandfather at the head of the table saying the blessing as he raised his wineglass, Mira admonishing the children to take a last look at the house and hold it fast in their hearts. These memories would be extinguished when Max and Victor died. They had never felt so close to each other.

Two days later Max took his brother to the airport. They embraced. Neither invited the other to visit. They both knew that they wouldn't write to each other, that they were probably seeing each other for the last time. But they were reconciled, and this late reconciliation forged a strong bond that needed no further proof.

Shortly before his departure for Europe several years later, Max got a late-night call and heard his niece's voice with its strong Israeli accent: Victor was dead.

Max's reputation as a sought-after interior designer often took him to other American cities, to Boston, San Francisco, Los Angeles. With a younger architect he had started a firm, with several employees and a group of suppliers and entrepreneurs under contract. The era when he used to climb ladders himself to test lighting effects on stucco ceilings was over, as was the excitement of entering a big empty house, the elation of watching a job take shape. If a client had different ideas, he no longer fought to impose his own. "After all, he's the one who's going to have to live in this abomination," said Max resignedly. "I can only offer him my opinion." Sometimes he'd buy a neglected house in an expensive neighborhood, renovate it without a client breathing down his neck, enjoy it for a while, and then sell it to someone he deemed worthy to live there. He didn't need to shop his skills around. People sought him out.

From time to time he grew weary of the city. New York tired him out, which Max took as a disturbing sign of advancing age. He was afflicted by the damp heat of the endless summers, the hectic agitation with which Manhattan always vibrated, without time to catch its breath, even at night. He was resigned to seeing clumps of filthy homeless people sleeping in entryways and on heating grates. They dwelt like cavemen, in cardboard shelters, under the scaffolding of construction sites. He felt helpless. He went out of his way to avoid the drug dealers and noticed himself going out less and less often. Max had never been able to see poverty as something that had nothing to do with him. He knew that he was one of the privileged few for whom New York laid out the rarest and most expensive of everything, and he was repelled by his privilege.

In the seventies, in the first euphoria of new wealth, he'd had the idea of buying ground-floor warehouse space in midtown Manhattan and installing a shelter for the homeless with dayrooms and bedrooms. Because he detested the ugliness of the purely utilitarian, he had furnished these rooms attractively. After a short time, the water faucets were removed; the bathroom fixtures were stolen half a dozen times before he gave up. The money Max had invested disappeared and the social workers took off. When he entered the vandalized rooms and saw the walls covered with coarse graffiti and every window broken, he gave up, embittered, depressed, a bit guilty.

"Sometimes," he confessed, "I hate this city."

From time to time he would leave New York, rent a house in a quiet suburb with pine trees and big, unfenced lawns that ran unbroken from one lot to the next. It could be somewhere on Long Island or in Westchester County, in Rye or Mamaroneck, close enough to the shore to see water. There the nervous energy that seemed to drive him even in sleep would gradually dissipate.

But it wouldn't be long—a few months at most—before Max would tire of the peace and quiet. Remembered images, smells, and tones of the city would reassert themselves: Pee Wee Russell's clarinet solos in a jazz club in Midtown, for instance, or the deep leather recesses of a lounge he had frequented with friends long since dead or living elsewhere. He thought of the bars scattered throughout the city, in the Village and on the Upper East Side, each with its own atmosphere and none he would ever visit again, assuming they still existed. He recalled the recent and the far distant past, like entering Grand Central Station with Eva for the first time or standing with Wallace Harrison on the evening they removed the last scaffolding from Lincoln Center. He longed for the sudden gusts of wind that sliced through his clothes at street corners and the smell of hot dogs and scorched oil mixed with gasoline fumes and the distant, salty sea air. It was his city and his memories reached back to the Central Park of his childhood, when the polar bear named Jake splashed around in his pool at the zoo. New York had been the site of Max's most unforgettable moments: the evening he first caught sight of Dana in the Russian Tea Room and the night more than thirty years ago when he picked her up after closing time and brought her home with him.

It would begin to annoy him that every excursion into the city had to be prepared, and that he didn't know anymore what movies were playing. He would miss afternoons among the endless rows of shelves in the Strand Bookstore, from which he emerged squinting into the sun, dizzy from reading all the titles and overwhelmed by the amount of knowledge he would never possess. He would imagine a Saturday morning spent strolling past the flea market stands between Canal Street and Orchard Street before eating the best knishes in Manhattan at Yonah Schimmel's on Houston Street. Once he'd started dreaming about food, he would soon find himself driving back and forth between Manhattan and his suburb, at first only to go to a restaurant or the theater, but after getting stuck in a few endless traffic jams, he'd decide to move back to his apartment.

He was unable to say when the burning pain and pressure in his chest had begun. They happened when he climbed stairs or something aggravated him. Soon they came whenever Max had to strain or exert himself. For the first time in his life he became conscious that he had a heart that no longer simply, effortlessly pumped blood through his body. On the contrary, now his heart was more like a delicately tuned gauge that would skip a beat and scare him if he let down his guard. It forced him to slow down his usual pace of life. Max had never thought about his body very much, he'd just relied on it. The only thing that had annoyed him about getting older was that other people seemed to regard him as an old man—his partner in the firm, construction workers, and most irritating of all, younger women, who reacted to his advances with amused surprise, as if they hadn't expected an older man to still find them attractive. A forty-year-old had told Max to his face that, as far as she was concerned, older men had absolutely no erotic appeal. And even when a seduction succeeded, he always had to fear that a sudden stab in his chest or pain down his arm would put a painfully abrupt end to a night of love.

When Max got the letter from Spitzer informing him that the last tenant had moved out of his house, which now awaited him, he'd already had his first brush with death. Max had agreed to a bypass operation and his life suddenly became governed by the hospital schedule. He was utterly absorbed in concentrating on his body: the heart struggling in his chest like a pounding motor, sending waves of pain flooding through his body, waves that ebbed under the analgesics before surging back with renewed strength. The letter reached him at a time when it seemed it must be meant for someone else. The only things Max could think about were to spare his body unnecessary pain, give it time to heal, and try not to groan aloud every time a careless movement sent searing pain through his sawed-open, slowly healing chest.

When he returned home after weeks in intensive care and rehab, he was depressed and, for the first time in his life, afraid to be alone. A longtime friend, a young architect he had met in Albany and helped get a job, had volunteered to take care of Max during the first weeks of convalescence. But she had brought her own work with her and sat at his desk, blithely absorbed in it, while he surrendered himself completely to his pain and the fear that life would never be the same again. Her unsatisfactory care and self-absorption annoyed Max, who grew impatient and peevish, remonstrated and made demands that she rejected, declaring that she wasn't a nurse. Finally she beat a retreat—not, however, before calling him a man who hadn't learned to age with dignity. That hurt.

Now his entire ambition became to regain his old physical stamina, and it was a triumph when Max could climb the six floors to his apartment without long pauses to catch his breath. Slowly, with a patience he had to learn, he regained his former life. But he had learned to recognize his physical limitations and accept his reduced energy.

On a milky blue winter day, Max felt for the first time the old joie de vivre flowing back into his convalescent body. It had been almost three months since the operation. It was December, and a blizzard had swept through the city. The snow glittered blindingly on rooftops and even the air seemed frozen. There were no colors except white and an endless bright blue. On this day Max went for a long walk in Central Park and felt reconciled with his life. He watched the sunlight glide up the tree trunks and the sides of the buildings on Fifth Avenue as the sun went down, and felt a kind of joyful expectation.

Max resolved to do all the things he had been postponing until later, until his retirement. He would move into his mother's house and there experience keenly, at least once, each season of the year. The time had now come. With age came a yearning for childhood memories, the smells, voices, the light and shadow in the rooms of that house at various times of day that he would recognize like images from a dream wrested from oblivion.

Chapter 9

As his plane started its descent Max looked down at the hilly country below, a bustling landscape with little patches of forest stretching their arms toward the rivers, sharply delineated fields and pastures, a quilt of little quadrangles, villages, market towns, small cities. It was the beginning of March and the earth still had something raw and naked about it after a long winter. On shaded slopes there was still snow.

The house stood empty. It belonged to him. He would move in today. He'd asked Spitzer to furnish it provisionally with the bare minimum. Its renovation would be his crowning achievement. Max brought plans that he'd already drawn up in New York and he was still brimming with ideas. It would be his final project, which he would watch as it grew and began to enclose him like a shell, completely attuned to his distant memories. The house would restore the magic of his childhood, recreate a serene present ignorant of the passage of time. He was convinced that he was returning to the place where he would die.

Max was fond of the sleepy atmosphere of small airports, the perfunctoriness of customs agents. Spitzer stood among the others awaiting the plane and, grinning impishly, held out the house key to Max before they had even embraced. They had seen each

other only once in the past eighteen years, when Spitzer spent a
week in New York. He'd finally taken Max up on his repeated
invitation to stay with him. Max had put himself out to fulfill
Spitzer's every wish. In the end, however, he got the impression
that Spitzer was glad to be going home again. Since then they
had exchanged greeting cards at the holidays. Occasionally Max
would phone, but his calls always seemed to cause panic. Spitzer
began every conversation by inquiring anxiously if something had
happened, if everything was all right, if Max was in good health.
Max feared that these calls gave his friend no joy, instead upset-
ting his equilibrium, and so after a couple of attempts he gave up
phoning.

Spitzer was sixty-seven. He was younger than Max but had aged
a lot and seemed to suffer from shortness of breath. They were sitting in the taxi and the luggage was safely stowed in the trunk, but
Spitzer's breath still came in an occasional asthmatic whistle.

Max suppressed his worried question, Are you sick?

The taxi stopped in front of Max's house. The deciduous trees
were still bare, but the tops of firs and spruces shaded the
housefront, where the flagstones had sunk deep into the soft
ground.

"They neglected everything the past few years," said Spitzer,
"but that was to be expected."

The old Nazi Party member had died a year ago and his daughter had taken her aged mother to live with her. That's all Spitzer
knew. He'd never understood why Max had refused to share the
house with his tenants. He supposed it must have something to
do with his sensibility to the atmosphere of a house. Whenever
Spitzer had stopped by to look after something for Max—to su-
pervise repairs or negotiate with the tenants—it was so quiet in
the house that Max could have occupied the second floor and the
attic in complete peace and quiet. But for Max it was unthinkable

to be daily running into people who had installed themselves here and fathered children while Sophie and Albert were being murdered and Mira was longing to be here more than anywhere else on earth. He couldn't forgive them, even if it wasn't directly their fault.

"It's good to have you back," Spitzer repeated as they stood at the front door. "Are you happy?"

In the failing light, there was an oppressive solemnity to this moment as Max went to open the new lock on the door. The key didn't work.

"A bad omen," said Max.

From time to time since the bypass operation, he was seized by a vague dread, like a premonition of evil. He'd known this unaccountable feeling of dread his whole life long: as a child riding the escalator down into a subway tunnel, later, sometimes in the afternoon, driving west out of the city or on some other highway into the glowing red sun so close to the horizon, or eavesdropping on Ben talking to himself in his room, listening to his voices and then answering them. But since the operation, this feeling often overcame Max for no reason at all, as though a protective covering had been pulled off the world and he could feel an implacable icy breath preparing to destroy him; he didn't know what to call it, if not the touch of death.

Max often caught himself listening fearfully inward, to his unreliable heart. It scourged him forward until he could hardly catch his breath, or it fastened a paralyzing iron clamp on his chest and shot pains through his body, pains whose reverberations he could hear like echoes of a distant explosion.

Spitzer finally succeeded in getting the door unlocked. In the hall it smelled of mildew. Diffuse light fell through the high stained glass window, casting red and blue arabesques on the wooden stairs.

"The kitchen must be here," said Max, turning to the right. They entered a bright, nearly empty room with a few pieces of garden furniture, a large, old-fashioned kitchen sink yellowed with age, a bulky refrigerator of similar dimensions, and a white kitchen cabinet missing its door. They must have been things from Sophie's kitchen, but they awakened no feelings in Max. It was as if he stood in the house of strangers.

"Do you recognize it?" asked Spitzer.

"Yes and no. The sink yes, the window out there on the landing, but everything is so strange and dead."

"I'm sure it will come back to life again once you've settled in," Spitzer reassured him.

The garden table at the window was spread with a white tablecloth.

"My wife got a few things together for you," said Spitzer, "so you wouldn't have to go out shopping right after your long trip."

Half a chicken in a frying pan, pickled vegetables, a loaf of bread, some dishes, all sorts of packaged food in the refrigerator and on the shelves, purchased by the wife of his longtime friend, a woman Max had never laid eyes on. He only knew that Spitzer's second marriage was to a local woman, a Catholic who led her own life separate from his. Maybe she was like Spitzer, Max thought, ready to help without a lot of talk and to-do.

Spitzer took his leave after explaining how the heating worked. From the door he glanced back at Max in concern. The suitcases stood in the hall like irresolute guests.

"No, no, just leave them there," Max reassured his friend. Spitzer had trouble tearing himself away from this doubtful, depressing homecoming.

Max walked through the rooms. None of them corresponded to what he had imagined all these years. They were small, while in his memory they'd always been large. And they were dark, shaded by trees planted close to the house, whose branches scratched against the windowpanes as if seeking entry. He wouldn't live in any of these rooms until they had been renovated and the moldy gray walls and unfaded quadrangles left by pictures and furniture had been painted over. The house was alien, inhospitable. He was disappointed.

Finally, Max carried his suitcases out onto the veranda that his Uncle Albert had enclosed and winterized. Despite multiple small window frames that fragmented the view of meadows and river, this was the brightest room in the house. Only wild grape would grow around the windows in summer. He imagined a large facade of glass, gabled with transparent glass bricks, a ship's bridge floating above the slope, sparsely and simply furnished in the way he recalled from childhood: a bed, a table, two chairs, a few shelves that would gradually fill like the shelves in his New York apartment: crowded with flea market purchases, house gifts from friends, things that people brought into his house even if they themselves soon disappeared from it, mementos of unforgettable evenings, the visible traces of fleeting moments, accumulating in his rooms like the sediment of his years. It was the principle of fortuity he found appealing: that every experience, every encounter, could be brought to mind by a particular object that bore the weight of memory. The older he became, the more he lived in symbols.

"Maybe you should rent a couple rooms out if you're not living in them," Spitzer had suggested. After all, it was a big house that could easily be subdivided into two rental apartments. Spitzer could recommend some tenants. But Max wouldn't hear of it.

He was oppressed by a peculiar weariness. He felt chilly, although the house was heated. Spitzer, who phoned every day or stopped by for a short visit, asked if he should send him a doctor—Malka, a member of the community.

No, no, he just needed some warmth, Max replied. The first weeks passed without any activity on his part aside from short walks. Some mornings, he awoke to the twinkle of a snow-covered landscape—every twig, every branch so white and strange that he couldn't remember right away where he was. Then, from one moment to the next, a curtain of black cloud would draw across the sun, a storm would blow up, tearing at the larches on the slope, thick wet snow sweeping across the valley and everything turning black again, and terribly bleak.

With many interruptions, Max had spent his entire life in New York. So much nature all at once seemed weird. He felt threatened by spring storms that blustered over the house on the slope, rattling its windows. Like a hotel guest who arrives at the wrong time of year and now wonders how he's going to kill time, Max gazed out onto gray-green meadows still wan from winter. Maybe his stay in this house was only meant to be a way station—who said he had to spend the rest of his life here, anyway? Each season at least once—he'd said that before leaving New York, he owed that to Mira's memory.

Chapter 10

ON FRIDAY EVENING, the prayer room was overheated.

"We're getting old," said Spitzer. "We get chilly easily. If we don't turn the heat up, Frau Vaysburg will still be wearing her winter coat in May."

Max knew only a few of those present from his first stay in H.: Frau Vaysburg, smaller than he remembered her, tough and fragile, like a feisty little bird with lively brown eyes; Steiner, a stocky seventy-year-old with a bohemian shock of white hair and a quiet, charmingly shy wife. Gisela Mandel had only been attending regularly since her husband died; it was so hard to spend Shabbat alone. Chaim Alter with his strong Polish-Yiddish accent was still a disputatious bachelor and no one was safe from his sarcasm. He must have been way beyond seventy but still had a pepper-colored brush cut and a face almost devoid of wrinkles.

Spitzer led the service. He prayed quickly, as if he wanted to get it over with as soon as possible. The younger people sat in the back rows: Malka, the physician, with her eleven-year-old son. In the first weeks after Max's arrival Spitzer had brought her to take a look at him after all, because he was worried about him, but Malka had allayed Spitzer's fears: the change of climate, the difficulty of adjusting to a new environment, the change of diet, whatever—at any rate, nothing to be alarmed about. Her short, sturdy physique reminded Max of Nadja, but she had a winning, self-confident smile. Her cheery optimism had the effect on Max of a salutary command to finally pull himself together and take his life in hand. Since her first visit, Malka called him frequently, as if he'd automatically become her patient. She asked if he needed anything, if she should stop by, as she casually described her house calls. This startled Max and he declined: no, no, he had everything he needed, thanks. He didn't quite know what to make of Malka. She was so thoughtful, so attentive, that she made him feel old and frail despite her reassurances, and her motherly sternness frightened him. He'd never liked taking orders from a resolute woman.

"Malka is lonely," Spitzer explained to him. "She lives alone with her son. Her husband left her." Spitzer couldn't understand why she was still alone after six years, a pretty young woman with such a positive outlook. In Spitzer's opinion they ought to send her off somewhere where there were Jewish men, maybe abroad, or she should live in a bigger city with a real community. "She needs a social life. She has a talent for bringing people together. She's even invited me to her house several times. On the other hand, it would be a shame if she left."

It hadn't occurred to Max that Malka might be lonely.

Malka and Daniel sat between Frau Vaysburg and the Barons, who in old age had come to resemble each other more and more. Both had the cautious movements of the nearly blind. Lea Baron still wore the same sand-colored wig she'd been wearing on Shabbat for twenty years. In some utterly strange way it made her delicate face look younger and led one to wonder how she would look with her own hair, or a different wig.

The others in the back rows, including some of the younger ones, didn't seem to Max to really belong to the community. They looked around inquisitively, as if they didn't know what was taking place or what they were supposed to do. But after the service they crowded eagerly around Spitzer, shook his hand, and thanked him.

"Who were they?" asked Max.

"Guests, people who are interested."

"Jews?"

"No, they come because they're curious. They're Christians interested in Judaism."

"Is there such a thing?" asked Max. "And so many of them?"

"Yes, it's obviously become fashionable to watch Jews praying."

They laughed.

After the service they all went to Spitzer's favorite café, the acquaintances from Max's last stay in H. as well as Malka, to drink a glass of wine in honor of Max and his return. "How long ago was it," Chaim Alter asked, "that you grabbed that shovel so energetically at the burial? Fifteen years?"

"Eighteen years," said Max.

They peered at him. How old might he be? And Max thought as he lifted his glass and said *L'Chayim*, they've all gotten old.

Back then they hadn't yet thought about old age, neither their own nor other people's. They all had similar life stories and no relatives except for the immediate families they themselves had founded forty, forty-five years ago, most of them here in this town, in a camp for DPs, in transit. They had ended up staying. Their recollections of earlier times had to leap over a longer and longer span of time. The life they told stories about lay far in the past.

They talked about those who weren't there. Their children and grandchildren lived elsewhere, and that was as it should be. Because of their grandchildren they had had to learn foreign languages in their old age—Hebrew, English—so they could talk to them. They passed around snapshots, the oldest grandson in an

Israeli uniform, the granddaughter in her wedding dress. They tried to figure out who they looked most like.

Daniel had fallen asleep on Malka's arm. He was one of the few children in the community. Wouldn't she rather move to Vienna, they asked Malka, if only for the sake of her child?

Then the talk turned to Nadja. Frau Vaysburg called her a restless soul. She was living in London now, had been married and divorced, and had finally managed to become a Jew. Somebody asked if she were going to come visit in the fall again; she always came for the High Holy Days. "She always comes back," said Frau Vaysburg, "but she never stays long. I just wish she could be a little more content."

Nadja, too, had become the object of memory and speculation.

"We're getting old, dying out," Spitzer said on the walk home. "We've gotten old together, the whole community."

They were headed in different directions, but Max offered to keep him company. "There's no Shabbat meal waiting for me anyway," Max said.

"Me neither," answered Spitzer, laughing. "People still find it disgraceful that we live here as Jews," he continued. "If I want to see old friends from earlier I have to travel to Zurich or somewhere else. They won't come here. I had to meet my cousin from New York in Frankfurt, in Germany of all places. He said he would never set foot in this country or this town again."

Max said he could certainly understand that. "They just don't want to have to see how the old Nazis who drove them out are growing old here in peace and prosperity without ever having been called to account."

"You've seen how small the community has become," Spitzer said. "There's hardly any from the next generation."

"But there were some young families with children there," Max objected.

"Yes, recently some Russians have arrived. We're glad to have them and we're trying to help. Most of them are young couples with children, a future for the community. But they don't stay, and why should they? And how are you supposed to know if some of them are really Jews? In the end it sometimes turns out that they just needed us to get a visa or a work permit and as soon as they discover that we don't have very much influence, they stop coming. People still believe we have some kind of secret connections, when really we don't even have the money to renovate the community house—only the synagogue. It will be finished soon, just in time for the High Holy Days, and we can't even scrape together ten men to take out the Torah. We have to request minyan men from other towns."

They had reached the river. The moon was a yellow, tattered fleck on the surface of the water. The stars hung twinkling in the blackness of the cold March night.

"It's going to snow," said Spitzer. "My joints tell me so."

"You've got a wife," said Max abruptly. "How come I've never seen her? Do you have children too?"

"A daughter, Helene. She's seventeen," Spitzer answered. Then he was silent and Max sensed that he shouldn't inquire further. They took leave of each other at the bridge. Max turned and walked up his hill. Spitzer might be a good friend, a kindhearted and selfless person, glad to look after other people's needs without expecting any thanks. But the dividing line he drew between his friends and his personal life was absolute. Max would have had to sneak after him to discover the house he lived in. He always said good-bye before they reached it, somewhere along the way. Who were the two women he called his family? You never called up Spitzer at home; you got in touch during his office hours. You met him at the coffeehouse, never at home, and you didn't ask any in-

quisitive questions because Spitzer didn't like that. He could easily fall into disgruntled silence.

In the course of the next few months, Max sometimes walked
through the city and found it almost natural that he was now here
and nowhere else. It was no longer the city that his mother had
known, nor the one from which they had once taken away his
relatives, but it was the shell enclosing all these other cityscapes
that continued an invisible life within it. And it had preserved
some unmistakable quality. It would never change fundamen-
tally, in its essence. It had long since ceased being a small town,
but would remain a small town nevertheless, even with half a
million inhabitants.

He knew that the town Spitzer carried around with him was
different than the one that his own eyes perceived. For Spitzer,
there were different absences that accompanied him through the
city like atmospheric layers or temperature zones. He had told
Max about how, as a child, he went swimming in the river with
other kids from the neighborhood and hadn't felt like an out-
sider back then. When he walked across the bridge on his way
home, he alone saw the place on the river and the ten-year-old
with his friends. And when he stepped onto the bridge, it was
always simultaneously the wooden planks of the old bridge too,
even if he didn't think of them every time. The Stadtplatz would
never be able to divest itself entirely of the red and black swastika banners, that's why he preferred to detour around it. Too
many memories were concentrated there. Nor was he able to pass
the synagogue, now restored, with a six-pointed star below its
ridge, without at least a quick glance. It was a reflexive habit he
could no longer break. To himself, he called the businesses in
the Hauptstrasse by the names of their original owners—Stern
& Sons, Schneider Paints and Varnishes, Schneeweis Clothing

Store—even when everything about them was changed, from their renovated facades to the floors that had been added on, to say nothing of their owners. Back then, in the early thirties, Jewish clothiers had hung their wares at the open doors of their businesses, sometimes even out on the sidewalk, and the newspapers had made a fuss. Their competitors were furious: the Jews were transforming the town into an oriental bazaar! Even then there were calls for a boycott and occasional acts of vandalism. And today, for the winter close-out sales, coats and anoraks again hung out on the sidewalk, but who besides Spitzer remembered what it had been like back then?

Max was eager to hear Spitzer's reminiscences. They were the same, almost the same, as those Mira must have had, but what Spitzer told him was always just fleeting impressions, short anecdotes he might break off in mid-sentence. Spitzer remembered the destroyed train station from right after the war, the cement ceiling sagging like a bent box top. Max's memory of the same location was of the rustic guest house, two-storied and painted Habsburg yellow. In its place now stood an office high-rise with a bank on the ground floor, and the park was no longer a remote appendage of the city but lay in the center of town, with manicured flower beds and a fountain.

The more life experience connecting a person to a city, the more manifold its layers became, invisible for others yet always present. Layers were deposited in one's consciousness like the annual rings of a tree, some lighter, some darker. A past catastrophe could perhaps only be divined in the irregularity around a deep scar. And Max thought it must be all these experiences and memories taken together that created in people like Mira and Spitzer that powerful sense of belonging that couldn't be transferred to any other place. When he walked with him, it seemed to Max that Spitzer had a separate reaction to every street and every part of town.

Sometimes he insisted on making a detour, or he became quiet, as if at a certain place he had stepped on a mechanism that transported him to another point in his memories.

In his peregrinations through the city Max discovered in the oldest part of town an arcaded passageway so narrow that one could span it with outstretched arms. In the curbstone of an arched entrance he thought he could discern inscribed, illegible characters. He traced them with his finger from right to left. Could it be a stolen headstone from a razed Jewish cemetery? He'd have to ask Spitzer.

On a desolate edge of the city he discovered a row of two-story houses that backed up against the restored castle, as rural and isolated as if they wanted to creep cowering back into a distant time. This street seemed to him like a passage into an uncertain past, almost as if its inhabitants had disappeared long ago, leaving behind only these houses with sunken roofs and little blank windows. Their romantic dilapidation appealed to the restoration architect in Max. But he guessed that these houses, too, were slated for renovation soon. They still had cushions of moss on their sagging roofs and the crumbling plaster had left scurfy wounds on the walls. Between the street and the dank foundations a strip of grass was recovering from the winter. In the back yards trellised fruit trees were showing the first green. An isolated residential neighborhood, almost a village, with narrow-chested houses huddling together in a dead-end street that took a sharp turn before it ended. At the end of the street stood a house that was bigger than all the others, with a massive wooden gate whose red paint was faded and peeling. There was an addition on one side—a gallery, Max thought—and Moorish windows. These bold windows seemed to him quite grand in such rustic, small-town surroundings. Couldn't he make out two niches under the gable, like open wings? Max was seized by the excitement of an explorer who stumbles across a precious treasure buried for centuries. Had he discovered a prayer house nobody knew about? He rattled the locked gate and looked for a rear entrance, feeling almost like someone rediscovering his own missing property, misplaced long ago.

Breathless with excitement, he barged into Spitzer's office. There, too, time had come to a standstill: the dark brown furniture, the creaking armchair with its cracking leather, even the brand of cookies that Spitzer pulled out of a drawer to offer him. Nothing had changed since Max's first visit here.

"I can't quite believe it," Spitzer said. "I'm sure I'd know about it if there'd been a prayer house in that part of town."

"What do you think of the idea of me writing a chronicle?" Max asked. "A chronicle of the Jews in this town, from beginning to end."

"What do you mean 'end'?" Spitzer asked in alarm.

"When we're not around anymore."

"Then there will be others around, younger ones."

Nevertheless, Spitzer was delighted with the idea. It would keep Max busy and give purpose and direction to his aimless rambles through the city.

Several times in his life, Max had attempted to write something, but never gotten beyond a lot of handwritten pages covered with marginal notes and footnotes. When his curiosity about a subject was exhausted, when the chaos of notes on his desk had become unmanageable, he put everything into one of his many boxes, shoved it into a closet, and turned to a new topic. It had always annoyed him that he lacked the ability to put his thoughts in order clearly and marginalize what wasn't important, as he'd always been able to do when designing surfaces and spaces.

Now, on many days, Max sat in the town library or the municipal archives, had manuscripts and yearbooks brought to him, read about conflagrations, births among the nobility, dukes and archdukes, their feuds and victories. He found mention of epidemics, floods, and murder trials, but about the Jews he found nothing. Only when Thomas—a young, effusively helpful librarian with a congenial, open face—came to his assistance and gave Max customs regulations and lists of tolls did individual Jews begin to appear—in sketchy, blurred outlines—in the nine-hundred-year history of the city.

What was he working on, Thomas wanted to know. He'd recognized him right away as a research scholar.

Max laughed. "So I look to you like a *Privatgelehrter?*"

Thomas laughed, too. He had a bashful, ingratiating smile that gradually spread over his entire face. Jews had always fascinated him, he asserted guilelessly.

"Always?" asked Max ironically.

Yes, always, since he was a child. He couldn't say why.

"Migratory birds always fascinated me," Max said, "how they get the urge to fly south at a moment they haven't figured out ahead of time and how they know their destination. I find it usually takes a lot more hard work to understand people."

Thomas turned red beneath his blond crewcut and apologized. He hadn't meant it that way.

In the beginning Max was surprised by Thomas's zealous goodwill. As he soon learned, he was a freshly minted Ph.D. in history. Max found his interest too hasty and unconditional. He kept his distance, waiting for the young man to reveal his motives or tire of being assiduous. But Thomas greeted him every day as if Max's arrival were a personal honor.

Max followed his leads with increasing obsession. Again and again he returned to the house with the mangy yellow walls and the Moorish windows. He never saw anyone entering or leaving the building. Spitzer showed him the buildings he knew to have been prayer houses in the previous century: middle-class houses with classicist ornamentation and without the least trace of their original purpose, not even any evidence of a cover-up. Like spring turf that overgrows the wounds of the previous year and makes them invisible, these houses stood among the others, repudiating their history. On the ground floor of what had been the largest prayer house before the synagogue was built, an antique dealer was offering for sale old chests of drawers, porcelain, objects made of silver. There were also candelabra—two-branched, seven-branched. Max entered the shop. No one could have told which direction the worshipers had faced to pray, where the ark with the Torah scrolls had been located. The proprietor knew nothing and just hoped Max would go away soon.

It was Thomas who showed Max the beautiful parts of the city: little parks with broad linden trees, secluded arcades, and Renaissance courtyards, facades and gables he had until now passed without notice. And steep, narrow streets from which one could look out over red tile roofs, carved wooden galleries with lace curtains, and over the city itself between forested slopes, cradled in the bent elbow of the river. Thomas had been born here, his parents had been born here, his grandparents, too. This family of burghers had lived for centuries in a house whose windows looked onto a side street of the pedestrian zone, and he loved his city. Its history was important to him, as was the confidence that there were no uninvestigated dark corners to it.

"My mother loved this town very much," Max said to Thomas, but instead of the delight Max expected, a strange, pained expression crossed the young man's face. Max had a premonition that he would have to listen to some sort of confession.

He assembled his furnishings at the Saturday flea markets, not to save money but because objects without a history were dead for him. Only memory, even if it were only conjectural or invented, made them come alive, but not for everyone. Because each object, once awakened to life, had a distinctive essence, an aura that made itself known only to certain buyers. Like the yellow house in the dead-end street to which Max kept returning.

Among beer steins and liqueur glasses he discovered two little silver-plated cups.

No, that couldn't be writing on them in the opinion of the young woman in the flea market stall, a pretty brunette with merry blue eyes. They needed to be polished, but she'd tried it already and it didn't help much. The curlicues were too deeply engraved.

How old might they be, Max wondered. She had no idea. It wasn't her personal stuff she was selling here. She didn't know where it came from.

"Could they be wine cups?"

"This small?" She laughed. "Maybe they're candle holders for thick candles." They were kiddush cups. Max read her the Hebrew writing she took for just an agglomeration of senseless squiggles. "The fruit of the grapevine," he read.

Startled, she assured him, "I get this stuff on consignment." After so many years these ritual sacramental objects had lost their owners for good. Nobody knew what they were for anymore. The really valuable pieces—the heavy Shabbos candelabra, the cut-glass wine goblets—stood in museums or perhaps as booty in living-room breakfronts, but the household effects of the poor had become orphaned. When they lost their meaning for the owners, they lost their value, too.

Who had ended up with the valuable pieces from Sophie's dining room, he wondered, the silver basket for the challah, the seder plate, the things she must have been so attached to. In which kitchen he would never enter were they standing now? Things were indestructible. His finds proved it—the *bessamim* casket he discovered soon after finding the kiddush cups, a heavily damaged piece missing the little bells at the top of the onion tower and on the four corners. Only the empty rings attested to the fact that they had once been there.

"That little tower's been standing around here for weeks. You can have it for nothing if you buy something else," the dealer said.

"There used to be little bells on it," said Max, pointing to the empty rings.

"Could be," replied the dealer morosely. "I told you I'll throw it in for nothing."

Max brought his treasures home, assigned them a place on the porch shelves, and decided it was time to renovate the kitchen. The house was still hanging on him like a baggy hand-me-down suit, musty and cumbersome, but certain rooms—the veranda, the bathroom, the kitchen—were starting to feel more comfortable, warmer, starting to take on an odor he considered his own. And upstairs, when the porch windows were open, he smelled the spring. It tugged at him a bit, plucked at his sleeve, made vague promises. The branches were still bare, but they had set moist, resinous buds.

Lately, since he'd returned to Europe, maybe since he'd been sick, Max had been feeling a diffuse longing.

On Friday evenings when he returned home after the service and it was still light (for it was staying light longer and longer), he thought that time stood still and demanded something of him. Then he would brood over his notes for the chronicle until late at night, tarrying over some terse marginal note in the annals that Thomas had unearthed for him, trying to imagine faces to go with the names: the Jew Friedlein, the first one mentioned as a homeowner in a

purchase document from the year 1306; Frau Rahel, whose gravestone had survived for seven centuries. Had she worn a white cap
with ribbons and long black skirts with hidden pockets in which
jingled the heavy keys to the pantry, as in the illustrations he had
seen in a cultural history of the rise of the middle class? Or had there
already been special sumptuary laws for Jewish women back then?
Rahel, the daughter of Markus, the spouse of Moyses, deceased in
mid-summer, on the twenty-second of Sivan, by chance Max's birthday. What might she have died from? In any event, she died in the
relatively long period of peace between the Ninth Crusade and the
accusation of desecration of the Host in the year 1338, so that Moyses
was able to put up a gravestone of red marble for her in the year
5098 since the Creation of the World, a durable example of the
stonecutter's art. Although the stone had in the meantime been
whitewashed and used as a cornerstone of a building beside a dark
gateway, one could still decipher the inscription. A piece of luck that
it hadn't bothered anyone, neither the builder nor the owner, to
lay the face of a Jewish gravestone into the foundation.

In the archives Max talked to Thomas about which pogrom it
might have been that supplied a nouveau-riche Christian with
Jewish gravestones as building material. Yet, in Thomas's imagination, the Middle Ages were a time when mysterious, wandering
Jews in romantic get-ups traveled the trade routes, unimpeded
by the knights faring to Jerusalem in sacred zeal to reclaim the
holy places of Christendom. He could recount anecdotes about
Richard Cœur de Lion as if he had been a hero of his childhood,
as well as amusing stories from the plague years. *Huius anni on
Saint Jacob's Day there arose a great dying in all the world, so
that a man got an ulcer and died on the third day thereafter. In
that same dying and in that selfsame year the Jews were slaugh-
tered and burned in all the lands of Germany,* they read in the
transcript of a page from a chronicle from the year 1350.

He hadn't studied that yet, Thomas admitted shamefacedly. There had been seven hundred years of regularly recurring murder and expulsion in his city, as if it had revolved in an endless present, and nobody had an inkling, nobody knew anything about it, nobody ever talked about it, neither in school nor at the university.

"That's hard to believe," said Max.

Chapter 11

SHORTLY BEFORE PESACH, new faces began showing up in the community, birds of passage who came to H. every year for two or three weeks, out of habit or homesickness. First to arrive were the Leafs, formerly Grünblatts, from Santa Barbara, California. Right after the war, they'd met here in a DP camp on the edge of town, and Edith Leaf had worked as an actress in the municipal theater for a few years. When they began to reminisce, Spitzer's eyes started to tear up and his face was transfigured by a smile like a reflection of another face he had put aside long ago. Then Chaim Alter and Gisela Mandel also got tipsy on the high-spirited mood, as if to say, we're not even here in your present or in your city that was never ours. And if anyone thinks we're just a couple of quaint old duffers celebrating memories of youth, let them go ahead and think so.

Malka invited everyone to the seder. The big table in her living room with its many little saucers of parsley, salt water, and *charoset* was too small. Max sat on the piano bench between Frau Vaysburg and a woman in her thirties whom he didn't know. But he'd been stealing glances at her since she paused in the doorway before entering the room. He'd maneuvered himself into the seat next to her. She gave him a nod and said her name, Diana, as matter-of-factly as if this meeting had been prearranged. She said her full name, but he called her Diana. No other name would have suited her so well. She was slim, elegant, aloof, yet very feminine and with a palpable nervous tension. Her surname was a common one in town, not Jewish, but familiar. He'd seen and heard it often. She parried his curiosity with a mysterious smile and captivated his interest—so much so that Spitzer had to shush Max to be quiet for the ceremony.

"I haven't been to a seder in years," said Max, "not since my mother died. But as a child I always looked forward to Pesach, because the whole family was together. What about you?" he asked Diana. "How was it in your family?"

She laughed and nodded, but said nothing.

Spitzer led the seder. As Max observed his concentration, he mused that Spitzer must be a deeply religious man. He'd never known such a person and didn't know what it meant to be deeply religious. But now, in this fleeting moment, Max felt able to understand it, yet couldn't have explained this to anyone.

Malka's Daniel sang the Four Questions. He had a lovely child's voice. He'd have to sing the questions for many years to come, just as Max had done in childhood because he was the youngest, until the Pesach when they stopped having a seder because Victor was with Saul in Washington and Ben was in the psychiatric clinic. Then Max had suddenly become the oldest, the only one left to take care of Mira and his sick brother.

Daniel would leave H. some day, but until he did, he'd probably always be the youngest. Malka was beaming. For these few moments she sat quite still and devout next to her son. But soon she would jump up again and rush into the kitchen, arousing Spitzer's disapproval.

Malka believes too desperately in goodness, Max thought. That's what made her so hard to take. And it put him in the wrong from the very start. He recalled an evening several weeks ago in this same living room. He had been invited along with other friends of Malka. She often invited people to her large apartment in a new development on the edge of town. Max had observed the others, who were strangers to him, and couldn't shake the suspicion that they were hiding something they were uncomfortable about. For quite a while, he hadn't understood the drift of the conversation because nothing was being said forthrightly. The word *ethos* was being bandied about quite a bit and he wondered if the other guests were members of a club, an ethical society. They were all preening themselves on their *heartfelt ethos*. They hinted that there were certain disadvantages they could expect because of it, that they'd even lost some friends.

"What ethos is it you represent?" Max asked the woman sitting next to him.

She looked at him in surprise. "Antifascist!" she said

"Doesn't that go without saying nowadays?" he asked.

Later the talk turned to disasters, a conflagration of thirty years ago that had reduced a church to ashes and of course the great catastrophe of the Second World War. Somebody recalled his father's return from a Russian POW camp. He related at length how as children they had to hang their clothes over the back of a chair before going to bed so they could put them on fast in case of an air-raid alarm. But most of them had been born after the war and talked solemn-faced only about the *unspeakable suffering* of those times.

"How did people actually react," asked Max, "when the Jews suddenly disappeared from their neighborhoods?"

They looked at each other in embarrassed inquiry. One of the guests had asked Max sympathetically about his own experiences and the number of his dead. Max fell silent—just as Spitzer always did—and waved the question away. For an uncomfortable moment no one spoke. When the guests had left Malka beseeched him,

"You've got to tell about your experiences. You could have been more accommodating to them. They mean well and they're decent people. You can only fight prejudice if you seek dialogue."

It was precisely the prejudices he had sensed, Max had replied—that and great discomfiture on both sides.

Max turned back to Diana now and started asking cautious questions, as one does with strangers. Her eyes were as transparent as amber.

She spoke as if trying to distract him. Her small, made-up mouth left a red edge on the wine glass from which she took only small sips while everyone else took swallows. The prescribed four glasses. Diana laid her hand over the glass, shook her head.

The wine had long since begun to quicken people's memories. When Edith Leaf made a celebrated appearance as Miranda in the first Shakespeare production since the war, her husband Eduard had thrown twenty-four red roses onto the stage, one for each year of her age, his long brown hair aswirl as he made the toss from his seat in the second row. Now Edith ran her hand tenderly over the toupee that stuck out over his ears and neck like a pelt. Back then he'd had beautiful hair, they both assured everyone.

Gisela Mandel heaved her considerable bulk out of the chair, raised her glass, and sang *Bej mir bistu schejn*. She too had memories. She'd been eighteen when she got married, with blonde braids, this long and this thick around.

"*L'Chayim*," cried Eduard and raised his glass.

The Mandels' was the first wedding after the war, he explained to those who didn't know it.

"Blessed be his memory," said Gisela Mandel as she sat down and reached for a handkerchief.

The young people listened and breathed the overheated air of the past. Chaim Alter had other memories. "Gretl Stern weighed 60 pounds and walked home from Mauthausen," he said.

And because she wouldn't marry him he had stayed single, everybody knew that, and also how jealously Chaim guarded the empty space next to her grave, reserved for him.

"I survived on snails," Herr Baron recalled. "They were crawling across the path, and that's how I discovered escargots!"

"We should be talking about something else," Spitzer reminded them and rapped on his glass.

Frau Vaysburg took photos out of her purse—her children and grandchildren. They were her life, far away from here. She spoke fluent Hebrew. She'd had to learn so many languages in the course of her life.

"Languages were always easy for me," she said. "I'm flying to Israel in May to visit them." She beamed. "My youngest grandson's going into the army."

Later, as Daniel was getting his prize for finding the hidden piece of matzo, Frau Vaysburg drew another piece wrapped in tissue from her purse. "This is from last year, and it brought good luck."

Max noticed that she spoke only to him, as if Diana were not sitting next to him.

"Do you know Diana?" he asked.

"Yes, yes, of course," she said quickly, as if he had brought up an inappropriate topic.

The others sang the traditional songs, laughed and corrected each other's mistakes, and, at the end, called out together in one voice, "Next year in Jerusalem!"

Max was unwilling to say good-bye to this woman he knew nothing about but nevertheless felt close to. Malka hugged her guests one after the other, shook hands, kissed cheeks with relentless cordiality. Was there a trace of coolness when she said to Diana, "Thank you for coming"?

"Where do you live?" asked Max.

She named a street just off the Stadtplatz.

"Would you like to walk a bit?"

She shook her head. "I should have been home long ago."

She asked Malka to call her a taxi.

"There's a bus stop in front of my building," Malka objected.

"That's probably faster," Max said, "and I could keep you company."

But Diana insisted on a taxi. When they were in the taxi and nearing the pedestrian zone, Max asked if he might invite her to a coffeehouse in a couple of days. She nodded, and without the least coquetry named a coffeehouse and a time: tomorrow at 7:30. She seemed already preoccupied as she distractedly said good-bye and quickly got out of the taxi, without looking back. Max continued on to his house.

When he set off the following evening, Max could feel his nervous tension, a mixture of stage fright and anticipation that made his heart beat faster. Then they were sitting across from each other in the coffeehouse. Diana looked at him as if she expected him to say something specific she had perhaps been waiting all afternoon to hear, something for which she had come here to meet him. They sat as if enclosed in a membrane, so that the noises of the café, the impersonal hum, the clatter of glassware, or an occasional call for a waiter reached them from far away.

"You're not a member of the community?" asked Max.

She shook her head. "I'm not a Jew," she said bitterly and stared at her cup. Then she visibly pulled herself together and looked him straight in the eye, as if challenging him to go ahead and ask his questions.

He was afraid of a confession, whatever it might be, that seemed to require so much fortitude. And so he told her about his house, about the first time he had come to H. as an adult, and how he had won it back.

"I live in a house like that," she said. "My father-in-law has owned it since 1939."

She looked at Max in fear and challenge, as if she expected a violent reaction. He was silent for a moment and looked back at her.

"Jewish ancestors?" he asked.

She nodded, "My father."

Max laughed out loud. "What does he think of his in-laws?"

"I never knew him," she said quietly.

She leaned back, exhausted, as if she'd told it all.

Max wanted to hug her or stroke her arm. He laid his right hand on her left one with which she was shoving the tray back and forth on the table. She pulled it back, picked up her cup with the other hand, and drank down her coffee in one swallow.

The mirrored columns reflected the lamps on the walls and individual faces. A man was watching them intently.

Diana rose abruptly, as if seized by a sudden panic she was desperately trying to keep in check.

"I've got to go," she said. Yes, there was panic in her voice.

"May I walk you home?" Max asked.

"No!" she said sharply, then got her voice under control. "No thanks. It's not far. I'll call you," she promised.

Then she went out quickly, without looking back.

The man in the booth by the window watched her go. Then he turned back and gave Max another long, searching look. Max changed seats, turning his back to the man. He read the newspapers for a while, then called the waiter over and paid. He thought he could feel the gaze of the stranger on his back as he went out the door.

It was already late when Max stepped into the street, and he felt light-headed. He didn't want to take the bus or a taxi home. He had the feeling that something had happened to him that was still too close to understand. A dry wind was blowing and it was oppressively warm. The wind rattled gutters and drove all sorts of trash through the empty streets. Tattered clouds moved across the full moon. For some moments a taxi cruised along beside him like a patrol car. As he was climbing his hill, he felt the little tightness in his chest that he feared. He had to stop and catch his breath. Now he regretted not hailing the cab. He lay awake half the night, listening to the wind and the branches scraping against the windows.

Max got up the next morning still feeling dead tired, tarried before the bathroom mirror, and asked his reflection the worried question, Am I getting old? He didn't mean in years so much as in his attractiveness to women. He'd always had a lot of confidence in it, but since the operation something had changed, something not quite palpable—an expression in his eyes, a faded look to his skin, his muscles grown flabby, as if the flesh hung more loosely from his bones. On the first evening he was invited to Malka's she took a picture of him. With his glasses slid down his narrow nose Max looked like a worried bird. Sure, his hair was still full and had stayed dark brown for a long time, at least from a distance, but now it had turned just as gray as his beard. His eyes lay in a skein of wrinkles and looked tired, as if they had trouble staying open.

On this morning, a spot on his right temple caught his eye, a light brown, thumbtack-sized spot. A melanoma? Max had taken off his glasses and was studying his skin with shortsighted intensity, inch by inch. Hadn't it gotten more blotchy, weren't the age spots on his forehead and cheeks spreading like lichen? He tore himself away from this disheartening examination: I'm just getting old.

Late that afternoon, he was watching the workmen lay the terracotta tiles in the kitchen, still uncertain what he would do with the ceiling, when Spitzer arrived. Spitzer seldom visited him, and if he did, then only in the evening. He brought a plastic bag full of groceries, a package of matzo, and a whole roast chicken.

"You've been losing weight lately," he explained. "You should eat more. This is from my wife."

From this woman he'd never met, whom Max imagined as stout and friendly, with an apron and thick legs.

"Spitzer," Max cried, "you're one of the Thirty-Six Righteous!"

"Then call me Arthur," said Spitzer dryly. "That's my name, you know. I don't call you Berman."

Max couldn't have explained why he didn't use Spitzer's first name, but he recalled that there had been women who never called him by his first name. It involved some sort of bashfulness, as if to use someone's given name presumed an intimacy one could not claim.

"I'll try," said Max, but he knew that he wouldn't be able to force himself to do it.

They talked about the seder, about Malka, who'd told Spitzer that Max looked tired and emaciated. He probably wasn't eating enough, or regularly.

"What do you know about Diana?" asked Max.

Spitzer nodded as if expecting the question. "You like her," he said.

"I find her fascinating."

"No wonder. She's beautiful and enigmatic. Her son's an altar boy in the parish church. Every Sunday she sits there in the first row, I hear. Friday evenings she comes to us—sometimes, not always. When she can get away without attracting attention. And why shouldn't she?" Spitzer continued. "She's not beholden to anyone. It's just tragic that she needs to belong so desperately."

Nine or ten years ago, Spitzer recounted, a young man had shown up in his office, a nice person, not one of those who fell into an imitation of a Yiddish accent the minute they entered the community building to make themselves understood. He'd been very matter-of-fact, laid a photo of Alexander Baranovits on the desk and asked Spitzer if he knew him. Because this man was the father of his wife and she wanted to know more about him.

"I told him she should come herself," said Spitzer. "I wanted to get a look at her for myself. She came the very next Friday—shy, very agitated, as if she had to pass a test. She brought the photo along, said her mother had given it to her. She held it out, filled with expectation. 'My father.' That's all she said. What could I say?" Spitzer asked. "When he showed up at the DP camp on the edge of town in '46 Alex was only nineteen, a completely feral boy. Lord knows what he'd seen and done. He never talked about it. But it was hard to keep him out of trouble. For him, the war wasn't over yet. I guess for him it never ended. He would go to taverns where former Nazis hung out, intentionally provoke them, and then start fighting with them. Many times I picked him up the next morning at the station house or from the hospital. He could never get his accounts settled with them; he just had too much rage in him. He had no relatives left. He had nobody. He was so desperate," Spitzer said, "that the most we could do was to keep standing him back on his feet."

Spitzer told how once he had got hold of a bicycle for Alex. Bicycles were not so easy to come by in those days. He rode over a nail, puncturing a tire; instead of pushing the bike home, he was so furious he tossed it over the rail of a bridge. Later on Alex dropped out of sight, only showing up again when he needed money. He was rebellious, demanding. Everyone ended up avoiding him.

"Why did he stay here?" asked Max.

"Yeah, once we even gave him money to emigrate to Israel," Spitzer recalled. "In half a year he was back. The worst thing was that he couldn't tell the difference between his friends and his enemies."

"Did he have work, a job?"

"He couldn't manage one, at least not for long. Before long he'd get into fights with his co-workers or his boss. And he had no training in anything. Maybe we're all responsible for what happened to him," Spitzer reflected. "We were helpless. The only thing he wanted from us was money."

"Who was the woman he had this daughter with?" asked Max.

Spitzer didn't know. He hadn't even known that Alex had fathered a child until this young woman showed up.

"Do I look like him?" she'd asked Spitzer. He couldn't remember exactly, but he said, "Yes, a little bit."

She beamed.

"What was I supposed to tell her?" he asked Max, "that he was a rebellious *schnorrer*, a troublemaker, so severely damaged that no one could have saved him?"

Then the young woman came back to Spitzer's office, demanding to be accepted as a member of the community. She reminded Spitzer of her father the way she insisted on it, wouldn't listen to his objections, angrily demanded something she had no right to.

"You'd have to convert," he argued.

"How come?" she protested. "I'm the blood relative of a Jew. I've already paid dearly for it."

He explained that it was the religion of her mother that counted.

"Okay then," she said, "I'll convert. Give me a date."

She didn't think much of having to study and wait, of being thrice turned away, as custom demanded. She'd read Sholem Aleichem. She knew that Jewish women didn't have to study anything, just run the household—and that, she could do. She had very peculiar ideas about conversion, Spitzer said, and was extremely obstinate.

Now she was thirty-two and her impetuosity had died down. "She has to think of her family," Spitzer said. "She's afraid of them because she's completely dependent on them. She comes to us when she can, behind the backs of her parents-in-law. They live in the same house with her. However," Spitzer said in conclusion, "you don't have to worry about her. She knows what's good for her and she can look after herself," he emphasized, giving Max a warning look.

"I'm not so sure about that," Max replied.

Diana didn't seem like a strong woman to him. Tough, maybe, but insecure, tormented, and lonely, someone forced to live at a great remove from her true self, in a coldness that might destroy her. He thought he had a sixth sense for women like her. He even thought he attracted them because he could recognize their imperilment, the despondency that overcame them because their lives seemed less and less their own.

"Stop trying to save her," said Spitzer. "You'll only hurt her."

After he said good-bye to Spitzer, Max went out onto the terrace. In the twilight its freshly painted columns seemed very white, as if they had stored up the last light of day. The sun had already set, illuminating some last red clouds that swam in the dull blue of evening. Suddenly all of this—the whole house, the sky, this entire country—seemed to him quite foreign and incomprehensible.

Chapter 12

MAX HADN'T REALLY expected Diana to get in touch, but she called him up, speaking hastily, as if she had to steal this brief moment of conversation.

That afternoon they met at the river, on the terrace of the same coffeehouse where years ago Max had sat with Spitzer and Nadja and she had told him eagerly about how she wanted to be a painter. Soon the moist shadow of the trees on the opposite slope fell across the empty tables and it turned cold.

"All my life I've been trying to establish roots by marrying into my husband's family," Diana told him, "since I've never had a family of my own. But I still lack that feeling of security everyone else has. The Christians think I'm a Jew and the Jews don't accept me. Oh, I can tell," she cut off Max's protest.

"Are roots so important?" Max asked. "What are we anyway, plants? What do we need roots for? I've got no roots either," he assured her. "It's exciting to be a rootless cosmopolitan. Wherever the people you love are, that's your home."

She shook her head, annoyed. "You have no idea what you're talking about."

"Could be." He fell silent, letting her talk. Maybe for her he was like the stranger in the railroad compartment to whom one tells what one has never revealed to a soul before.

"I had a terrible childhood," she said. "I was given away as a baby."

"All childhoods are cruel," he argued, "almost all, in countless different ways. Mine was terrible, too, in many respects."

Her clear amber eyes darkened angrily when Max contradicted her.

"But my childhood has to be kept secret," she said defiantly. "It's like an illness I'm not allowed to talk about and nobody's supposed to know about. Others can put their awful childhoods on display and demand sympathy, but not me."

There were rings on the fingers with which she was now snapping toothpicks in two in intense concentration. "I suffered more than anyone else," she insisted, and Max stopped trying to contradict her.

For reasons he couldn't guess, Diana had decided to tell a stranger what was threatening to suffocate her otherwise. She talked with an imperious urgency, as if she'd been waiting for him—for someone like him—for a long time. And as she talked, she began to shiver from the cold.

"My name is really Dina," she said. That's what her father wanted to call her. It was his mother's name, but then on the birth certificate they put "Diana," and that's what everybody had called her ever since.

She told about the two brief encounters she'd had with her father. The first time was in some bleak public room when she was five. The foster mother who had raised her was there. They were drawing blood from Diana. She had to take off her shoes and socks. They inked the soles of her feet and her fingers, then pressed her toes and fingers one by one onto a piece of paper. The stranger—

her father—must have been in the room the whole time, but she hadn't noticed him. When she started to cry he was suddenly there, but not near enough to touch her. He was stretching out his open hand to her, squatting on his heels before her chair and smiling. Diana couldn't remember what he offered on his outstretched palm. Chocolate? A little toy? Money? It had all happened so fast, because her foster mother had pulled her away and rushed out of the room. The woman had been angry, outraged, tugging Diana away as if she had to rescue the child from this man. "A bad, bad person," she'd said when Diana asked her about the man. But later, when she was older and couldn't forget the encounter, her foster mother had admitted, "That was your father." He'd refused to pay support, had denied being the father. The bare office had been in the courthouse.

"I didn't know him," said Diana, "but I was absolutely certain I had seen him once before and had recognized him in that office, but I couldn't remember where. Later, when I was in a deep depression after the birth of my son, I was in therapy. I tried again to recall my early childhood, but it was as though everything before my fourth year was locked away behind a door. Only that one time when I saw him was like a ray of light, the certainty: That's my father. And then the door slammed shut again and try as I might, my memory can't retrieve anything from behind it.

"There must be a kind of memory," she speculated, "that only preserves feelings—before images, long before thoughts. That's where my intuition must have come from when I saw him and knew he wasn't just some stranger, but my father."

She told how a few more memories had surfaced during therapy, memories she couldn't place chronologically. The image of a meadow, wet grass and a shallow stream, everything very sunny and bright, and yet this memory filled her with inexplicable dread. Her mother was there with a man, but she didn't know if the man was her father or her mother's subsequent lover whom she eventually married. After her mother's wedding she was sent to her foster mother, an unmarried relative. Those years, on the other hand, she could remember very well. There was another image from her early childhood with her mother: the brown bars of a crib through which she could see a kitchen, painted white, and two people sitting at the table—her parents, she was absolutely sure.

She had seen her father one more time, when she already had his photo and so could recognize him. She saw him by chance. She was fourteen and riding the bus home from school. He was standing on a corner waiting for the green light. As she rode past, she twisted around to watch him until he disappeared among the other pedestrians. But he must have recognized her, too, because their eyes had met and he stopped to watch her ride by.

For quite some time Diana had been shivering as she talked, even though they had long since left the terrace to sit in a small dark room with a bar. Her teeth began to chatter. Max took off his jacket and went to put it over her shoulders, but she refused. She wasn't cold, it was just nerves. She looked very pale and drawn, as if the exertion had exhausted her.

"I have my hairline from him," she said and pulled lightly crimped, wavy hair away from her forehead. "They say that a high forehead is a sign of Jewish intelligence," she said without a trace of irony. "You think I have a high forehead?"

Sometimes she seemed so vulnerable and credulous to Max that it pained him to be a witness to her self-revelation.

"You know," he said, "that stuff about high foreheads and Jewish intelligence—that's just prejudice."

Whatever people had seen as her defects she had transformed into distinctions, precious signs of belonging.

On the way home through the chestnut allée along the river and across the bridge, Diana told him about her mother-in-law's garden out in the country, where only native species were allowed to grow. She talked about the battles they had fought with each other for years over every single plant, about how much she would have liked to plant tamarisks on a slope protected from the wind.

She could plant tamarisks and anything else exotic she wanted to in his yard, Max offered. "I've got no talent in that direction anyway," he said. "I'm a city person. I've always loathed houseplants and pets."

He was suddenly seized by a wave of excitement there on the bridge, a powerful happiness on this cloudless spring evening. So there was a life for him after all here in this town—new people, unexpected things that could happen, adventures, maybe a new love and, if not, then at least friendship with this troubled young woman.

Diana said she would be glad to help him plan and get a garden started. She stopped abruptly, held out her hand. "I go a different way than you." She didn't want them to cross the Stadtplatz together.

"I'm so happy we've met each other," said Max, almost against his will. He didn't want to scare her.

She smiled. "Next time we'll buy seedlings and flower seeds . . . soon, before the end of the month."

Every day he waited for this next time, from morning till evening, but without being conscious of doing so. He was now seized by new ambition to press ahead with the house renovations. The kitchen was soon finished and now resembled an old Italian pantry. The terrace was finally as it had been in Max's memories. For now, the living room was sparsely furnished, a large room created by joining two smaller ones, with a dark parquet floor, tall, narrow windows, and sparkling morning light into which the young leaves of a large walnut tree stretched fingers of bright shadow.

Diana arrived in her car, bringing two nursery flats full of young plants in moist, dark humus. She wore jeans and her unruly hair was knotted on the back of her head while ringlets escaped at the curve of her forehead. She seemed to him even younger than before, younger than her thirty-two years. She was so beautiful that Max wanted to look at her all the time but didn't dare to. She seemed inviolable.

The earth was dark and heavy from the rainfall at the beginning of the month. All by himself, Max dug over the beds the tenants had allowed to go to seed. He was intoxicated with his new life. He'd never before held a garden spade or shovel in his hand, had never tilled a garden. Together they planted clematis below the balustrade and a vine of pale *Glyzinie* in a corner protected from wind, between the house wall and the terrace steps.

"In America *Glyzinie* is called wisteria," Max told her, describing the heavy purple racemes blooming on the wall of friends he'd often visited with Elizabeth. Elizabeth has been dead thirty years, he thought to himself, and here I am planting wisteria and looking forward to them blooming.

Near scraggly looking black currant bushes that Diana predicted would bear lots of fruit they lowered the root balls of individual flowering shrubs into the ground, supporting each seedling with a broken-off branch tied to it with a strip of red woolen yarn. They squatted next to each other in the clingy dirt and sometimes their hair or their shoulders touched. They both pretended not to notice and didn't move apart.

Max never asked about her husband or her child, nor about her other obligations, as if he could thus extend her visit by a spell that obliterated everything else.

It was she who started talking about them. About being constantly haunted by the fear that something could happen to her husband, for then she would be completely alone in the world.

That was one more reason she'd wanted to convert to Judaism for a long time, so someone would be there for her and her child. But Spitzer hadn't considered that an adequate reason. She said Spitzer hadn't been able to imagine the panic she felt, this fear of being abandoned without a soul to look after her.

"It's a fear from your childhood," Max replied gently.

She was lucky to find her husband, she said, but she didn't sound happy about it. He was a good person, sensitive, completely different from his parents, only weak. He was afraid of his mother and that's why he wasn't able to protect her, Diana, from his parents. But he understood how important the connection to the Jewish community was to her. He had also agreed to let their son be baptized with the name Alexander.

"I know I'm not doing him justice," she said remorsefully. "I'm impossible to please. I have no reason to be unhappy, yet I am. I'm always afraid of being abandoned. He wouldn't stand in the way of my conversion, but he'd never let Alex become a Jew."

She told Max that when she started lighting candles on Friday evenings, her husband said nothing and acted as if he didn't notice. But when Alex asked what she was doing, he'd quickly replied that lighting candles was a nice custom, before she had a chance to say anything. On the other hand, he sometimes gave her something Jewish—an illustrated book, a Jewish calendar, a book on Judaism.

"Do you love him?" Max asked abruptly.

She looked at him thoughtfully. "I don't know . . . Yes, of course," she hastened to add, "I'm very fond of him."

She said little about her son. She didn't seem to have the same need to do so as other mothers. Instead, she talked about the parents-in-law who spied on her and about her own mother, whom she had never forgiven and whom she despised. She talked about her foster mother, too, a bigoted, narrow-minded woman who hated everyone who had a better life.

When you listen to her, Max thought, you'd think she was surrounded by enemies. But around him she was self-confident. When they worked in the garden together she told him what to do and decided when he'd done enough. He couldn't detect a trace of timidity or servility in her.

He could have looked up her number in the telephone book but he didn't do it. Why should he? He shouldn't call her up, he told himself, no matter how much he longed to hear her voice.

She showed up and left again, usually without warning. She explained neither why she came nor why she hadn't come, even if she didn't come for an entire week. And Max asked no questions, required no explanations. He persuaded himself that there was a certain appeal to living in a state of constant expectation. Even when Diana was present, something of this expectation remained. Even when they were sharing a laugh she projected a cool reserve, sometimes even a sense of absence, as if she routinely played the role of someone else.

Between her visits, on sunny days, he watered the young plants regularly. From this ground would soon emerge shoots and leaves in a profusion of undreamed-of colors and forms.

The blossoming trees were almost shamelessly luxuriant this year, but just when you could hardly see the branches and the emerging leaf buds any longer for all the white and pink blossoms, there was a cold snap, snow buried the meadows, and the blossoms fell from the trees.

Diana usually came in the early afternoon. When she arrived, her first glance was always into the garden. She inspected the tamarisk that she had supported with a bamboo stake and the soft, smooth lances of the iris; stood a long time before the still tightly closed rosebuds; bent down to the tender seedlings springing from the earth, whose mature form Max could not guess. She brought cloves of garlic to repel root voles and Max admired her talent and knowledge.

"If you weren't looking after things here," he said, "I'd probably let the garden deteriorate into a wilderness again."

"You're doing that anyway," she said, laughing. "You've never weeded even once!"

But he professed not to be able to tell the weeds from the plants they'd sown until he could see the blossoms.

Despite the apparent ease of their interactions, a distance remained that inhibited him from addressing her with the familiar *du*. She ignored every compliment and there was always a slight unease between them.

Once Diana was sitting on the stone pediment of the terrace, right where the little Venetian lion of his childhood used to sit up on its hind legs. Max was coming up through the garden and raised his head to look at her.

"Are you happy?" he asked, and she nodded.

After that she said *du* to him, without further explanation, abruptly, just as she did everything.

But when she left, he didn't dare ask when she would come again. He also didn't know for certain that his garden wasn't the main reason for her regular appearances.

"You just come to inspect what progress the sunflowers have made," he said, only half in jest.

"I'm not about to leave the sunflowers in the lurch," she answered.

But on many afternoons they also sat on the terrace or, if the weather was overcast, on the veranda overlooking the river. Diana never brought any food along, as Spitzer and Malka always did. She came to talk and often began to tell him something even before they had sat down. It was mostly about her childhood, and she admitted that much of it she'd never told to anyone before. She didn't say this in gratitude for his interest, however, but rather as if she were granting him the privilege of her trust.

Diana told of her strict Catholic foster mother's hardness and primitive fear of God. She'd been too ugly and too rigid to take from life what others were granted without any effort on their part, and for that reason she'd hated life and hated love, too, a love she'd never experienced. And yet love for this strange child, the fruit of her relative's youthful indiscretion, had somehow gained entry into this woman's heart and took the form of worry about the girl entrusted to her. Shortly after Diana moved out, her foster mother had died following a short illness, as if her life's work had been accomplished.

"And your mother," Max asked, "what's she like?"

If Diana was to be believed, her mother must have been a monster of female vanity, lusting for status and money.

"Doesn't she have any good qualities at all," asked Max, "not a single one?" What about the apprenticeship to a jeweler that she'd arranged for her daughter? Or the fact that Diana had lived with her and her husband for the two years of the apprenticeship?

"Do you know what other parents do for their children?" she asked angrily. "I'm an abandoned child," she repeated bitterly. "I have no good memories."

"Not even one, no moments of happiness?" Max asked. "Think it over."

Why did he always get the feeling when he listened to Diana that she was trying to make a specific impression and was hiding something?

But he also could sense how she was torturing herself, and he wanted to help her discover the lightness and joy of life.

Yes, she admitted, she had enjoyed the apprenticeship and the way her boss had praised her for the first pieces of jewelry she had designed by herself. Then she'd met her husband and gotten married.

"Have you ever been out of this town?" he asked.

Oh yes, once to a training course in Vienna, but she'd been glad to get home again.

"Then you don't even know what it would be like to live somewhere else?"

She thought about it. In any event, it would mean being alone, she said, or not being able to make yourself understood. "I'm afraid of being alone," she admitted.

"We could travel together," he hazarded the suggestion.

She shook her head, "I've got a husband and a child and parents-in-law. My place is here." She smiled. "When I come visit you, that's as daring as I can afford to be."

At night she often lay awake, she told Max. Since she was a child she sometimes hadn't been able to fall asleep until the early morning hours. At such times what she most wanted to do was to tell somebody about every pain, every hurt, everything down to the last detail. But when she started to tell her husband all this, it ended up being a completely different story and the most important parts remained unsaid. The little she had told him was subtly used against her; every conflict with her parents-in-law was laid to her childhood. Since then she didn't tell him anything anymore.

"And now you've told me everything," Max said.

She shook her head, "Not by a long shot."

She looked at him thoughtfully, as if formulating a difficult thought. "I always feel like I'm different, but I don't know in what way."

"Why should you be different?" asked Max.

"Because of my father and because of my childhood."

"Did your husband have a happy childhood, then?"

No, she admitted, not with parents like that. "He's completely different from them. He's always been tyrannized by his father. But he's also completely different from me. We try, but there's always something that one of us doesn't understand about the other."

"Aren't there any happy people in this country," cried Max. "What kind of country is this anyway?"

"They made my father *kaputt*, too," she said after a pause. "They wouldn't let him exist."

"Who told you that?" Max wanted to know.

"Otherwise he would have stayed with us . . . for sure."

It was drizzling when he walked Diana to her car, but it was still light, a strange twilight that made colors flare up one last time before dying out.

"Would you mind calling me Dina?" she asked at the garden gate. Without waiting for his answer, she went down the steps and out to the red Toyota waiting in the road.

Chapter 13

BACK IN THE spring the light green leaves at the high windows had still let the sun in. They had tossed and turned in the wind, showing silvery undersides. As summer progressed, the days grew darker in the ground-floor rooms, transforming them into cool aquariums. The isolated dapples of sunshine allowed in by the dense foliage flitted across the walls like will-o'-the-wisps and then winked out. Only from the veranda was there still an unimpeded view. Here and there a serrated leaf of wild grape shimmered through a window, but spread out before him were the unmowed meadows, their grass and wildflowers already waist-high.

Max sat at his old portable Olivetti typing up his notes. He couldn't recall a time when he had felt so light and clear-headed.

During the pogrom of the aristocrat Rintfleisch, he wrote, *who marched through southern Germany with the mob of social misfits he had stirred up, Albrecht the First attempted to protect his Jews as well as he could. After all, they were his best source of income. But the clergy took such offense at his partisanship that they ceased to pray for him in the churches. That, however, Albrecht could all the less afford since his feud with Adolf von Nassau made him dependent on the support of the clergy and the people. He was thus temporarily compelled to withdraw his protection from the Jews in order to prevent even worse from happening, namely, losing land to the Kaiser.*

How devoted the Duke was to his Jews could be seen from the fact that after his victory he forthwith restored their freedom of movement, at least to the few who were still alive. They also got their houses back so that he could immediately begin to levy taxes on them. Already by the year 1321, his successor, Friedrich the Handsome, was collecting a considerable sum in silver. At this time they had exactly fifteen years left until the next massacre. Of course, there was no way for them to know that. They mourned their dead from the last Crusade, built houses wherever and whenever they were permitted to, procured money for the Duke so that he would remain well disposed to them, and could be certain that this respite only postponed the next wave of murders.

Max had a dictionary lying next to his typewriter. It surprised and irritated him that he lacked so many expressions and words. Several times in each sentence he would have to look things up. He never possessed the blind assurance of someone who has always lived in one language that the word chosen from among several other possibilities was exactly the right one. In conversation he had never been aware of this uncertainty. There were always plenty of possibilities for saying something, and they didn't have to reflect precise nuances, only convey the approximate sense of what he wanted to say. After each long interruption in using his mother tongue, he had always been able to retrieve it effortlessly, astounded every time at how many words he thought he had lost would automatically materialize when he needed them. But now, in the act of writing, turns of phrase in English would block his path and absorb all possibility of expression. He had to search for the German idioms and had a difficult time deciding which one was appropriate. He would ask Thomas how his writing sounded to a native speaker's ears.

He wondered how the Jews had been able to live with the burghers of the town after the massacres. Did they have personal or only business contacts with each other? Was there mistrust and

fear on both sides? The fear of the one group for their eternal souls
if they suffered unbelievers in their midst, the fear of the other
group for their possessions and their lives?

The patience of the Christian townsmen finally wore thin, Max continued, *for their debts to the Jews—including the debts of the church—
had grown considerably. Even the monastery outside the city walls had
had to pawn a golden monstrance and thought that it was high time to
take it back by the force of the faithful. It had been twenty years since the
last murders.*

That's how long it takes a generation to grow up in peace,
thought Max. The memory hasn't faded yet, but its traces are
blurred. Those who were children during the Crusade of 1308 had
children themselves twenty years later, but probably could still feel
the terror in their bones. Something as harmless as the process of
oxidation in a monstrance, which had perhaps been pawned intentionally with this in mind, brought the unstable peace to an
abrupt end.

*Bloodspots on the Body of the Lord, only Jews could have con-
ceived such an abominable martyrdom. On a Sunday after Mass, inflamed
by the sermon and strengthened by Communion, the believers armed themselves with axes, shovels, flails, and pikes, and forced their way into the
houses of the Jews while the bells of the city sounded the alarm. Sunday
morning was a well-chosen time, for the Jews were almost certain to be
found at home. On Sunday mornings they were under curfew so that they
would not disturb Sunday tranquillity by their presence.*

There were moments in which he stopped to ask himself, Why
am I writing this, anyway? Who's going to read it? And why in German? Then he thought of Thomas and how little he knew of the
suppressed history of his hometown. As for himself, this history
was his only connection to H.

In his transcription of a page from the chronicle, Max found
the word *butchered.* Nothing more. No numbers, neither of the

dead nor of the survivors, only that they had been *butchered* in their homes. How was he supposed to write a chronicle when he lacked the necessary powers of imagination, when he was brought up short before this word as before a wall? In 1328, Rahel was already lying beneath her gravestone, but Moyses and their children were still alive, perhaps her father Markus and her unnamed mother as well. How many people had fallen victim to the armed citizenry on that Sunday? Max had found only three purchase documents. Were there more houses owned by Jews? He knew the part of town where these people had lived. The lanes must have been very narrow back then, alleyways that could be blocked off by a horse cart. People would have had to hug the walls when passing each other. In these lanes there was no escape, and fire could spread quickly. For a while after this there were no more Jews in the city.

Max reserved space for more narrative, searched for other notes, continued writing, wrote himself into a fury that always expressed itself as sarcasm: *After the pogrom, in gratitude for the debts that had been discharged with divine help and the recovery of the impawned monstrance free of charge, the burghers of the town erected the Pilgrimage Church.*

The annals kept by the Town Clerk wasted few words on the pogrom, but had fulsome praise for the builders of the church: *It emerged that the bloody monstrance could perform miracles. An imaginative Franciscan had this idea and it earned the town money. From everywhere, the afflicted began to come and spend money on indulgences and votive tablets, to say nothing of the room and board they paid during their stay. Throngs of pilgrims populated the city. They streamed in from all the parts of the country that had as yet no miraculous relics of their own, and they turned a formerly mid-sized trading town on a river into a center of piety. It expanded so quickly that it soon burst through its original ring of defensive walls. The Jews who had escaped the massacre—one or two always survived—sold their houses within the city walls. . . .*

Sold? When had Jews ever been able to sell anything during or after a pogrom? Max reached for his copy of the document. Certainly someone had made a purchase, but he had purchased from someone else about whom the document said he *acquired the synagogue and the Jewish school "kristlich."* Why bother to buy the house of the Jew Hirschlein when he could take possession of it *in a Christian manner?*

Max imagined to himself that the remnants of the community had later settled behind the protective back of the city wall, in a row of small houses. He saw blue irises proliferating on the patches of grass between the house walls and the lane, saw vegetable gardens and fruit trees growing out by the fields of the peasants, and a new prayer house at the end of the street. If they had to stand surety for each other even for the tiniest of infractions, then it made sense for them to live close to each other. But that was all just a fantasy; the houses he was thinking of had been built much later, at a time when there hadn't been any Jews in the city for centuries.

The plague years as well as their attendant persecutions were documented by a Town Clerk who had, in fact, taken the trouble to count the dead: *For the sake of the souls whom conscientious clerics were attempting to rescue from the fires of hell, this time they locked the Jews in a barn for a whole month in the hope that at least a handful would allow themselves to be baptized. In addition, the townspeople demanded ransom money from richer Jewish congregations, but they had their own worries. Nothing came of the ransom money and no one wanted to be baptized. And so no other course remained open to the city fathers,* Max wrote, *but to set the barn on fire. At the same time, the first Jewish cemetery was leveled and the gravestones—including Frau Rahel's—were re-used in the construction boom that followed the plague years. The chronicler counted five hundred Jews: three hundred imprisoned and two hundred slain. Many children were baptized and brought up in monasteries. No traces of the baptized led out of the monasteries again. Most of them must have forgotten where they came from and become pious monks. But finally, even the survivors and the returnees were expelled. By the end of the fifteenth century there were once more, once and for all, no more Jews in the city.*

Word for word, Max read in the chronicle: *All the Jews together were utterly done away with and driven from the land.* Where had they been driven? Onto pyres, as usual? Beaten to death, as usual? Destitute, deprived even of what they could carry with them, on foot, eastward, to Poland where his grandmother had lived and died, no one knew how. Or still farther, to Podolia, where his grandfather had grown up. Driven away, outlawed, with no rights, no letter of safe conduct.

Max took off his glasses to ease the pressure emanating from his shortsighted eyes. His thumb and forefinger sought the spot at the bridge of his nose that brought him relief when he pressed it with his fingers. He'd been sitting at his typewriter for hours. The table was strewn with photocopies and notes, the centuries were starting to become confused in their repetition of the same story over and over again, in their circling around the predictable calamity, predictable yet inevitable, worth only a marginal note from the chroniclers, while he was trying to extract a story from lapidary dependent clauses—the story of the Jews' love for this unworthy town, a love they had borne through the centuries, unrequited, a love the town could only think to requite with rape, plunder, and murder.

But next morning Max was already on his way to Thomas again with a long list of questions and requests for documents, dates, and facts he needed. Thomas would know where to find them. Thomas was very precise. Historians had no business speculating about undocumented events, he declared. Spitzer, on the other hand, relied on his own experience. For him a sales agreement could be the occasion to describe to Max generations of the history of one house or another.

"Did you know that Diana is co-owner of a house that the owners were never compensated for?" he asked Max. It was a corner house with ancient vaulting along the rear facade. Its arched gate on a side street was so wide that at the turn of the century people could drive horse-drawn wagons through it into the courtyard, while the windows of the upper stories, where the family lived, looked onto the Stadtplatz.

"Diana can confirm this for you," he added ironically. "She lives above the arches of the arcade."

Abraham Pevner had been one of the first businessmen to whom the town had granted a license for retail trade in textiles. His sons had purchased the corner house and it had been in the family for seventy years. In the thirties they started selling ready-to-wear clothing, which had enraged the competition and raised calls for a boycott. Spitzer recalled how popular the store had been among the poorer classes. It must have been a particularly desirable prize when the *alte Kämpfer* divided up the loot among themselves, he speculated.

When Spitzer returned from Palestine after the war, the business had a new name. Many businesses had new names. Witnesses to the name change couldn't recall when it had happened. But they had experienced much worse things that they remembered precisely: nighttime air raids, the sirens, often several times in the course of a night, the collapse of the Nazi regime, the hunger after the war. They'd told him about it reproachfully, Spitzer remembered. "You simply can't imagine what we've been through," they said, "just be thankful you didn't have to live through that."

People in town still spoke respectfully of Diana's father-in-law. A capable businessman, an imposing figure of a man, big and imperious, he looked down on anyone who approached him—a patriarch. It was his wife who ran the business, sold bolts of cloth herself from nine in the morning to six in the evening, and nothing escaped her attention. People said she was the soul of the business. It was she who went to trade fairs and bought new stock. You could find her in the store at any time of day. You could chat with her. She was very friendly to Max as well. Despite her fashionably elegant wardrobe she had a down-to-earth directness that made a solid impression on customers.

"You know, " she confessed to Max when he entered the store out of curiosity, "Jews dominate the fashion industry." She gave him a conspiratorial look. "You develop a sixth sense for it . . . Don't get me wrong."

He got her right. She had sized him up and let him know that she knew. Years ago a relative of the Pevner family had shown up in H. to see what had become of the house she recalled from childhood visits. Diana's mother-in-law had sized her up right away, too, as someone who could be intimidated. Her name wasn't even Pevner and she wanted to see their living quarters! The mother-in-law was outraged, felt she was within her rights, and her employees and even the customers were outraged right along with her. A stranger who presented no identification, a foreigner speaking bad German, wanted to see her house. They threatened to call the police; the salesgirl at the register was already reaching for the phone when the stranger beat a hasty retreat. "A mental case," said the owner whenever she told the story.

From Spitzer the stranger had obtained the key to the cemetery. She was granted access to the graves of her ancestors. Except for her, nobody from the Pevner family had ever returned to H.

Sometimes Max saw Diana in town. He didn't call out to her if she didn't see him or didn't want to see him. He understood. She was a woman from local high society who had a reputation to lose—the reputation of her parents-in-law. One Friday morning he happened to see her walking among the stands at the farmers' market. It was strawberry season and she stood a long time by the boxes of berries, took her time choosing the ripest ones, walked on, exchanged greetings with acquaintances, lingered by a stand with long-stemmed cut flowers in buckets. She was obviously familiar to the proprietor. She chose daisies and pale blue crown vetch and moved on with a cordial farewell. She strolled through the market, filling up her basket with purchases: the morning of a housewife in harmony with her life, wearing a blue suit that looked good on her, accentuating her dark hair. She was a pleasure to look at. How could one know if she felt at home here? Who would presume to distinguish appearance from reality? And if you could? Max knew her other side, and loved both equally.

Diana sat down at a coffeehouse table on the edge of the flower market and set her full basket down beside her. Her stockings shimmered as she crossed one leg over the other. She gave the waiter a dazzling smile and the man hurried into the interior of the café with its reflection still on his face. For a brief moment in which she was alone with herself, a weary, discontented sadness lay over her features—perhaps only in the eyes and the corners of her mouth—a moment of melancholy she allowed herself. Max walked up to her table, intending to greet her in passing like a slight acquaintance. She gave him a smile, too, but her eyes looked slightly startled. "I'm meeting someone here," she said, "but in the meantime . . ." She gestured to the empty chair. He could see in her eyes the worry that he might sit down.

He shook his head, "I'm in a hurry."

"See you soon," she called after him, relieved, "nice to see you."

She's a woman who fits this town to a T, it occurred to him as he continued on his way, and he decided to remember this sentence for Spitzer. Spitzer would ask which characteristic of hers he was thinking of and Max wouldn't know how to answer, not

wanting to speak ill of her to Spitzer or say the words that sponta-
neously occurred to him: conceited and dishonest. No, he protested against his own judgment, that's not true. Because what had
just happened, the brief encounter, the friendly brush-off, would
gnaw at her conscience as unjust. That was the difference. She
would come to him as soon as she could slip away to explain everything to him, maybe with an excuse, a white lie, what difference
did it make?

She came the next afternoon, again wearing the blue suit as if she
hadn't changed in the meantime. She was a bit embarrassed, a bit
out of breath, without a car. He waited patiently for her to shed
her sprightliness, the manic breathlessness that ran on awhile
longer, as if her engine were still turning over after she had turned
off the key.

"It's a small town," she finally said as if in explanation.

"I know that," Max replied, "you have nothing to apologize
for." There was unconcealed fear in her pale eyes. "They've got a
hold over me. My mother-in-law knows everything."

"About what?"

"About my background and that I sometimes go to the prayer
house and also that I often drive up here to your house."

She totted up her misdemeanors like a criminal on the run, and
you could clearly read in her face the punishment she feared most:
being disowned.

"None of that seems so objectionable," Max said matter-of-
factly.

She looked at him in surprise, as if an unexpected perspective
had just opened up.

But her mother-in-law had said things in the course of the past
ten years she couldn't expunge from her memory. Accepted with-

out protest, they had become a kind of truth. She'd told her son, "You've brought a cuckoo's egg into our house." She'd said it at a holiday gathering of the family. Everything got talked about at these reunions, never directly, but circuitously, with a suggestive grin, like when you need to find a polite word for bowel movement. Was Diana too kosher or not kosher enough? they quipped. And her mother-in-law puzzled over where her son got his penchant for the exotic, not from her at any rate, because she never had felt any attraction for *other races*. And Diana sat there silently. Her mother-in-law once asked her if she thought it right to have sneaked her way into a prominent family like theirs under false pretenses. They had assumed that her mother's husband was also her father.

Max took off his glasses and pressed his thumb and forefinger against the bridge of his nose. "Stop it," he said, "that's all stupid crap. How can you take that seriously?"

"Because everything I do, and the way I do it, and also what I fail to do and say—everything gets observed and interpreted," she said, "and everything they don't like or can't understand gets traced back to my Jewish heritage."

Max nodded. "Don't you sometimes show off with it, too?"

"What if I do? What's it to you people?" she asked angrily.

"What people?" Max asked in amusement.

There was a childlike pathos to her helpless rage, an innocent egocentricity. He wasn't able to take her completely seriously.

She told him about a Yom Kippur years ago when she didn't get there until *Ne'ilah*, the closing prayer, because that afternoon she'd had to lend a hand in the store. Then she'd picked up Alex from his riding lesson and run to the prayer house in jeans and a pullover, without having time to change.

She'd felt rebuffed although no one had said anything to her. After the service there were sandwiches, she related, but no one offered her any. She felt shabby and out of place, but the only reason she didn't change was not to waste any more time. "I could feel the rejection on all sides and I didn't deserve it." She broke into tears.

"Yom Kippur," Max explained to her, "is the highest Holy Day. Even non-religious Jews observe it. You either take the whole day off or you don't go at all. Maybe they were disturbed by the fact that you showed up as if going to the synagogue was just another appointment in your day."

She clutched her crumpled-up handkerchief in her lap and said nothing. From nearby the sounds of a piano could be heard, the same phrase from a sonata movement over and over again, always breaking off on the same note.

Diana looked expectantly at Max, and when he could no longer resist the challenge in her eyes, he stood up.

She stood up as well and took a step toward him. If she was thinking what he thought she was, it wasn't the right moment. They had often been much closer to each other. Everything had a time, and recognizing it was the secret of success. That's what his experience told him. But she had wept and aired her secret grievances, and she must have felt so exposed and vulnerable that the only thing she could think of was this daring step into his arms. Cautiously he approached the face that she offered him with a gesture of resigned surrender. She was utterly silent, not even a sigh, as if she had come to a decision and was now waiting for it to be carried out. He kissed her and she let him do it. She also let him slip her suit jacket from her shoulders, unbutton and remove her blouse, and then her skirt. Twilight had long since absorbed all color from the room and began to obscure the outlines of things. He could no longer see her face clearly. He saw only that her eyes were closed and took her silent readiness as consent. Her clothing fell to the floor while they kissed, at length, again and again. But when he took her by the hand to lead her to the bed, she started up as if she had just woken up. "No," she pleaded, "I can't." In her voice there was such wild panic that he let her go. He helped gather up her clothes and was careful not to let their bodies touch again.

In the harsh light of the ceiling lamp they stood facing each other. Out of the corners of their eyes they saw each other's embarrassment in the black mirror of the window. She asked him to call her a taxi, and without a word they went down to the garden gate.

"Diana," he began, "I'm sorry, I wanted to . . ."

"Dina," she said, "call me Dina."

"I can only be your lover," he said, "not your father."

She looked at him aghast. Then she walked down the street toward the approaching taxi without a word of farewell.

Chapter 14

ON THOSE ENDLESS early summer evenings when Max sat on his veranda after sundown and watched the surface of the river turning into a blank mirror that merely threw back all remaining light, or the storm clouds on the horizon erasing the glittering stars from the sky, he was overcome as never before by the loneliness of old age. His days passed monotonously—quickly, yet paradoxically, in unending slowness.

Over the course of many days, a peony below the terrace slowly unfolded its blossoms. Until they opened completely a dark, nocturnal color lingered long in their shadowy centers. For a while he measured the progress of time by the petals developing and changing from day to day. Then, one by one, they dropped to the ground. It was as if with each dying blossom nature were closing a chapter.

Max hadn't yet completely unpacked the boxes that had been sent from New York: the books he thought he couldn't live more than a few weeks without, clothes, mementos. Now it seemed to him that even without them the past was looming all too large. Things long forgotten were constantly appearing before him and taking on new significance they had never had before. The future was becoming small and dark. Soon he would arrive at the point where the future was no longer imaginable.

Hadn't he wanted to restore the house in order to return to the past, to revive his mother's dreams? But the house of his childhood was not retrievable. The further his renovations progressed, the more the old images faded. Memories tired him out, but at the same time they were all that remained to him on these lonely evenings. Time was slowing down, just as he had once wished it would, but its stagnation was like a paralysis.

What made Max uneasy was the gradual withdrawal of his vitality, his failing memory, the creeping deterioration of his body, and the waning of his curiosity, even toward other human beings. The unexpected events of his life had been repeated too many times to astonish him any more. Every new encounter reminded him of something in the past, and he already knew how it would turn out. The brief adventure with Diana—predictable, disappointing. As he expected, she had disappeared without explanation. But there was nothing to explain. He was a paternalistic friend, and she had indulged in his admiration. Sometimes when he passed her in-laws' store he saw Diana standing behind a narrow table and unrolling bolts of cloth. He didn't even pause but continued on his way without regret. He was offended by the heedless way she had moved on, even if he had experienced this often enough in the past that it didn't come as a surprise.

He could just as well have spent these warm sunny days somewhere else, he mused, in the mountains or at a lake. Suddenly he would be overcome with a powerful longing for the ocean, for Neponset Beach, south of Brooklyn, where Mira had taken them as children and they had dreamed in minute detail of the house far beyond the horizon, the house in which he was now sitting.

In the end, Max thought—and the end was long since determined and awaited him—he would have only accomplished, experienced, read, and thought a fragment of what he had wanted to in his life. And it would possibly turn out to have been the wrong things, things he had never intended.

Calls came from New York. Every Friday he talked to Mel, his partner. Friends said they missed him. Whenever he went to the archives or visited Spitzer, he tried to be back home by three o'clock in the afternoon. That was when they called, in the morning, six hours earlier, before they went to work in New York. He didn't call New York until after midnight, when he could reach at least those of his older friends who had begun leading more sedate lives. "When are you coming back?" they asked, "What are you doing there, anyway?" "Not much," he said. "I'm renovating my parents' house. I live in the country and enjoy the peace and quiet."

"I don't believe it," responded his old friend Eva. "You're incapable of enjoying peace and quiet. You're a city person. Don't give me that about the idyllic rural life. You could enjoy peace and quiet just as well right here," she urged, "I've discovered a romantic little inlet not far from Neponset Beach."

Precisely the place he'd been thinking about recently, Max admitted.

They told him about openings he was missing, shows they said were fantastic. These nocturnal phone calls made him restless and stirred up longing for the life he was used to.

"How can you live there with those people?" Eva said reproachfully, "I've never gone back even once."

"I don't actually live with them," Max explained. "I see them on the street. I only know a few of them. Actually, I'm living in the past of this town. I've only provisionally alighted on its surface."

"You're talking nonsense," she said. "You're just making excuses."

Eva wanted to force him to decide, as if it were somehow immoral to feel a sense of belonging to two places at once. She was right. The greater part of his life bound him to New York, but H. and Europe were also a part of him, part of his memory.

"What are you trying to find there?" she persisted.

"I don't know," said Max, "something invisible, beneath the surface. I haven't found it yet." How could he explain it to her when he himself had difficulty understanding his various allegiances and sense of rootedness?

"You must be really lonely," his friends guessed. "Aren't you bored in such a small town?"

All their objections were justified from their point of view, but still they had nothing to do with why he was in H.

———

In the middle of June, on his seventieth birthday, Max spent the entire day within earshot of the telephone, waiting. He knew it was absurd to wait because no one could know it was his birthday, and besides, when had he ever needed to have people crowding around to congratulate him? Finally he gave up pretending that he hadn't stayed home just to wait for a call. He listened to the stillness in his house, the distant murmur of traffic in town, the wind in the trees, the birds, the sound of a nearby piano. The few birthdays in this house he could vaguely remember had always been occasions for celebration: long tables set out on the terrace and guests he remembered only as a motley flutter of bright girls' dresses, children's voices like the chirping of startled sparrows, and on the tables, bowls of red strawberries, for his birthday came at strawberry season.

In the evening Max called Spitzer, complaining that he had just spent his seventieth birthday alone. Maybe it would be his last one. An hour later, Spitzer and Thomas appeared with a bottle of wine and a half-eaten cake. He had called up too late for them to scare up an entire birthday cake.

They stayed up long into the night, talking about all the projects Thomas had in mind to carry out with them, with the community. The renovations on the synagogue would be finished in six months at the latest. They'd have to get the municipality involved; they needed ideas for how to celebrate the occasion with appropriate dignity. Thomas sensed the resistance of the two old men. To a certain extent he could understand their reluctance, he conceded, but he tried to convince them that it was misplaced. For too long they had been invisible, beyond the pale. Many people nowadays were interested in Judaism, he said, his eyes full of fervid intensity. They wanted to learn more about Jewish rituals, symbols, ways of life. That was a welcome change, wasn't it?

"Yes, yes, of course," Spitzer reassured him.

"You're young," said Max. "You believe that change is possible. And that's good."

Things were changing all over the place, Thomas replied enthusiastically: the bookstores were full of books on Judaism, on Jewish art. There was a great backlog of demand for them, at last, after so many years, and he wasn't the only one who felt this way, who wanted to find ways to publicize the Jewish cause.

Max asked, "You think that'll change things in the heads of people who are not as enthusiastic about Jews as you are?"

Max liked Thomas, and not just because of his helpfulness in the archives. There was something unsullied about him; in earlier times one would have called him chivalrous. An upright goy, Max had once called him in conversation with Spitzer.

"You shouldn't always call them *goyim*," Spitzer had warned him. "It's an insult; they're Catholics."

From then on, Max called all non-Jews Catholics, even those who insisted they were nonsectarian.

There were also Christian sects whose members regularly came in large groups to the services. They were interested and eager to learn more, and Max avoided them because they asked so many questions he didn't know how to answer. He referred them to Malka, who took the time to explain things at length. What annoyed Malka was that, in the end, these people had their own ready-made answers; all discussions of religion always led to accounts of miracles and moments of illumination that could be hers if only she would convert.

"Why didn't they say right away who they were?" Malka asked irritably. "It would have saved time. They know everything better anyway."

Max, who had just been writing in his chronicle about burning barns and the Middle Ages, laughed at Malka's indignation. "We've already resisted much more determined attempts to convert us."

By contrast, Thomas had no ulterior motives and no proselytizing zeal. His entire passion was focused on reporting what he found fascinating about everything Jewish.

"Why us, of all people?" Max asked.

Because his grandfather had been a *Gauinspektor*. Thomas was tormented by the thought. He confessed that he was sometimes paralyzed by guilt. It threatened to suffocate him, like an awful fear that something horrible was after him, but it was only the reflection of past horrors.

But then why did he resist thinking about this grandfather, Max wanted to know.

Thomas had always avoided questions about the *Gauinspektor*. It depressed him, he admitted. He couldn't stand it. When he thought about it for too long, he was disgusted with himself.

"Have you talked to your grandfather about those years?" asked Max.

Thomas shook his head. "Not really. I couldn't. He always got furious. I was too young. He asked me once just what I had in mind when I used the word 'resistance.' The entire population of our town had been *deutschnational* since the First World War, if not before. You couldn't just bow out of society, not if you had an important position in town. Everything he said sounded logical," Thomas recalled. "He loved me and I didn't want to upset him. I cared for him more than for my father," he reluctantly admitted. "I was his first grandchild and I looked like him. He came to my *Matura* party even though he was already very sick. He died a week later."

So is this how the *Gauinspektor* looked in his youth, thought Max? A confidence-inspiring, unsullied young man with smooth, almost noble features and the same earnest, eager eyes?

"It's all so hard to explain," Thomas said in great discomfort.

They fell silent as each pursued his own thoughts about the *Gauinspektor*.

Thomas wondered if they would be willing to take part in a panel discussion if he organized it.

"Not me," said Spitzer, "I'm no public speaker."

"Depends on the topic," Max said.

"Judaism today?" Thomas suggested.

"Let me think about it," Max answered evasively.

It was getting late; Spitzer looked tired and worn-out. "I shouldn't have had any wine," he said, "I'm not used to it." He had difficulty getting down the steps to the car. His face looked gray and his forehead was sweaty.

"I don't feel well, but it will pass," he tried to reassure them. They left in Thomas's car, Spitzer slumped down and staring vacantly, concentrating on his pain.

A few days later, Thomas sent Max an article he had written for the local newspaper, "A Lost Son of Our Town Turns Seventy." He meant well, and it was a courageous thing to do. It had surely not been easy for him to write that Max's relatives had been murdered rather than that they had died, to talk about plunder and larceny, when words like "aryanization" and "dispossession" were available. But could this dreary, woebegone figure, this stooped fellow with weary eyes reflecting deep sadness and ennobled by suffering, this man whom his young friend portrayed with such loving sentimentality, really be him? A Prodigal Son? Would Thomas describe his own father or the jaunty *Gauinspektor* this way?

Max knew that Thomas was too proud and also too shy for him to be able to talk about the article with him, but every time their eyes met, Max would see in his eyes the unspoken question as to how he had liked it.

"That was a nice article, very nice," Max said as he entered Thomas's office. "I enjoyed it."

Thomas beamed.

Max didn't try to explain that he shouldn't have portrayed him in that way. Maybe it was the futility of it all that often stopped him in the middle of an explanation—a sudden insight into the ambivalence of feelings, the multiplicity of motives, or a new sense of charity, a yearning for peace because it wasn't worth getting excited about. Maybe it had never been worth it.

These days, Max quickly grew weary reading documents. His whole life he had been convinced that you had to be patient and gather enough experience before you could say something meaningful. Now he feared that he had waited too long and was no longer up to the task. For every entry that made progress, there were piles of books and documents that were a waste of his efforts and a strain on his eyes. Sometimes it seemed to him that he was researching the blurred traces of a legendary tribe that had left behind hardly any evidence of its existence.

"You're writing the chronicle in German?" Thomas asked. "Not in your mother tongue?"

"German is my mother tongue," said Max. "We spoke German at home until the war started. It's my private language. I always hear my mother's voice in my ear when I use it."

Thomas found Max's written German a bit stiff. "You have a very literary style," he ventured diplomatically.

When Max returned home after half a day in the dusty air of the archives, he was as tired as if he had been performing heavy physical labor, and he lay down to rest. Just for a few minutes, he would think, but every time sleep robbed him of a large portion of the remaining day, and the sun had long since reached the farthest limit of its daily journey across the room and was setting aglow the saturated green of the grape leaves.

Max went down into the garden to watch the last light touch the cool and distant river with metallic fingertips before bathing the needles of the larches near the house in flames. The sunflowers Diana had planted were developing strong stems and raising their heads. They were almost as tall as he, nodding toward him their heavy yellow blossoms. Diana had broken her word after all and left them in the lurch.

When the long twilight had given way to a starlit night Max sat down at his desk and pulled from the box of index cards his notes and citations on the fifteenth century: statistics, decrees, uncontested charges, judicial decisions, confiscations of the wares of Jewish traveling salesmen. He wrote:

The armed raids, instigated by officials of the City Council, were carried out by enraged proletarians who lacked all understanding of their implications.

According to the annals, on Maundy Thursday 1426 a child disappeared. The town scribe noted with surreptitious admiration with what dignity and defiance the Jews had died for a crime that had not been proven against them. The body of the drowned child was later found—too late—in a pond.

Once the town became a bishopric, dress codes were sharpened: peaked hats, a round yellow spot to be clearly visible, otherwise there would be fines or, at the discretion of the authorities, torture.

To his mind's eye appeared the blurry faces on the photo in front of the house, the dark suits and light dresses with lace collars. This was the image he had always had of the deceased. Now he suddenly pictured Sophie in a dress that reached to the floor, without the lace trimming or jewelry reserved for Christian townswomen; Hermann in the Lódz ghetto, an old man marked with a yellow spot. There were seldom photos of bad times. In her later years Mira, too, had refused to let herself be photographed. She wanted to leave behind no visible testimony to her misery. She would remain in people's memories as the twenty-eight-year-old on the terrace of her house. There were occasional snapshots from the first years after they emigrated, but they soon ceased. After her forty-fifth birthday she fended off in panic every camera pointed at her.

The Jews had their own baths, Max wrote, *their own cookshops. They kept to their own streets, celebrated their weddings and carried out their funerals furtively, so as not to attract any attention or give any offense. The palace of the bishop stood in another, newer part of town. The Jews had no reason to go there.*

It was a neighborhood of old trees behind the walls of former monasteries, baroque bay windows and facades beneath which the austere structures of the late Middle Ages had disappeared. Back then, the narrow one-way streets must have seemed like boulevards, promenades made for Sunday strolls beyond the town walls.

The Council had forbidden Christians, Max wrote, *to purchase groceries from the Jews or to have any association with them, whether as neighbors or as friends, or as one would with human beings who live on the same street, breathe the same air, get up and go to bed at the same time as oneself. The clergy forbade every contact under the threat of the tortures of hell that were more real than life itself, for what was life but the continual attempt to hoodwink Satan and secure for oneself eternal bliss? But now the embodiment of Satan's temptation was to be found among them, earmarked and branded, and the slightest friendly saluta-tion could have eternal damnation as a consequence. It caused a strain on one's nerves that smothered every trace of human compassion.*

Max hesitated. Wasn't that too much interpretation? Who were these people? How should he imagine them to himself, and was that even possible? One thing was fairly certain, at any rate: you wouldn't find any Jews at inns or public baths; they weren't to be seen at dances or celebrations. On holidays they were under cur-few. That was a documented fact. *There they sat in their houses,* he wrote, *hoping that nothing would ignite the hatred of the Christians or incite them to mischief. The Christian bourgeoisie, the high society, flaunted its wealth in the center of town as it had always done. In those days, just like today, it probably consisted of only a few hundred people, a few dozen families. Their houses stood along the commercial streets of the New Town, near the Bishop's palace, or in the lanes of the Old Town that had been widened since the pogroms of the plague years. All the Jewish houses from back then had new owners.*

Max often worked late into the night, until the stillness became so deep and uncanny that he felt like the last witness to the his-tory of mankind. Then he couldn't sleep, asking himself why he was spending his last energy on discovering that the history of his generation had been repeating itself for seven hundred years. It had taken more than twenty years to build the cathedral next to the Bishop's palace. Was that the town he wanted to live in? Sure, the house, the garden, had gradually begun to feel familiar, so that he spoke without hesitation of his house, his garden. If he could have packed them up and mailed them off, the city wouldn't have held him.

Chapter 15

IT WAS DECIDED to honor Max's seventieth birthday retroactively. The mayor placed a large cross on a corded ribbon around his neck. He had to stoop down, as the mayor wasn't very tall. Thomas squinted into the flashbulbs of the photographers, proud and earnest. He had taken Max by surprise, luring him to this ceremony under false pretenses. Now he stood next to Max for the group picture, like a loyal son.

In the first toast the mayor vaguely referred to Max's achievements and hoped that many Jews would return to the town; this was a beginning. And he raised his glass to Max. But somehow people around the table couldn't seem to get in the mood. At the far end of the table Frau Vaysburg whispered with the Barons and Gisela Mandel. The mayor leaned alternately toward Max or toward Spitzer with a well-considered question and the addressee would stop eating and respond at length. The mayor's assistant chatted with Malka about mutual friends and the hospital where she worked. A press photographer sidled around the table, on the lookout for photo ops.

A stranger to whom Thomas had yielded his seat next to Max avoided saying his name by briefly glancing away. Then he asked Max if he was feeling at home in H. yet.

"I was born here," said Max.

"I know, but I mean, do you feel like a native?"

Max was silent.

"What camp were you in?"

"What?" asked Max. "When do you mean?"

"In what concentration camp?"

"I took part in the liberation of Dachau," said Max, "and I prevented the murder of one of the guards. I often regretted it later, but back then I still believed in some kind of higher authority, and that a man has no right to personal revenge. Then I set out to find my relatives, but not one was left. On a train, a German once asked me if I was visiting relatives. 'They were all murdered,' I said. 'How many?' he wanted to know. 'Forty or so,' I said. He gave a knowing nod. 'That's about normal.' That's when I regretted placing my twenty-three-year-old self with my rifle in front of that guard."

"So you were a soldier in the American occupation," the man concluded. "Do you think that anti-Semitism could make a comeback in this town?" was his next question.

"You mean," Max corrected, "under what circumstances do I think it would become violent again?"

The other nodded.

"If times change," said Max distractedly, "any time at all."

Max never read the local newspaper, but if he had, he would have seen this headline on the following day: *As Long As Full Employment Guaranteed, No Danger from Right, Says Jew on His Birthday.*

"Why did they feel compelled to give me a cross, of all things, for my birthday?" Max said to Spitzer as he took it off and stuck it in the pocket of his sports coat. "I can't even hang it on my wall."

"You made Thomas enormously happy," said Spitzer.

They were making a detour to Spitzer's office in the Färbergasse.

Beneath the scaffolding, the synagogue was beginning to assume the original contours it had in the photo in Spitzer's desk drawer. Spitzer told how one day, after the construction workers had gone home, he'd clambered into the interior over piles of lath and mortar. In the middle of the room he had stood in a pool of light falling onto the stone floor from the windows just beneath the newly completed dome. It was like no other shaft of light he could remember. He would have described it as pure or sublime if he weren't so mistrustful of exalted words, but basically there was no adequate word for it. Maybe it was just because the window frames were still empty, or the walls were only weatherboarded, but for Spitzer it wasn't the old synagogue anymore. "It's not like it used to be," he said with resignation, "and it never will be."

The shadows of history, the mayor had said, as if echoing a previous speaker, would now be dispersed, the synagogue would shine with a new brightness.

They watched wheelbarrows full of debris being rolled away. "From now on," the mayor had said, "reconciliation and joy must reign."

Spitzer had asked a young cantor to come see him. His name was Eran and he had a beautiful tenor voice. "The women will fall in love with his voice," he said. He admitted to Max that lately, leading the prayers had become too much of a burden for him. With the High Holy Days approaching, it was time to look for a replacement.

For weeks Spitzer had been sitting in his office every afternoon, writing long letters, then locking them in his desk drawer before going home. He didn't tell anyone about them, not even Max. The letters were to the young woman who had showed up unannounced at the beginning of the summer, a university student barely older

than his own daughter. Her idea was to write about the expropria-
tion of Jewish homes during the Nazi era. Spitzer had a whole file
cabinet full of documents about suits to recover stolen property.
No one, except for a few returnees and their lawyers, had ever
asked him about them. Spitzer had always let himself be guided
by his spontaneous impressions of people, and was still capable
of placing enthusiastic and unqualified trust in someone whom he
considered the messenger of a higher power. It had happened to
him with Nadja, and now again with Margarethe.

"I can't help thinking," he wrote, "that our paths have not
crossed by accident." It was one more letter that didn't get mailed.

Spitzer held to the cabalistic theory (which he simultaneously
regarded as a superstition) that some Jewish souls stray into foreign surroundings—into Christian families, for instance—and for
as long as it takes, they must search until they find their way back
to the surroundings they were destined to inhabit from the start.
But his feelings for Margarethe weren't amenable to such a banal
explanation. It was something intangible, more of a spark from
one pole to another, most comparable to love, but to call it that
was also too simplistic, too profane.

"I come from a Nazi family," Margarethe had said, looking at
him as if she expected to be shown the door.

Spitzer said nothing and looked at her inquisitively.

"I can't help you there," he said at length.

"I just thought you ought to know that up front," she explained.

Spitzer nodded. "You were right about that."

All summer long they sifted through the documents. He read
them to her, explained what they meant, and she sat beside him with
her notebook in her lap, filling pages with her notes. She seemed to
be listening to him with her whole body, which exuded the slightly
bitter fragrance of some climbing vine that was familiar to him from

somewhere, but he couldn't remember its name, only this bitter smell. He missed it on the days when she didn't come.

Sometimes Margarethe interrupted him to ask direct questions others would never have dared to ask.

"Why did you come back?" she wanted to know, pulling in her head and looking up at him as if expecting a rebuke.

He tried to explain his feeling that he couldn't just turn his back on everything—the dead, the destruction, the memories. "I'm a very loyal person," he said.

And what was it like to come back after the war?

"They avoided us," Spitzer told her. "It was embarrassing for them. My brother was older than I. He returned with the victors, with the English. That increased their hostility. One time, outside a DP camp in a small country town, the population staged an uprising. People gathered in front of the camp barracks, threw stones and screamed, 'Kill the Jews!' That was in 1947."

"Then why did you stay?" Margarethe persisted.

"Maybe I believe in the possibility that people can change," he said.

Spitzer went to the cemetery with Margarethe, showed her the tall marble monuments of the Kafkas, the Kohns, and the Edelsteins. She found names that were familiar to her, names of acquaintances of her parents, of contemporaries who had sat next to her in confirmation class. He showed her the plot where he would be buried, next to his first wife Flora. She'd been dead for thirty-eight years. He told Margarethe how he and his brother had tried to get his parents' cabinet-making business started again after the war. The four of them—the two brothers and their wives—had worked day and night.

"In a town like this," Spitzer said, "if they don't want you, it doesn't matter how hard you try: nothing works. Then Flora died,

my brother left for Israel, and I was left in charge of the community. Maybe that's why I stayed."

He looked around for a pebble to place on Flora's grave.

"Maybe because I buried her here," he added, "in a town she
had nothing at all to do with.

"You can study the whole history of the Jews of H. in this cemetery," he said as they walked along between the rows of graves,
"better than elsewhere. Here it comes alive." They walked hard-
packed paths among the black marble monuments, in the shadow
of tall trees. In the damp twilight of luxuriant ivy the past seemed
crystallized into a cool, otherworldly peace. But on the other side
of the central path was a different past, crude and contemporary,
in the shadowless midday sun. The earth of the paths was soft, as
if undermined, and the gravestones small and irregular, like loose
teeth. Those who lay here had died young, and the dates of their
deaths were pregnant with history: March 1938, November 1938
at the age of fifty-eight, at the age of thirty-four, at the age of thirty-
two, three people from the same family on a single day in March
1938. Young people lay in these neglected graves. Of those who
had had to abandon them, not a trace remained in this cemetery.
And beneath many stones no one lay; only place names were inscribed on them: Theresienstadt, Treblinka . . . Others mentioned
only a birthplace: here lay people from Kovno, from Lódz, from
Szeged and Budapest, people who had come here to die. They had
survived the war just long enough to become individuals again,
entitled to their own gravestones. That distinguished them from
the five hundred murdered along the roads and buried in a mass
grave. They had neither names nor birthplaces, only the year of
their deaths.

"I could tell you stories," said Spitzer, "and maybe I will, some
day. Now I'm a bit worn out."

But the usually so reserved Arthur Spitzer became still more communicative, even downright foolhardy. He walked through the streets of the town with Margarethe, in broad daylight, calling in a loud and audible voice every formerly Jewish house by the old name that had been expunged from the registry of deeds. He pointed out the houses with outstretched arm, told their histories to his listener: "Pevner's textile store, and there above the clock of the jeweler was the office of the lawyer Doctor Leeb. This corner house with the projecting bay window and the little tower belonged to the Poirisch family. They had a dry goods store on the ground floor; now it's a jewelry store." Spitzer walked through the town like a judge, his head held high, as if with this public declaration he were reinstating the property rights of the original owners.

"In just a few days in the spring of '38," he said, "the houses and businesses were expropriated. And how many years did my brother and I have to fight to retrieve our parents' house! But to date, no one has gotten back any of the money paid for the so-called *Reichsfluchtsteuer*."

They turned into a small park behind the courthouse. Spitzer had to sit down. With his handkerchief he wiped the sweat from his forehead and neck.

"I'm a bit out of breath," he said in an exhausted voice. "Let's take a little breather here until my heart calms down."

She watched in helpless worry as he struggled for breath.

"I'm okay again," he said after a while. "It was all the excitement of my first guided tour of the town. Now I can die in peace," he joked.

That evening at six o'clock Spitzer didn't go home as usual, but up the hill instead. A humid evening in July, a light breeze that failed to cool things down, and shadows growing longer on the lawns. It was very quiet; the neighbors summered in the mountains. Spitzer found Max in the garden next to the fully opened sunflowers, concentrating so intently that it seemed he was in conversation with them.

"Are you talking to them?" Spitzer asked.

Max laughed. "I'm seeking their advice, but they have none to give."

They sat outside while the evening illuminated the landscape—the trees, the house, and everything in the garden glowing red, so that it appeared that they had only one side that was turned toward the setting sun. Then darkness fell, the trees rustled more loudly, and Spitzer shivered.

"The weather's going to change," he predicted. "My shoulder hurts and my whole left side. Lately I've often longed for more rest. It's all getting to be too much for me, at the office, too. And this melancholy I feel sometimes—I never felt that way before."

He looked at Max inquiringly.

Max nodded. "I've felt that way, too: longing for rest and at the same time impatience. What's there to look forward to at our age?" he asked. "To death? You can't look forward to death. How could you look forward to your own extinction? It goes against nature. So what are we waiting for?"

Spitzer shook his head. "I'm not thinking about death yet. I have a daughter who's seventeen; she's turning eighteen this fall. And the community, what would happen to the community? It's probably the summer that's getting to me. I've never been able to take the heat, not even as a young man on the kibbutz. Another reason I came back."

"If you weren't here in this town," said Max, "I'd be very lonely. Maybe I wouldn't still be here at all. It hasn't turned out the way I thought it would. It's completely different, but I guess that has its own charm."

Spitzer was reticent and gloomy. At some point in the course of the evening Max took a close look at him. Spitzer's weary, gray face worried him.

"What's wrong with you?"

Spitzer told him about his walk through the city with Margarethe.

"You know," he said, "what was so astonishing was that nobody took the least notice of us. I showed her our grave," he continued, "and she laid a pebble on it."

"Are you in love with her?" Max asked.

"I should certainly hope not!" Spitzer laughed. It had grown so dark that Max could no longer see his face clearly.

It began to rain. They waited for a taxi under the trees in front of the house. The wind swept through the treetops and rustled in the hedge.

Later, Max remembered an impulse to keep his friend there. He felt an unwarranted panic that lasted several minutes, contracting his stomach and constricting his chest—a sensation familiar from his operation. He didn't connect it to Spitzer.

They waved to each other in the darkness, then Max climbed the stairs back up to his veranda beneath the glass roof and listened as the rain from the thunderstorm soon eased up.

———

The last time he saw Spitzer was at the panel discussion Max let Thomas talk him into. Spitzer sat in the last row of the sparsely populated hall and watched the three panelists with concern. On Max's right sat a religious Jew, on his left a man in his mid-sixties in a traditional Steiermark jacket of gray loden material with green lapels and staghorn buttons. Thomas had clearly chosen them in order to display three different kinds of Jews to the audience. With some satisfaction at the surprise value, Thomas explained in his introduction that the pious Jew had been raised a Catholic and the grandfather of the man in the folk costume had been a rabbi. The audience craned their necks. The panel discussion was brief and polite. How did they live their lives in a Christian society? Quite well. They muddled through. They talked about the limits to assimilation. The man in the Steirer outfit told family stories, the history of his emigration and return. He clearly enjoyed telling stories.

Max spotted Diana in the audience, sitting next to a distinguished-looking man with an alert, intelligent face. They smiled a greeting to each other. Her husband also smiled and nodded, without suspicion. He must be very sure of her.

Thomas invited the audience to participate in the discussion. A married couple raised their hands. One knew so few Jews, said the man, it made it hard. How would they like to be treated, the Jews?

"Normally," said Max dryly. "I'd like it if people would treat me normally, like anyone else, like a Catholic." He looked at Spitzer and grinned.

Older gentlemen in the audience offered convoluted analyses of the difference between guilt and shame. One emphatically rejected the concept of collective guilt. Thomas declared that no one had said anything about that.

Max's secular co-panelist was asked if he considered himself an Austrian.

"Why? Is there a law against it?" he responded.

The audience laughed politely. Thomas shook his head and looked threateningly at the questioner. Then, despite encouraging gestures from Thomas, there were no more questions.

"I don't know if that was very productive," said Thomas in disappointment as he handed Max carefully from the stage. He asked Max if he might introduce him to a man Thomas had admired since he was a boy. Max shook hands with the priest, and when he could get away again to look for Spitzer, he had disappeared.

Four days later, Malka called. Max had just been brooding over his chronicle. He was listening to Chopin on the radio and was annoyed at the interruption.

Spitzer had died of heart failure.

Around Max, it grew as quiet as if the world had collapsed into nothingness.

Part IV

Chapter 16

THE COMMUNITY WAS not prepared for the news of Spitzer's death. Who would see to everything on the High Holy Days? Who even knew what needed seeing to? Was Spitzer's death the end of the community? Who could lead it forward? Who would ever again think of the rundown building in the Färbergasse the way Spitzer did—as home? The others always felt like guests in a well-ordered house. The center of their lives lay elsewhere—with their children living abroad, in the past, in their own households. Or they were en route to somewhere else and regarded what this place had to offer in the way of Jewish life as a way station they would remember fondly. Only for Spitzer was the community house the center of his whole life, an unbreakable contract. He was the custodian of their heritage. Would it all now come to a standstill?

They buried Spitzer on a warm autumn day. Across the cemetery paths Indian summer spun gossamer threads that shimmered in the sun. Many people came whom Max didn't know. Frau Vaysburg knew them, and they greeted her with the respect due the widow of the last rabbi.

The proceedings were very simple and peaceful beneath a high, pale blue sky: the bright pine coffin, the open grave, the prayers. Spitzer's brother said kaddish. He was bigger and more powerful, but he had the same fine features. I'm next, thought Max, and started to perspire as he had twenty years ago shoveling dirt into a grave. When it's your turn, he said in silence to Spitzer, at least you don't have to shovel.

No more talks in Spitzer's office, no more walks together on Friday evening after the service, no more unannounced visits. Whichever way he turned, the words *never again* loomed in his path like a watchman before whom his thoughts turned aside.

Seeing a homemade cherry pie in Spitzer's office early in the summer Max had said, "I guess I won't get a look at your wife until I go to your funeral." Now she stood by the grave next to Spitzer's brother. Spitzer's wife and behind her his daughter, two slender women with reddish-blonde hair, the daughter's a little darker, both looking withdrawn, as if not wanting to share their pain with anyone. Max shook their hands, said who he was, and thanked the wife for all the meals she had sent him. She nodded silently. Somewhere deep in the gentle and harmonious features of her round face lay an unbending resoluteness.

Max turned down Thomas's offer. He had no desire to make predictable small talk about Spitzer during a comfortable car ride home. He wanted to be alone, climb alone up the hill, pause halfway up at the curve by the cemetery and look down on the town in its fall color, peer over the cemetery wall at the wilted wreaths and the swaths of smoke stubbornly hugging the ground.

When his father died he'd had a similar feeling of having failed to do something. But then, above all, the feeling had been sadness at having taken so many years to understand his father that he'd barely gotten to know him. The last time Max visited him in the hospital—a shrunken old man with sparse, shiny white hair standing out against the almost black age spots on his forehead and temples—he had been seized by vertigo as if in a strange dream. This decrepit old man he was helping out of bed while the hospital johnny tied at his neck parted to reveal a pale, emaciated body was his father, and Max knew nothing of the high and low points of his life, his dreams and disappointments, not even what his sons had meant to him. He asked about the hospital food and about his pains, about the doctors and whether he was able to sleep at night, and the silence between them had been almost unbearable, a silence it was too late to break.

When he got home after Spitzer's interment, Max went into the bathroom and washed his hands. Looking in the mirror felt like he was staring blankly at a stopped clock. The leaves of the chestnut tree beyond the window obscured the sun and chased dapples of light across the mirror. In summer this room was always a bit shadowed, even in the morning, and from this twilight, as if from the depths of a dark painting, an old man with a mousy beard looked out—searchingly, contemplatively—and finally smiled at him. That was some consolation. Max found him congenial, this sad old man.

He wandered aimlessly through the house, the garden, without finding peace. The sunflowers were withered. One afternoon in August, after a week of rain and cold, their faces, now black, had turned toward the ground. They made him think of Diana and that it had been two months since her last visit.

She had phoned two or three times, and he was happy to hear her voice. But neither his questions nor the hearty intimacy he tried to put into his voice was successful. Her perkiness kept him at a distance. She chatted about trivialities until it was time for the stock formulas of good-bye. "Will I see you again?" he asked. She promised to call again, and he wondered if she was being overheard, if she was under observation in the big house on the Stadtplatz. If so, Max thought there was a chance that not all intimacy between them had been broken off for good. When he tried to imagine her face, he saw her sitting motionless, as in a photo, at the base of the balustrade.

During the following days, Max continued to live in a sort of daze, as if time were hesitating, in a state of suspension in which nothing retained its former validity, or as if a piece of the ground beneath his feet had broken off into the abyss. And the air seemed a bit colder than before. He watched the birds gathering for migration. They appeared in sudden flocks over the river valley. They had been living here, but he hadn't noticed them.

———

Nadja's call was unexpected. She had to say who she was. He hadn't recognized her voice, and even her name came to him as if from a great distance, haltingly taking shape as an image in his memory: a young woman with sleek shoulder-length hair, wearing a bulky purple sweater he had given her, standing in the leafless Central Park of early spring, shivering, with hunched shoulders and red cheeks. He tried to reconcile this new voice with that image, the direct, somewhat brusque manner of that twenty-five-year-old with this dark, quiet voice. With what determined possessiveness she had tried to make him hers and move in with him!

The woman to whom he opened his front door two days later was a stranger with dark hair tightly pulled back and a cool gaze that seemed to miss nothing. Everything about her was slender and severe—the hair held in place by a barrette at the nape of her neck, the figure clad in black from top to bottom. He thought he detected something like an amused gleam in her eye. "Good to see you again," she said and offered him her hand. There was an awkward clumsiness in this gesture that awakened a vague memory. He raised her hand to his lips in a pantomime kiss, something that had always amused her as a young woman. Her hands were still as cool as glass.

"I wouldn't have recognized you on the street," he said. "It's clear you've found your own style." She gave a snort of laughter.

And because he was afraid he'd offended her with this remark, he added, "You're completely grown up."

He noticed that she was staring at his mouth. He felt uncomfortable beneath this keen, appraising gaze. Was it his teeth? Had the implants altered his smile, his bite? They had been well done, tedious and expensive and almost identical to his original incisors, with the same narrow gap between his top front teeth, only more smooth and regular. Over the years, the incisor that had died when he got punched in the face as a boy had begun to darken more and more. About ten years ago it had broken off. The new implants had never attracted anyone's attention before.

She seemed to notice his discomfiture. "You look good," she hastened to say.

"For my age," he answered with an ironic smile.

"I heard you were sick?"

"I had a bypass operation, but that was quite a while ago." He gave her a tour of the house. "The renovations aren't finished yet," he said apologetically. "Beautiful," she said, pointing to the ceiling moldings and the window recesses in the living room. "I see plasterwork is still your passion."

"Yeah, but I can't find the right furniture to go with it."

A long table of black lacquered wood with narrow high-backed chairs gave the room the severe look of a refectory that contrasted with the green of the garden just outside the windows and its shifting light and shadows.

Then he led her upstairs and out onto the veranda, jutting from the house like the bow of a ship stranded on the slope above the river, alarmingly exposed to the forces of nature. He had never before seen the room in which he worked and slept as he now saw it through her eyes, so exposed, solitary, and audacious.

"This is where I live," he said. "This room was ready from the start, as if it was expecting my arrival. I only had to simplify the windows to let in more light."

He suddenly saw the room as a last outpost.

"I once took a series of lighthouse pictures," said Nadja. "Somehow this reminds me of them."

For a moment she looked at him keenly, then she turned toward the windows and looked out at the slope, the valley. It seemed as if she wanted to avoid facing him directly. When she turned back into the room, she bustled over to his desk in an almost exaggerated way. Papers and index cards in various sizes and colors were jumbled together on it—books, a water glass, empty coffee cups.

"You're working?" she asked.

"I'm writing a chronicle of H."

"A chronicle?" She raised her eyebrows in astonishment and he noticed the horizontal lines in her forehead and also two deep folds that descended past the corners of her mouth to her chin.

"Actually, I've come up with a special form of historiography for myself," he explained and tried to dampen the enthusiasm in his voice. "Not an accumulation of facts that I discover in the annals and documents, but life stories, the fates of individuals that are illuminated for a mere moment when measured in historical time, sometimes only at the moment of their death."

He told her the story of Frau Rahel and her gravestone and lost track of the fact that they were facing each other after all and she was watching him attentively as he spoke.

"That sounds like a historical novel," Nadja said.

"No, not a novel. More verifiable facts, more attention to real people and the traces they leave behind, fleeting traces that show up in some document or other, only to disappear again. The problem is," he said, "the town scribes hardly ever mention the Jews. They simply weren't part of the history of this town. It's the suppressed history of H. that I want to write, the things that traditional history has ignored so thoroughly that their absence is not even noticed."

"Who are you writing it for?" she wanted to know.

"I've often asked myself that question," Max replied. "Maybe it's just a pretext for being here, or maybe I'm writing it for the Jews who will live here in twenty or fifty years. Just so people know that there were Jews here from the very beginning. So they can't forget it any more."

She was silent.

———

Later, he prepared a supper of cheese, bread and salad in the kitchen, and as they went through the motions of setting and clearing the table together a new, cautious closeness was established. Afterward they sat across from each other on the veranda in the fading light and Nadja told him about the stages of her career, avoiding any reference to their former relationship. She said, "After college, when I lived in Manhattan for a few years." She didn't say, "After you threw me out," or "After I left you." She talked as though she hadn't even known him back then, told about her first successes and how later her career stagnated and she suddenly found herself back in advertising again, like her first job in the printing shop in H.

"I was married," she said, and seemed to expect him to be surprised at this piece of news.

"And where's your husband now?" he asked with an ironic smile.

"Probably still in Pennsylvania," she said. "At least, that's where I saw him last."

"What was he like?" Max asked.

She laughed. "A real homebody."

"That's what you wanted, wasn't it?" he said inadvertently.

"Yes, that's what I wanted," she said without taking offense at his innuendo. "And it was very nice for a while. I was utterly secure in his love. The only thing was, I had to share it with the small town in Pennsylvania where he'd grown up. We moved there right after he graduated."

"Fairfield?" Max asked.

They both laughed and it seemed that now they could talk about the past.

"No, Pottsville."

"*Potts*ville!" cried Max with an exaggerated emphasis on the first syllable.

They laughed.

"And what did this *potz* do in Pottsville?"

"He was a pharmacist. We had a drugstore and pharmacy. We sold everything you need in a small town late at night when the shopping center is closed."

"You waited on customers?"

"He and his mother did that. I developed pictures for the customers just like in my first job in New York."

"You must have loved him very much," Max concluded.

"Yes," she said, returning his gaze defiantly. "I still love him, but I couldn't stand it there any more."

"And then?"

"Then I went back to New York, and then I got a commission in London. I still take portraits now and then," she said and added with a smile, "As you know, that's my specialty."

"How did you decide that Pottsville was so unbearable you had to leave your husband even though you loved him?"

Nadja replied that Ofra had come for a visit. "She was as beautiful and free as she was back when we were still kids. And I'd put on weight, since there's not much else to do in Pottsville besides eat, and his mother was a good cook. Ofra's first question was, 'How could you let this happen?' In her opinion, I was letting myself go. And suddenly I saw myself through her eyes: lethargic, frowsy, and overweight. At some point, I would have realized it on my own."

"But up to then you were happy?"

"Up to then I was grateful," said Nadja. "He gave me security and a real home."

They fell silent. It was a long, uncomfortable silence during which Nadja looked out the window. The early twilight blurred her features and her voice sounded like it was coming from outside as she said offhandedly, "At first you always think that nothing can leave a mark on you."

He turned on a lamp and Nadja returned to the desk where a coffee spoon still lay from breakfast. Whether absentmindedly or nervously, she picked it up and twirled it in her fingers. And as she asked him how his life had gone, her voice wavered as if seeking a neutral, disinterested tone.

"There's not much worth telling," said Max. All his relatives and many of his friends had died, but he'd never told Nadja anything about them, so why should he start now? He didn't want to boast about his professional successes and he certainly wasn't going to tell her about his women friends. Instead he said, "I still live at my old address."

The table lamp made her eyes look larger and deeper, and the black shadows transformed her face, so that it seemed to him strange, inchoate, neither the girl he had known nor the woman of just a moment ago.

"Haven't you ever felt the need to come back here?" Max asked.

She shook her head, "That would have meant defeat."

They talked about Spitzer and his sudden death.

"He was more of a father to me than my own father," Nadja said. "He was always there for me. It's unthinkable that he won't be sitting in his office any more."

They fell silent.

Finally Max said, "It was a mistake." And then he yielded to the compulsion to finally confess what had been tormenting him, although it seemed totally irrational. He felt that he had spent so many lonely hours here in this house contemplating death that he had attracted it and diverted it to Spitzer. "I know it's absurd," he said, "but why did he die precisely the death that I've been expecting for myself?"

"Are you afraid of death?" asked Nadja.

"Not afraid exactly. I sit up here on the bridge of my ship, on the lookout, and sometimes it's so near that I could touch it with my fingertips, I can almost see it tarrying at the edge of a fog bank. But when I struggle to understand what sort of presence it really is that I think I'm sensing, my mind goes blank, my thoughts get even more sluggish than usual, and I give up. I tell myself there's nothing there and there never was."

In the course of the evening Nadja also talked about her fears. "I've been photographing faces for so many years," she said, "and I still don't understand other people. I find them more and more alien and I'm getting more and more fearful of them. Sometimes I think that what I'm really taking pictures of are my own dreams— or nightmares—superimposed on the faces of strangers. The only time I lived without fear was back in Pottsville, when I was married, but then I couldn't stand how limited and predictable it was."

It was midnight already. Nadja looked at the clock. The spell was broken. They were back in the present, where it was difficult to speak of intangible things. Before he opened the house door, Max quickly bent down and kissed the back of her neck. She let it happen, as impassive as if she hadn't noticed, as if it hadn't occurred. She tucked the folder full of typed pages he had given her to read under her arm and with her free hand touched his cheek, then ran down the steps to the street where the taxi was waiting.

In bed, before falling asleep, Max got out the same pages and read them with another's—with Nadja's—eyes: *Once during the decades of the Inquisition, a pogrom was sparked off by a proselyte. He was a town scribe and monk and was learning Hebrew from the Torah scribe Aaron in order to read the Old Testament in God's own language. They must have continued for many years, for at the time of his conversion he was already an old man. He must have known that he would be carted off to the stake as soon as he had undergone circumcision and the ritual immersion. His superiors in the order would hardly have left him in the dark as to how his apostasy from Christianity would be received. But had he also taken Aaron's death into account; did he realize that he would burn at the stake along with him? Was his conversion worth the murder and exile of people having nothing to do with him and his change of faith, who didn't even know about it?*

Thereafter the church renewed the prohibition against any contact whatsoever between Jews and Christians. A casual conversation could develop into a discussion of religion. Franciscan friars regularly delivered sermons on conversion to the Jewish community that was forced to assemble before their pulpits by order of the City Council. They must not be allowed to remain in ignorance with regard to their crimes, above all the murder of Christ, and the torments of hell that awaited them. When the Christian missionaries cried, Ye shall burn!, the Jews could have no doubt they meant it literally.

When the entire city burned down a year to the day after the massacre, there were whispers among the folk about God's judgment for burning the Jews. . . .

Late at night, in solitary stillness, Max was suddenly horrified at the thought of dying and being buried in this town. He found no comfort in the proximity of Spitzer's grave. I'll sink like a stone here, he thought, and the memory of me won't have time to cause a single ripple before I and my chronicle are swallowed by oblivion. Who's going to read it, after all? Who's still here to read it? He should have written his own autobiography, he told himself, and the story of his parents, and not in German but in English. Instead, he was wasting the final years of his life in a foreign city, writing in the language of a people to whom he was just as indifferent and unintelligible as everything Jewish down through the ages had always been.

In the days that followed Nadja often came by, sometimes first thing in the morning, usually early in the evening.

She had missed Spitzer's burial, she said, so now she wanted to stay somewhat longer than usual because Ofra was in H., sitting shiva. Max didn't remember seeing Ofra at the burial but Nadja insisted she'd been there.

Nadja was hesitant to say for sure how long she would stay. She was staying with her father, living in her old room above the shed. She said her father had completely withdrawn from active life. Since his failing eyesight no longer allowed him to read Russian novels, he sat in his living room and listened to Bach cantatas. His wife had died young; his son was living in another city. His suspicion that human communication was impossible had obviously hardened into a conviction, said Nadja. He didn't even pretend to be pleased when she came home. He'd lost interest in life. His indifference no longer made her unhappy; it hardly touched her.

On that first evening, there were moments when she and Max had felt quite close to each other, and Max had hoped that a new intimacy might develop between them. But when Nadja came to see him, it seemed that she did it against her own better judgment and as if every time might be the last one.

Nadja made it a habit to take the shortcut along the river and across the meadows to Max's house. She laughed at the joyful surprise with which he waved his arm back and forth at her from the windows of the veranda, like the captain of a foundering ship.

At first she was a small, bright point in the distance, then a slender figure recognizable by the unique, determined gait that was sure to leave an imprint on the soft earth of the meadow. The wild grasses and pale late-blooming weeds of fall brushed her calves as she approached.

One day Nadja suggested that Max visit her in London for a few weeks, but when he declined, saying he didn't want to interrupt work on his chronicle, she didn't press him. She only asked what made H. so important to him. She couldn't imagine that he was happy here.

"Don't kid yourself," she said. "Neither of us has any roots in this town."

"This chronicle is something like the appointed task of my final years," said Max. "I want to finish it. Remembering the past is the only thing we have left in the end, and sometimes the past goes back further than our own personal memories."

Since Spitzer's death, Max hadn't attended Friday services. He said he wouldn't be able to stand not having Spitzer there. When Nadja started bringing guests to his house after the service he was a little skeptical at first, but the second time he began to take pleasure in the idea and by the third Friday he suggested feeding the guests himself: she didn't have to bring along food any more. At first it was only Frau Vaysburg, Malka and her son, and the Barons who came, but soon they were joined by Eran, Gisela Mandel, and Chaim Alter, and his living room lost something of its lonely, brooding vastness. When he lifted his wine glass Max remembered how his grandfather had blessed the wine in this room and how lonely Mira had been in the last years of her life, when he was the only one who came to see her on Shabbat. Suddenly he felt very happy, as if he had accomplished something significant or been given something he'd been lacking for a long time. They ate like a family—intimately, informally. They talked while they ate; they laughed. Max could sense the affection they felt for him.

No one from Spitzer's family came even though Nadja had invited her friend Ofra and the two Spitzer women. Max's guests conjectured that they might want to be alone. Maybe it was the same constraint that had kept them away from the prayer house all those years.

"Who sat shiva for Spitzer?" asked Max.

"His brother and Ofra," said Nadja.

"In his apartment?"

"In their apartment," Nadja confirmed. From the silence that followed Max gathered that everyone was thinking in perplexed embarrassment of the two women. None of them had wanted to disturb the wife and daughter they didn't know, force them into the rituals of Jewish mourning—so they'd left them alone.

"It's only a shame there's no one to say thirty days of kaddish for him," interjected Frau Vaysburg.

They were silent, following their own thoughts, everyone for himself. Perhaps their thoughts touched in the stillness. Helene, Spitzer's daughter, would have children some day, thought Max, and maybe one or two of them would bear a resemblance to their grandfather. But sometime or other in the course of the next sixty, seventy years, his memory would grow dim and finally expire completely in the following generations. The awareness of belonging that had been the essence of Spitzer's life would disappear even sooner. Perhaps a great-grandchild researching his ancestors would come to stand, astonished, before Spitzer's grave in a strange cemetery in a city where hardly any Jews lived anymore. And what if the great-grandson or daughter were to decide to turn back, return to their Jewish roots with nothing in hand but a stubborn claim, as Nadja had done? It would be a long haul with no guarantee of success. The Torah said, *The fourth generation will possess the land*, but how many generations did memory survive?

Chapter 17

SPITZER'S DAUGHTER WAS the last person Max expected to pay him a visit. That's why he didn't understand who it was at first when the young voice on the telephone said her name was Helene Spitzer. She wanted to come see him; she had some questions and wanted to show him something.

It seemed to Max that in his generosity and concern, Spitzer was sending him a gift from beyond the grave: his daughter.

She's beautiful, Max thought as he greeted her at the door, and she wasn't even aware of it. He saw Spitzer's features like a delicate outline beneath hers: the gentle hollows, the tentative smile that gradually rose toward the eyes but seldom reached them. On the veranda Helene sat down in the armchair that stood in the sun. Her dark blonde hair shimmered in a glistening palette of reddish highlights that he watched in fascination.

"My father told me you were working on a chronicle. He gave me the job of bringing you this file, in case he . . ." She fell silent but didn't cry. She merely held out a portfolio with a marbled cover, the kind Max had seen in the archives, the kind of portfolio you couldn't buy anymore. It was Spitzer's family history, the dead whom he had already set out to find as a young man right after the war, first with Flora, then alone, traveling to the razed

ghettos where they had starved to death, to the forests on the edge
of Riga and Minsk where they had been shot. Spitzer had not been
satisfied with official reports or death notices. He'd gone in search
of them the way one goes to a dying friend, to be with him in his
hour of need. And the ancestors of the dead—his ancestors—were
recorded in the file too, with documents and references to their
names in registries of births all across Bohemia and Poland.

"He only told me a little bit about this," Helene said. "He was
very reserved. He only talked a lot about it with his brother. He
said he didn't want to burden us with these sad stories. But his
silence could be a burden, too, sometimes."

How could someone who wasn't directly affected ever understand the lifelong sorrow for murdered loved ones? But Max didn't
say that.

"Of course I knew that he'd lost his family," Helene said, "his
parents, his grandparents, his younger siblings. But they were his
dead and he kept their memory to himself, jealously, so that
they've always been strangers to me."

"He certainly did it with the best intentions," Max assured her.
"He was an extremely considerate person."

But who was he actually protecting, Max wondered as he silently contemplated Helene's face. His wife and daughter from too
much painful knowledge? Or was he protecting his dead loved ones
and Flora, who had died from the effects of a concentration camp?
Where did his secret lie, or did he have one at all? Who was being
protected from whom?

"We have photos and mementos of dead relatives buried in our
cemetery—the Catholic cemetery," she said. "My mother often
talks about them. My grandmother died young; she was only thirty-
five, and an uncle of my mother's died in the Second World War
when he wasn't much older than I am now. We often visit the
cemetery."

Helene's mother came from an extended family of craftsmen living in villages in the vicinity of H., a family that stuck together, celebrated anniversaries and honored its traditions. The sense of belonging created strong bonds among them, and her father hadn't belonged. So he kept his distance from the family and went his own way.

"Why did he keep you and your mother hidden from us?" asked Max.

"I think they decided right away that I should be raised Catholic. He respected my mother's wishes. And she respected his spending so much time with the community. There were never discussions about it, but I've come to think that it would have pleased him if I'd shown more interest in his world. I just didn't think very much about it until now."

"He waived his rights to that part of your upbringing," said Max. "He probably thought it was better that way."

And thus Spitzer had turned the child over to her, Max thought, so that it would feel at home in *her* town and *her* religion, so that it could have roots. And when he prayed, "And these words, which I command thee this day, shall be upon thy heart; and thou shalt teach them diligently unto thy children and shalt talk of them," what was he feeling?

"It wasn't always easy for us," Helene said, "that he had another life, one we knew nothing about."

"It must have been a very special relationship to survive that stress," Max ventured.

She nodded. "They trusted each other. I had a good childhood."

On Friday evenings, Spitzer often persuaded those who had no family to come to the coffeehouse with him. "We'll just drop by," as he used to say. On the holidays he postponed going home where everyday life awaited him. But he never said a word about it.

Every day Spitzer lived out the conflict between religions in his marriage, in his calling, in his human kindness, without ever being dogmatic or unfair. Maybe he only succeeded by being quiet and withdrawn.

"Did you know his first wife?" Helene asked cautiously.

Max shook his head.

"She must have been very beautiful. I've seen a picture of her, but he never talked about her, either. Mom was always jealous of Flora anyway. To this day she believes he loved his first wife more, that she was closer to him and they had more in common. And now he's lying next to her, as he wanted to. And later on, we'll lie in the plot of my mother's family, on the Catholic side of the same cemetery."

"Those are things," said Max, "that only he would have known how to answer. But maybe there wouldn't have been any clear answers. That was his secret and you've got to respect it."

"My mother," Helene continued, "was horrified at the meagerness of my father's interment: no flowers, that pathetic pine coffin, no music and no speeches. She said it was scandalous and didn't think he would have wanted it that way either. Aesthetics were so important to him—a nicely set table, good manners."

"He was buried as a Jew," Max explained.

After a while Helene quietly said she had to go. He went to the door with her. Once more the light from the stained glass window on the landing fell on her hair. He suggested walking part of the way with her, but she said no, she had to hurry. But she'd come back again; she had a lot of questions.

"Come as often as you like," he called after her.

He went back into the house and couldn't calm down for a long time. A restless happiness drove him into the garden and beneath the trees whose tenuous and withered leaves swayed, ready to fall, in the autumn wind. Nothing was over. Something new and un-expected was beginning.

***

There were days that from early morning on came wrapped in their own festiveness. The New Year for instance—Rosh Hashanah—had never lost the aura it had held for Max since earliest childhood. Even in the years when he didn't celebrate it, he could sense its demanding presence as well as its loss.

From the windows of the veranda, floating above the morning fog, the sky looked high and glassy while down below, white fog blanketed the river and the town. A feeble sun picked at the fog. Before noon it would penetrate it. The sun had already taken possession of the church towers and sparkled from their spires as Max walked down his habitually quiet street in his best suit. A gentle wind rustled the dry leaves in the beech hedges lining the road. A dog and a man in a sweatsuit and disheveled hair were coming toward him. The dog looked at Max inquiringly, but his owner had already seen him and looked the other way. Max had long since learned that you didn't say hello to the people in this neighborhood. They seemed to feel threatened by it.

In town, a normal weekday was underway: people going to work, hurrying off to shop, while he—differentiated only by his dark holiday suit—strode toward the prayer house. He felt self-conscious yet privileged, as he had in his childhood when they returned in their sprucest clothes from Brooklyn to the Bronx on a Saturday afternoon.

They were already assembled in the prayer room: Malka bustling about like a hostess, Daniel looking freshly washed and combed, Gisela Mandel, short of breath and bursting with news of everyone who couldn't come: Chaim Alter, who had recently suffered a stroke; Lily Leaf, lying in a distant California hospital with a fractured femur. Herr Baron stood a bit apart with his gentle wife and both smiled sadly at Max. Frau Vaysburg was talking with Nadja and appeared even smaller and more fragile than usual next to her. Thomas was there, too. He hurried over to Max, pleased and re-lieved, to tell him about a plethora of new plans. But Max couldn't concentrate on what he was saying. Diana hadn't come, and why did Nadja give him only a quick glance and a fleeting smile? And Helene? Why had he had the absurd hope that Helene would come?

Instead, there were people there he had never seen before or who came so seldom that he recalled them only vaguely. There was no reason for that to trouble him, but it seemed that the fes-tive brightness of the day had lost a bit of its sheen. Eran, the young cantor, appeared in a white prayer robe and tallis with a minyan of strangers, refugees on their way to somewhere else, emigrants waiting for a visa. They stood around waiting, didn't mingle with the locals, and only their wives sometimes talked about their former life in Iraq, Iran, showed snapshots to the other women, speculated about what awaited them in America, where they were all headed. The men prayed and read the Torah with a confidence that clearly came from having watched and practiced since child-hood. They were the actors, the others the audience.

Eran came from an inhospitable region of Kurdistan. He had told Malka all about it, and she'd immediately taken him under her wing. Malka repeated his story to others and mixed up all the exotic de-tails he'd told her in his tangled welter of languages: the poverty he'd grown up in, sometimes amongst wild Mongolian or Ossetian tribesmen, in a wooden house on stilts beneath which his father, a horse dealer, kept his livestock. She said he'd wandered the forests as a child, imitating bird calls, and that the family had only wooden utensils at home. When he was twelve he'd emigrated to Israel with

his parents and siblings and had studied in a yeshiva. But in Malka's
eyes he remained a lonely, feral child from the Caucasus.

Eran's piety was in some doubt. It was rumored that he often
ate at McDonald's or at snack bars. People had even seen him
eating Vienna sausages. But Malka defended him: he was a fun-
loving guy, childlike, pious in his own way; you just couldn't help
liking him. And beyond a doubt Eran was in love with her. When
he entered the prayer room, the first person he looked for was
Malka, and anything served as a pretext for him to turn toward
her. He'd been shadowing her for weeks, casting devout glances
into her bedroom when she accompanied him to the door after
a Shabbat meal, and persuading her to come with him on hikes
into the surrounding countryside. He gushed over every bird-
call and moss-covered stone and called Malka by nicknames with
no regard for the astonished looks of their fellow hikers. Eran
knew an enormous amount and had a huge need to communicate it, but only rarely could one make sense of his sentences,
for he used too many languages simultaneously and without
differentiation.

Max sat between Herr Baron and an unapproachably silent
young man completely wrapped in his tallis. Baron told Max that
he and his wife and their children were going to move to another
city where one could live as a Jew, with a minyan in the temple and
kosher shops. He'd been retired a long time, and now that Spitzer
had died, what was there to keep him here? "Spitzer was our soul,"
said Baron, "Now everything will fall apart, just wait and see."

Max nodded. "Well then, I guess these are our last High Holy
Days together."

During the Torah reading, his thoughts caught on the sentence,
And she was in bitterness of soul. He stopped following along. After
all, he was familiar with the story. He knew that God would agree
to Hannah's offer of a trade and give her the longed-for child

Shmuel. But Max lingered over her bitterness. If there was no one to entreat or curse for something you hadn't gotten, what then?

Had it been forty, forty-five years ago? In his mind's eye, Max saw Dana in her greenish-yellow summer dress as clearly as if no time had elapsed. He saw her slim back and how she had held onto the edge of the table with both hands, so tightly that her knuckles turned white, as he said, "It's not about getting married. I don't want this child ever to be born in the first place." He could no longer remember how they had split up on that day, but he could clearly see the pattern of her summer dress and her white knuckles. How do other people stand this, he wondered. Everyone who gets to be my age has something that's close to driving him crazy, a moment he can't retrieve, no second chance to reach a different decision. How do other people get through their sleepless nights? When you can't adduce any more reasons why, when the circumstances no longer seem so compelling, but those moments, frozen implacably in memory, allow not the slightest mitigation or change? And after such a long time, whom could one ask for forgiveness? When almost an entire lifetime has passed since then, all the years that can never be made up for, and that distant love has long since been transformed into hatred or indifference?

The first blast of the shofar, mournful and archaic, tore Max from his reverie. For a moment, more fleeting than a thought, he felt he had been heard. As if he had complained that life was an illusion in which you cheated and got cheated, and someone who was responsible for it had simply said, Yes, I know.

At the taxi stand near the prayer house Max got a cab and felt morose and guilty for his laziness, as though he had thereby single-handedly brought the Holy Day to an early end. But he had never observed religious commandments anyway.

He arrived just in time to find Helene at his front door. She was leaning hard on the doorbell. She'd brought him a present, a package of matzo from last Pesach, because today was a Jewish Holy Day, wasn't it?

He laughed. "How sweet of you," he said.

He made some cheese sandwiches, washed some grapes, asked her what she'd like to drink. They ate at the kitchen table. There was a consonance between them, a harmony he feared would be dissipated if he said a word.

"Next Monday is my birthday," she said. "My father told me I was born on a *Shabbat shuva*. Apparently that's something special."

"It's the Saturday between the New Year and the Day of Atonement, the Shabbat of turning back," Max explained. "Spitzer was a mystic." He thought to himself: maybe he hoped that because of the hour of her birth, his daughter would someday arrive in his world.

"What's so special about it?" she wanted to know.

"It's hard to explain," said Max. "It's got something to do with religious conviction. By the way, I have a story for you. I've been studying your father's file and I wrote down a story for my chronicle. But first let's go to my room."

Max always called the veranda his room, as if he were only a guest in the other rooms. The slice of nature he could observe from up here seemed to him a sufficient sample of the world. He could measure the progress of the seasons by a single wild cherry tree on the slope. When he had arrived here in late winter, the black lines of its wet branches reminded him of a pen and ink drawing; now the leaves that had first appeared as a light green shimmer in the spring sun were turning brown again. And here he was in the midst of life with this eighteen-year-old, and he was supposed to explain her father to her. That was now Max's task, to reveal the side of her father that he had never turned toward her. Otherwise she would remain fettered by her belated love her whole life long.

On his mother's side, Max read aloud, *Spitzer's family came from Susice in western Bohemia. At some point in the predictable succession of generations of tradesmen, merchants, and peddlers there was a black sheep. He and his vile deed make only a brief appearance in the history of the family, then are expunged from it along with all his descendants. His name was Samson and he was a thief. But as luck would have it, this Samson earned an entry in the town chronicles of H. He had joined the gang of the Jew Hirschel who stole horses from aristocratic estate owners, then drove them a few towns away and sold them. There were Christians in the gang, too, even a woman, Mariam Sommer, whose religion was not recorded. Samson was a man plagued by bad luck. He'd tried his hand at all sorts of trades—he'd sold goose feathers for beds, been hired out to a wagoner—before he threw in his lot with Hirschel. And barely had he joined them when they were all apprehended. The three Christian horse thieves got off with a thrashing, a fine, and banishment from the county. The Jews were tortured and sentenced to the gallows. Hirschel was hanged; Samson had himself baptized. It's not known whether he then got married and had children, or how he earned his living. He stayed in the town and wasn't banished. That was his reward for converting. But from then on he was one of the defectors, avoided by Jews and Christians alike, despised by both sides, especially by the Christians. In any official mention, a "baptized Jew" was especially noted. One was never allowed to forget that he was suspect. In those days there was a small number of baptized Jews in town. Other Jewish merchants had to obtain a permit and a license to be allowed to trade on market days.*

A hundred and some years later, a Jewish community was founded anew in H. The founding fathers—the first to obtain licenses to build a prayer house and later a mikvah and a kosher cookshop despite the opposition of the clergy and the leading citizens—stayed to themselves. They lived in two or three streets adjacent to the new prayer house, far removed from the first synagogue from the Middle Ages, of which they may have known nothing. Here in this neighborhood most of them also had their offices and businesses. Years later, the town sold them a few acres of land outside the city limits for a cemetery so they no longer needed to cart their dead sixty miles through snow and wind and the heat of summer to the nearest Jewish cemetery.

In the late 1880s, a Samuel Spitzer married a certain Marianne Samson from an well-established family of local Christians. The union was probably not a very welcome one. Marianne must have become a Jew and been married by the rabbi beneath the chuppah, for her children were Jews. Nothing is known about her. But her son was one of the founding members of the new synagogue. He must have been well-to-do, for he donated a splendid Torah curtain of blue velvet embroidered in gold. Others donated ten Torah scrolls with silver crowns and embroidered covers.

"Your father found the remains of the last Torah scroll in a dumpster," Max told her, "and when Marianne's grandchildren were in school, their future murderers were already sitting at the next desk, earnestly preparing for the obligations of adulthood. Her second son Menachem founded the Choral Society. He must have been musical like your cousin Ofra. You see how intertwined the paths are."

"A fascinating story," Helene said, "but what was your point in telling it to me? You think I should convert like Marianne Samson?"

"I don't know," was Max's startled reply. "No, I don't think so."

"All these categorizations depress me," said Helene. "Once a couple visited us. I don't know who they were—Americans, friends of my father. The woman waited until no one was in the room except her and me, and then told me that she couldn't understand how my father could have done such a thing as coming back and having a child with one of *them* to boot. She felt compelled to say that to *me*. Why?"

Max was silent. He laid his manuscript pages down on the table and looked out at the autumnal landscape in the summer-like afternoon heat. Elsewhere, in Brooklyn for example, everywhere in the world where Jews were celebrating the New Year, they were going down to a river before the sun set to throw the sins of the past year into the water. In his childhood they went to the East River, and seagulls in mid-flight had caught the breadcrumbs that were supposed to symbolize their sins. Back in Brooklyn, the days of Rosh Hashanah were always hot late summer days as well. A warm breeze off the ocean had carried the breadcrumbs far out over the water. There was something barbaric, frightening in the screeching of the gulls. This morning Max had resolved to go down to the river toward evening and strew breadcrumbs on the water.

Now the opportunity had passed.

"I only want you to come to understand your father better," he said wearily, "nothing more than that."

"I know it would have made him happy if I had gone to the prayer house with him sometimes," Helene admitted. "But when I was a child I didn't know what it was all about, and later I just wanted to be left alone. All those topics that raised unexpressed tension from time to time: religion, holidays, where you belonged—I just wanted to stay out of it."

"And now you're sorry?" he asked.

She nodded, "A little bit. For his sake."

Suddenly Max was tired, immensely tired. How could this young girl who listened to him with such interest ever understand how much he had to struggle against this weariness, this diffuse malaise that washed over him in waves? But he didn't want to worry her; he wanted to be alone with his body. How far removed everything else became when one's body called attention to itself.

He didn't walk her down to the door. He just told her to leave it unlocked.

Late in the afternoon on the day before Yom Kippur, Nadja came to pick him up. She was wearing a light-colored suit and looking hale and hearty. She gave him a probing look. "You've lost weight. Don't you feel well?"

"Sure," he said patiently, "I'm just getting old."

From the stairs of the community house they could already hear an unusual chatter of many voices, a babble that sounded more like a theater at intermission than the subdued, solemn stillness of Yom Kippur. Men and women filled the prayer room, laughed, greeted one another, obviously knew each other already. Malka had ascertained that they belonged to a Christian sect that had been founded in America and called itself *God's Friends*. They had shown up here several times before, but never in such large numbers. They repeated how dear to their hearts the Jews were, chatted with each other, and were quite cheerful. Diana sat among them while two of the women talked to her earnestly; she was visibly uncomfortable. She ignored the women, looked over toward Max, tried through persistent, friendly nodding to attract the attention of Frau Vaysburg and Malka. She was obviously falling between two stools once again.

The regular members of the community kept a perplexed eye out for familiar faces. The new visitors were waiting for things to get underway, full of eager anticipation, as in a theater. They put their heads together, whispered and nodded knowingly. An uneasy tension filled the room, a distractedness that even Eran's voice launching into the Kol Nidre could not recall to attention. Not a trace of abashed contrition nor fear of divine judgment, impossible even for a moment to tear one's thoughts away from the disconcerting banality of the situation: here sat members of a

Christian sect on the highest Holy Day of the year, come to a dying community to watch the Jews in prayer. Their curiosity had a certain macabre lasciviousness to it.

"Please take me home," Max said to Nadja, "I've got to get out of here."

There was a sudden cold snap in the days that followed. The wind swept up the slope across the leathery, worn-out green of the meadows. They were days on which it barely got light, so deeply did rain-heavy clouds hang over the valley. When it cleared up a week later, the sun's strength seemed broken; thin streaks of cloud blew across its pale disk like wisps of smoke.

Every morning Max began his work full of new energy. By midday, however, it was already dissipated. Feverishly he worked at his manuscript, especially now that he had an audience for his stories: Helene. Writing it was like talking to her—answering her objections, dispelling her doubts. Now that I'm old, he thought, and I could hand on a bit of knowledge, maybe even some wisdom, I lack the strength and stamina.

The ancestors of the Spitzers and the Walches, he wrote, *came from northwest Bohemia. They logged many hours with their horses and carts, traveling to weekly markets in the surrounding towns. They probably rode through the forests on smugglers' paths, for on the main roads they would have had to pay such high tolls that their trips wouldn't have been profitable. Levi Walch, a maternal ancestor, acquired a letter of passage in the year 1573 allowing him to conduct trade in the archduchy, with the proviso, however, that he must at all times wear a visible yellow spot on his clothing. Whoever sought to conceal the spot would have his wares confiscated. After two warnings, he would be banished if it happened again. His grandson Jakob Walch and other Jewish traveling tradesmen rented storehouses outside the limits of the towns. During Holy Week in 1677, the Jewish vaults in H. were plundered and destroyed by seminarians, prospective theologians, supposedly in revenge for deicide.*

Max learned from the documents in Spitzer's file that the Walches had all been traveling salesmen. *Constantly exposed to weather and the highhandedness of the authorities,* Max wrote, *dependent on the good will of customs officials and the inattention of highwaymen, praying that the narrow paths they freqented would not turn into roaring spring-time streams that would carry away their wares. Even when the town for whose weekly market they had to show a license was already in sight, this by no means meant they were no longer in danger of losing their wares and their freedom, maybe even their lives. They were held liable for each other. For the town council, one Jew was as good as another. Thus the flight of one Jew, the most trivial misdemeanor, could randomly cost any other Jew his freedom. If one was bankrupt, the wares of another were confiscated. Nor did it require a breach of the law to be tortured. At the discretion of the district court, Jews could be tortured by officials "using their best judgment," as the regulation put it. That reaped a significant income in bribes. Jews were also tortured if they had the misfortune to be discovered still in town after the weekly market was over. That didn't change much for two hundred years. However, it was in the Bohemian towns that they left behind visible traces,* he wrote.

Maybe I'll take a trip there with her next spring, Max thought enterprisingly. He didn't consider the difficulties of getting to those villages and small towns, he just imagined them driving through a gently undulating landscape, between fields of dandelion and past shallow lakes over country roads that led to towns with baroque churches and widened into market squares in the center of the villages. He'd never been to Bohemia, not even to Prague, but Mira had been born in southern Bohemia and spent her childhood there. Once, visiting relatives, she'd seen Saul for the first time. That's where they met each other, not in Vienna, but in the shade of a tree in a village later inundated by a post-war dam project. Max had always had a very clear, slightly fairy-tale image of this scene. It was as ingrained in his consciousness as if he had seen a photo of it. And his maternal relatives were buried in the cemetery of a small town in Slovakia.

He would suggest to Helene that they take a trip there in early summer, before it turned hot. For in the meantime Max had come to understand that he would have to lead her to those locations and show her how she could find a place in the part of her father's life that had been turned away from her, a place where she could feel his love.

Chapter 18

WHEN NADJA STOPPED by these days, a sense of gloom sometimes hung in the air. It was as ephemeral and impalpable as the melancholy of aging that occasionally descended on Max for no reason. They never talked about the past nor about concrete plans for the future. Sometimes he caught her in the act of contemplating him as if she wanted to find out something about him, but didn't want to ask. The only intimacy between them was that their hands often touched, apparently by accident, and Nadja would then smile at him as if to confirm the contact.

For three weeks Nadja came by often, almost every day, but every day might also be the last one. When Max asked when she had to leave, she said, "Soon. I've already stayed here too long." But she wasn't more specific than that. Ofra had left again, and Nadja wasn't close enough to the other members of the community to stay longer for their sake.

"You're postponing your departure because of me," Max said, satisfaction audible in his voice.

She was silent, looked out the window, said something inconsequential about his garden.

"Stay," he said. "For me."

She turned around abruptly, astonishment in her face, "Do you need me?"

For the length of a heartbeat he hoped she would take the few steps over and embrace him. She raised her arms slightly and her eyes lit up, but only for a fraction of a second. And when she smiled, it was as if she were dwelling on a thought or a memory. Her smile was too distant for him to dare stepping across the space that separated them. When he walked her down to her car, she stopped next to the two larches in front of the house where a spider had spun its web among the delicate yellow needles. She started to say something, but then turned to go.

Now it was up to her how much intimacy there would be between them. She would only allow chance physical contact. If he held out his hand to her she turned away. Then she sometimes looked as if she would start crying. Max was paralyzed by her reserve.

Sometimes she brought another visitor with her—Malka, who said his attacks of exhaustion were masking depression.

Thomas came, too. Max could tell that he didn't like Nadja very much because she wanted to be included in their discussions, but Thomas was not very talkative in her presence. He had founded a Society Against Racism and Xenophobia and now had to listen to Nadja's criticism. She told him she didn't feel included in the goals of such an organization. He told her irritably that if she liked, he could think up another name, but you could see from his face that he denied her any right to an opinion in the matter.

The Friday evenings around Max's table didn't become habitual, even though when his guests took their leave, they always said they should all get together again soon. He guessed that when Nadja departed, his house would become quiet again. Nadja was taking pains to bring order and variety into his life. She provided conviviality, Shabbat dinner parties with people who gathered for conversation and were fond of each other.

When Max was alone again, in the evening or late at night, he wondered whether she loved him. He was almost sure—but the next day or the next time they were together he would grow discouraged again. This brooding over the nuances of her behavior, over hidden meanings in her sentences, and the fact that he didn't dare to ask about them, was making him dependent. Did *he* love *her*, after all? Or was "love" not the right word for the melancholy friendship that bound them together? When Nadja was away, the tension he felt in her presence fell away and he could think about her more objectively, interpret her sentences and gestures more accurately. Often for no reason at all, while he was performing some banal act, she would occur to him and he would linger over her image or a conversation with her. In the act of remembering her, he felt happy and alive.

It was October and the river, the forested slope on the other bank, the town on the extreme edge of his view over the garden, seemed very far away in the pale colors of autumn. As she did almost every evening, Nadja came up from the river and across the meadows.

Max had always enjoyed the pleasure of her gradual approach, the feigned surprise and exaggerated wave with which he greeted her in a ritual they repeated almost every day. Now she was getting ready to leave. He heard her open the door from the terrace, then her steps, and he was already there in the hallway to meet her.

He had cooked dinner for her, and the table in the kitchen was already set. Potato pancakes with applesauce, her favorite, just like Mira used to make them for Chanukah. He drank tea and watched with satisfaction as she ate. Lately, he himself had little desire to eat. "I'm old," he countered when she asked him about it, "I only need one meal a day. I ate at noon."

It was quiet as only an autumn evening can be, as if there was no more to be said or done.

"I don't want this fall to end," said Nadja.

Max said nothing.

"You know the feeling that you're doing everything for the last time?" she asked.

He nodded, smiled. "You're too young to be feeling that way," he replied.

But she shook her head.

"Maybe it's the first sign of getting old," he said. "That's how it starts. Later the feeling of ending goes away again. It becomes a matter of indifference how many more times you'll do something. The end loses its novelty value."

They went up to the veranda. Through an open window the sky shone clear as glass. Before she had a chance to sit down, Max took Nadja's hand.

"I've been thinking about us," he said, "and it would be a shame if we just parted like this."

They stood facing each other, very close, and he thought he could detect consent and relief in her face.

"It won't be easy," said Nadja.

At first the joining of their hands, the rapprochement of their bodies seemed like a cautious slide back into a distant, lost intimacy. But the self-consciousness remained despite the gentleness of their caresses. He could sense his failure and didn't want to think about what was causing it. For all his disappointment he was also a bit relieved. So nothing remained untouched by time, and the body was incapable of storing memories and keeping them fresh. The woman in his bed was a forty-year-old with a lovely body still barely touched by age who was offering him an almost impersonal opportunity for pleasure.

"I'm sorry," he said.

She smiled and ran her finger along the jagged scar on his sternum. "Here's where death touched you," she said quietly.

"There are other ways I could satisfy you," he said, changing the subject.

She shook her head. "That's not the point."

"Then what is the point?" he asked wearily.

"The time that's gone by. You can't just wipe it out."

He looked at her inquiringly.

"It's too late now, Max," she said gently. "A lot has happened in the meantime."

"I know, I'm an old man," he said bitterly.

"It's not that easy. We'd always be thinking of back then, but that can't be repeated. It's over and done with."

"Maybe we're more ready to love each other now," he objected.

She was silent, and he suspected that she said nothing rather than saying something that would hurt him.

"Do you have a lover?" he asked, and felt a pang of jealousy.

She gave a laugh. "Even if I did," she said, "that would be another story."

They lay next to each other for a while, both absorbed in their own thoughts. Later, they dressed quickly, each turned slightly away from the other.

Max walked her to the front door. "Will you come again?" he asked.

"Of course," she said, "I'll phone you when I get to London."

Max was unable to fall asleep for a long time. He'd always liked the way Nadja smelled, and her scent lingered on his pillow. Some time later he went into the bathroom, stood before the mirror and studied his body: the scar—a frayed, dark red bolt struck across his breastbone; the white hair on his chest; the yellowish-white skin; the slightly rounded shoulders; the torso a slack question mark if allowed to assume its natural position; the skin folds left by a belly he had gotten rid of. He'd always had a good reliable body, broad-shouldered, athletic. Even the doctors had asked with respect what sport he played. "None," he answered, "I get enough exercise on the job."

This is just how we old guys look under our clothes, he said to his reflection. Not really so bad, considering all we've been through. He hadn't subjected his reflection to such a thorough examination in a long time and he didn't want to be reminded of the past right now.

The night air was still. The leaves that had rustled continually all summer long lay on the ground. It was as quiet as if everything beyond the house had ceased to exist. Max listened anxiously to the stillness, feeling if he made a sudden movement or a loud noise, it would collapse on him, burying everything beneath it.

After a long absence, Diana showed up again, unannounced and unexpected as usual. She explained that the garden had to be prepared for the winter, as if no more than a week had gone by since her last visit. She got right down to work pruning the roses whose blossoms she had never seen. She bustled about so much that Max wondered why she had come if she intended to avoid him.

"The sunflowers faded without your seeing them," Max called. "That's how long you've been away, since the end of July."

She couldn't come, she explained earnestly. She needed time to pull herself together.

"And now?" he asked. "Are you all there again?"

"I'm still in therapy," she said and gave him a meaningful look.

"In therapy? For what?"

"This relationship, this relationship you and I were starting to have—it triggered the whole thing."

"We had no relationship," he said in a voice that sounded unnecessarily harsh to him.

"Whatever it was," she replied quickly, "it was too much for me."

They loaded the withered leaves into the wheelbarrow. Under her instruction he layered them on the compost pile. Max was glad to be doing something with his hands while trying unsuccessfully to catch her eye and interpret her look. But she avoided looking him in the eye.

"Why did you come?" asked Max.

"Because it's important for me. That's what my therapist says." Diana gave this explanation without a trace of self-consciousness.

"Aha!" he cried, "this visit is part of your therapy."

"I have to learn to accept myself," she explained. "I have to confront my specters."

"That's not you talking." Max was annoyed. "I want to hear you, not your therapist."

She told him about phobias she used to have and said that because of him, an old conflict had broken out again.

"What old conflict?" Max wanted to know.

"A transference neurosis," she said almost proudly.

He shook his head and waved her remark aside. "I know that jargon." Max looked at her leaning her shoulder against a pillar on the terrace. The same hair curling at her rounded forehead, the amber-colored eyes, near enough to touch yet armored with alien words, a look of blank challenge, and a self-control that had her vibrating nervously like a taut string.

"Are you happy, at least?" Max asked, recalling that he had asked this question once before and since that moment they had said *du* to each other.

Uncomprehending, she looked at him and said nothing.

"My husband knows I'm here," she said instead of answering. "He saw you at that roundtable discussion."

"I remember seeing him," Max replied.

"My mother-in-law knows you, too," she continued.

"So the whole family helped get your head straight. They must love you a lot," said Max sarcastically.

She didn't react.

"I'll start visiting you regularly again," she said, "if it's okay with you."

"With pleasure. Come as often as you like," Max exclaimed.

"Just once a week," she said firmly.

And that's how they left it. From then on, she drove up to his house in her red Toyota almost every Tuesday afternoon and greeted him with a cheery *Wie geht's?* Sometimes Max suspected that she came to visit him the way one visits sick people in nursing homes to relieve their loneliness. In Diana's amiability Max clearly sensed the arrogance of young women who think their presence is a privilege they bestow on those to whom age has left only memories and helpless yearning for lost youth. He found her conventional conversation tiresome and felt patronized by her cool friendliness. She sat across from him, elegantly dressed in custom-tailored suits, sipping at her cup of tea. Nothing she did seemed natural. They had forbidden her to be the person he had known— driven, searching, and she hadn't succeeded in reinventing herself. She crossed her legs, looked at him. Her artificial behavior was irritating. Was she trying to please him or did she reject his desire as an inappropriate aberration? There was something offensive about these scenes. She wouldn't allow any serious conversation and refused intimacy, and when she left, Max felt despondent, as if he had failed.

The first snow flurries arrived unexpectedly early this year, and with the snow the last fall leaves went whirling through the sharp air. Max was unprepared for this winter. The garden chairs still stood on the terrace, snow gathering on their surfaces. Only in the hard, glassy light of clear evenings and in a few nights of frost could one have guessed that winter was on its way. The wind knifed through the cracks and seams of the old house. It had become drafty and uncomfortable on his veranda.

Sometimes Max went to the coffeehouse late in the morning, sometimes he paid Thomas a visit in the archives, but on many days he was so depressed by the knowledge that Spitzer was not in his office in the Färbergasse that he avoided going into town altogether.

One evening he was so sick that he called Malka in the morning. Malka ran ahead of him up the wooden staircase to the veranda, suggested that he hand over the front door key to her for future house calls, and announced that he had the flu. No need for concern. Max wasn't concerned, he was only exhausted, and Malka's admonition not to leave the house was superfluous. A week later she diagnosed him with pneumonia.

Thomas frequently sat by his bedside, Malka nursed him, Helene came to visit, but he longed for Nadja, wished she would be sitting by his bed when he awoke and never leave again.

When he regained his strength, Max wanted to get back to work on his chronicle. You never know how much time you have left, he told Thomas. Instead he wrote to Nadja almost every day, the way one keeps a diary—letters that he didn't mail. She called up often, but on the telephone they talked about everyday things and afterward he was dissatisfied, as if they had wasted precious time on trivialities. After he had hung up the receiver he would write her a long letter because once again he'd neglected to tell her about any of the things he was really thinking about.

Malka scolded Max for letting himself go; he needed some exercise. But he liked this weariness that sometimes allowed the days to merge into a single unending day. Doubtless one day he would reemerge from this fog, but he sensed that something in his body was changing, and he was letting it happen, full of anxious curiosity. Was this the way a final, fatal illness announced its arrival? He sat in his cane chair on the veranda in the falling twilight. Nature had retreated. The trees around the house had been reduced to their smallest volume, to naked skeletons. Was this the right place for him?

His past rose up before him and blocked his view. Everything had happened so long ago—thirty, forty, fifty years ago. Ben had been dead fourteen years, Mira for more than twenty. They were all dead: Elizabeth, Victor, Spitzer. Sometimes he felt like someone who's escaped the Angel of Death. That cheered him up and reminded him that he'd always loved life, even during bad times. There was still too much left to be done: the chronicle he still intended to supplement with the history of his own family, the trip with Helene. And Nadja was not yet a closed chapter in his life. Max yearned for Nadja. Now that he had no more power over her, he often wondered what she was doing at this very moment and whether she was thinking of him.

Malka's visits awakened longings completely new to him. She usually brought along a supper she had prepared and warmed it up for him, clattering awhile in the kitchen. She ran lightly up the stairs to the veranda, set the tray down in front of him, sat with him while he ate, and plumped his pillows. "I'm going to come visit you even when you're not sick anymore," she teased. Later she washed the dishes, called out a good-night to him. Then the front door slammed and he heard her car start. For the first time in his life he experienced being alone as being abandoned. He'd always refused to let women move in with him. Marriage struck him as restrictive, a constraint that suffocated love and joie de vivre with monotony. Yet now he longed for Nadja's presence.

For almost a month, Max hadn't left the house. He found something reassuring in his lack of movement, while the daylight and friends with their familiar noises came and went: Thomas's conscientious scraping on the doormat and cautious footfall, Malka's car jolting to a stop and her energetic stride. She banged open the front door like a policeman, as if expecting to find some gruesome surprise in the front hallway she would have to confront with courageous determination. She drove off just as abruptly after a visit and then quiet would return, as if noises were only a pretext to deepen the stillness.

The one person Max could still impress by staying bedridden for so long was Helene. Malka had long since instructed him to take walks and go window-shopping in town. Helene's blue-gray eyes looked at him with such concern that he had to comfort her: "Not to worry. I'm fine, just a little tiredness that comes in the winter. Malka even claims I'm malingering."

When Helene looked worried, she looked most like her father.

They talked about Spitzer. That made both of them happy.

"I never told him even once how much I loved him," she admitted gloomily.

"He knew you did," he comforted her.

She told him that as a child she had to recite Heine poems to which her father listened devotedly.

She wore a Star of David on a thin leather thong around her neck.

"Where'd you get the star?" Max asked.

She blushed. "I've had it for a long time. Ofra gave it to me."

"But you just started wearing it?"

She nodded, looked out the window. "It's easier now," she said, "nobody asks questions any more."

"In the spring, we're going to Bohemia together, where your ancestors came from," he promised and noticed with surprise that he suddenly didn't feel tired any more and had forgotten himself completely in his eagerness to find ways of transforming her sadness into happiness some day.

When she had gone, Max sat for a long time looking out into the blue afternoon, the slow twilight on the snow. It was as still as though the world had lost its voice or he his hearing. He opened the window. The cold air tasted bitter and metallic. Before the colors withdrew for the night, a reddish shimmer spread over the snowy meadows and the sky, a translucent veil in whose depths the evening light lay like a promise.

Yihyeh tov, Spitzer used to say: It's going to be okay. Maybe.

Chapter 19

AT THE END of April, Nadja returned for a brief visit. She was preparing for a trip to eastern Europe, to Slovakia, Poland, and the Ukraine. She was tense and preoccupied with background research. It was her first big assignment since starting to work for the photo agency in London.

She was seeing Max for the first time since his recovery from the flu, and she was alarmed by the sallow white of his cheeks and deep blue-black shadows beneath his eyes. In London she had toyed with the idea of inviting him to come along on her trip but now was relieved she had decided against it. She had changed her mind because of Bogdan. She was going to meet him in Krakow and they would travel together to eastern Poland and the Ukraine, where he had spent his childhood. It was unthinkable that Max and Bogdan should meet. Her relationship with Bogdan was the sort of thing Max had warned her about back then, many years ago—the hasty urge for instant gratification. He was wrong; brief, impetuous encounters also left their traces behind, although the wounds were more superficial, mere abrasions that didn't leave permanent scars.

When Nadja showed up, Max was dressed to go out (the suit hanging loosely on his body), and he seemed very happy to see her. He led her back into the house as if he had been expecting her.

"I'd hoped you would stay longer," he said.

"How long?" she asked, smiling.

"If you would even consider it: forever."

She looked at him in astonishment.

"I'll set up a room for you," he suggested, "so you won't have to stay in that maid's room at your father's house anymore."

"Let me think about it," she said cautiously. "Maybe we can talk about it when I return."

"Whenever you like," he said.

She'd brought two photos to show him: the one she'd taken of him without his knowledge, sitting in front of the Waldorf Astoria, and a snapshot on which one could barely see his face, only the dark blue duffel coat he used to wear, with a hood and staghorn toggles. She recalled the sunny winter day when they first went to the park with her new Leicaflex. It was so clear in her memory that she thought she could feel again the biting cold and crunch of the snow, see white clouds of condensation from their mouths, feel the warm wool of his coat against her cheek. She only had to look at the snapshot.

"When was that?" he asked.

"Sometime in the winter, in Central Park." She pretended not to remember exactly.

"And this one?" He looked at the photo in which he held his narrow spectacles in his right hand while wearily pressing the fingers of his left hand against the bridge of his nose, almost as if in pain.

"A good picture," he said approvingly. "Did I know you were taking it?"

"No," she said. "It was two years afterward."

"I'm very proud of you." He opened his arms and then let them fall again. She was standing too far away for him to hug her, and she made no move to come toward him.

"By the way, you stole a couple of photos from me," Max said mischievously. "Don't think I didn't notice."

"The woman with the four faces?" Nadja asked.

He laughed. "Is that what you call her?"

Her expression became withdrawn and she dropped her eyes so as not to betray the glitter of the tears she held back.

He put his arm around her shoulders. "Please forget about her. It's been years since I've even heard from her."

She knew if she asked him now whether he loved her, he would say yes. But she didn't ask.

On the last afternoon before her departure, just for the pleasure of approaching the house from below, Nadja came the way she had in the fall, up from the river and across the meadows in wet shoes. They sat on the terrace for a long time. Max told her about Spitzer's file and the names of the towns where his ancestors had lived and might be buried.

"Bring back some pictures if you get to these places," he urged her. "Maybe you'll find traces of my family, too. Are you going to Przemyśl?"

She was counting on it, Nadja said. There was someone there she hoped to visit.

"Go to the cemetery, look for the Berman graves. It must have been a big family, Berman and Schammestik were their names."

Max recounted that his great-grandfather had been a foundling. His parents were supposedly Sephardim who had been murdered aboard a train on the frontier between Turkey and Russia. Max's paternal grandmother was from Przemyśl where his grandfather, who had grown up in Lemberg, had settled. It was a love match, something unheard-of in those days of arranged marriages. Max had never known these grandparents nor the siblings his father had left behind in Poland. He'd never even seen any pictures of them. His father's oldest sister had emigrated to America as an adolescent and a second sister had followed her there. Both settled in Chicago. There'd been occasional contact with them when he was a child, but that had broken off after his parents' divorce. "The rest who stayed," said Max, "must have been murdered. After 1941, no more letters came. Please take pictures of the graves," he impressed upon her.

Then both of them became absorbed in their own thoughts. It was not a tense silence, but instead like a pendulum swing from talk to stillness.

Nadja contemplated his face as if memorizing it for later. His narrow, haggard features gave Max a look of ascetic abstraction that didn't suit him. He sat like that for a long time, his eyes closed, turned toward the sun. She couldn't tell if he'd fallen asleep, but she almost wanted to touch him to make sure he was warm and alive. She thought that perhaps this was the way death announced its approach, by settling tentatively on a sleeping face and transforming it.

When he opened his eyes he saw her look of concern and laughed. "I'm still alive."

But she sensed that he knew what she had seen and needed to fend it off, because solicitude had always made him uncomfortable. At the same time, she also sensed that her mute concern made him happy.

Later, when it turned cooler, they sat for a while in the wicker chairs beneath the ceiling of glass bricks. The clouds almost directly overhead reminded them of sand dunes, so soft and fluid. It seemed to her as if she were lying exposed beneath the vast sky, washed up by time, and she felt an overwhelming urge to be carried out again into a timeless eternity. They were as close as they could come to each other, but the longing within her was still not assuaged. It was no longer love she wanted from him. He was prepared to give her that. It was something that had to do with earlier, but it wouldn't have been enough for him to ask for her forgiveness. The love he was now offering her came nineteen years too late, and his earlier refusal still weighed more heavily than his dependence on her in old age, which aroused her pity. If he had asked her what she wanted from him, she would have had to say, "That you turn back time to that April afternoon after the snowstorm, and that from then on everything turns out the way we wish it had."

At the front door in the hallway, they kissed, and, without warning, for a moment, the past was present with all the nuances of sensuous perception his kisses had once elicited.

"Won't you stay after all, even just for one night?" he asked.

"No," Nadja shook her head, "I have to get up really early tomorrow."

By the next morning Nadja was already driving through the villages Max had mentioned to her, through small market towns with crumbling middle-class houses whose baroque facades suggested an earlier prosperity.

She photographed a frieze over the entrance to the Discotheque Calypso: between two lions in bas-relief rearing up on their hind legs you could read the inscription in Hebrew letters *Beit tefila la-y'hudim*, Prayerhouse of the Jews. Later, when she developed the film, she would match the photos to the towns; for now she wrote them down in her notebook.

The towns often lay at the end of allées of huge old trees, but seldom fulfilled the expectations aroused by such grandeur. Sometimes the road was little more than a track between boggy embankments. Willow stumps leaned over it and distant villages were swallowed up by fields.

Near a village in Slovakia she found the cemetery where Max's maternal ancestors were buried. It lay in the middle of a sparse grove of deciduous trees. An old man emerged from his dwelling as from a crypt. Without a word he removed the padlock from the rusting cast-iron gates and shuffled back into his cottage. Woodruff and luxuriant bunches of young ferns grew along the paths. Gray lichen and moss had eaten into the inscriptions on the gravestones, making them undecipherable. No one had been buried here for many years. Young beech volunteers impeded the way to the more distant graves. The forest was on the verge of reclaiming the cemetery, lifting and toppling gravestones from their foundations. It was a cemetery forgotten by the living.

On a forested slope with hairpin turns she came upon a truck with its cab rammed deep into a splintered tree trunk. A fractured branch was sticking out of one of the cab windows. A police cruiser stood guard at the scene. Two or three kilometers farther on, a village lay in the sun. Men in work clothes walked across the village square, unshaven and emaciated. They looked weary and disheveled. The accident in the forest was as far removed as if it hadn't happened, and if they knew about it, what could they have done except to go about their business in the village?

Beyond the Polish border the landscape flattened out. Between the fields lay pine woods with tall yellow grass under the trees. Between brush-covered banks, rivers cut deeply into the land.

Bogdan was waiting for her along the highway leading east out of Kraków. When she saw him standing at the turnoff to Nowa Huta in his tight jeans and cowboy boots, attractive in his way, she almost felt like driving on past him. He put his forearm on the car and leaned in through the window on the driver's side. His laugh had always felt to her like a challenge. The mop of dark hair falling over his forehead, his strong white teeth and nonchalance— or was it indifference?—seemed to invite her on an adventure with no predictable outcome. He thought talking was a waste of time. She had disavowed their relationship to her friends, fearing it would be too obvious that their only bond was a strong physical attraction. So now, for no particular reason, she reacted coolly, almost gruffly, when Bogdan told her to slide over to the passenger side, she must be tired and he wanted to drive.

"I'm driving," she decided, rolling up the window.

He shrugged, tossed his duffel bag into the back seat, sat down next to Nadja, and lit a cigarette.

"We'll drive to Lwiw today," he declared. Even after ten years in London, his English still retained a strong Russian accent.

"No," said Nadja calmly, "we're driving to Przemyśl."

Then they were silent for a long time, a tense, peevish silence.

"I'm not about to spend the night in Poland," he resumed after awhile, but Nadja didn't answer.

Silently, he smoked his unfiltered cigarettes. Once when she was unable to get past a tractor he said, "So would you just let me drive now?" There was suppressed rage in his voice.

They drove straight east past Tarnów, a belt of bright apartment blocks on the hills. It felt like they were going to run off the edge of the world, where the broad fields of the plain met the drab sky. Lilacs were blooming in the villages, giving the tottering, wind-blown cottages a romantic touch. Orchards surrounded the villages, as if to protect human habitations from the immensity of the steppe.

The wooden houses turned their longest sides to the road and reminded her of old photographs of Jewish houses before the war. When they drove through the small towns, middle-class houses with cast-iron balconies and front doors level with the ground also awakened vague recollections of something she had seen pictures of somewhere, or heard of, or maybe only read about. The names on the road signs—Jarosław, Lublin, Bełzyce—were designations of extermination.

From time to time Nadja stopped, shot pictures: fountains on town squares, the broad crowns of chestnut trees in bloom, balconies, hand-carved window frames, recessed doorframes of dark wood. Later, when she developed and enlarged them, she would look for the faint traces of mezuzot on them. She photographed the melancholy of these lonely streets in the late afternoon and hoped it would be visible in her pictures.

"I can't imagine what there is to take photos of here," Bogdan complained and stayed in the car, smoking. "We'll never get to Lwiw today at this rate."

She was silent and ignored him.

More clearly than the cheap apartment blocks in the postwar suburbs, more visibly than the isolated cows and horses in the lush pastures, the German tanks appeared to her mind's eye and the columns of people torn from their daily lives and marched to their death.

Toward evening a storm blew up, hiding the sun that shone its final lurid light onto the sides of the houses, bathing the pastures in an unnatural, poisonous green. Then it was swallowed by the blackness and they sat in the clatter and roar as a cloudburst came down upon them.

"Drive faster," Bogdan demanded roughly.

She was familiar with this ruthless side of him as she was with his capacity for great tenderness, and she knew that everything he did had a purpose, even if it sometimes looked merely whimsical.

Signs for Przemyśl appeared.

Bogdan lay tilted far back in his seat. "It's only an hour and a half more to Lwiw," he said.

Nadja said nothing and turned off toward the center of town.

"You're going to regret this," he threatened.

She stopped the car to show passersby the address of the woman she wanted to look up. From their complicated answers she understood only *proste*, straight ahead. She took a wrong turn, in confusion tried to follow people's waving hands that seemed to point in all directions at once. Bogdan spoke Polish; that had been one reason why she'd brought him along. But he wouldn't help her. He sat next to her in silence.

It was dark by the time Nadja finally found the right house in an unlighted dead-end street. She gave Bogdan some money to find himself a place to stay and told him what time to meet her at the car next morning. Without a word, without looking at her, he walked off.

Irina was a relative of one of Nadja's oldest friends. She knew Nadja was coming and said she'd been expecting her for hours. She was a stocky woman with a full head of dark, unruly hair. But what struck one about her first of all was the prominent facial hair she seemed painfully self-conscious about.

"Where's your friend?" she asked Nadja.

"I sent him away. He hates me."

Irina cooked pirogi and they sat up late into the night looking at family photos: women in black shawls with long fringes, women in fur jackets standing in front of their houses, proud-looking women in wedding pictures with straight backs and narrow waists, women in wide skirts with children decked out in ruffles sitting in their laps. Only an occasional man, standing a little apart from his wife and children, gazing into the distance. Wedding parties. A round-shouldered, gangly groom with a mustache, standing next to his bride, a bundle of white material from which a small, frightened face peered out.

"My friend told me that some of your family were Jews," Nadja said.

"My great-grandmother was Jewish," Irina corrected her, "the mother of my maternal grandmother."

"Then you're Jewish, too," Nadja declared.

Irina gave a laugh. "I'm Polish. I don't know anything about Jews. Even my grandmother was brought up Catholic."

"Are there still Jews in Przemyśl?" Nadja asked.

Irina shook her head. "I'd know if there were. There are some people who had Jewish ancestors, but you don't talk about it. Other people know about it if they know who your parents were, your grandparents, but the descendants themselves don't make a fuss about it. It's just not something you talk about. Nobody knows about my great-grandmother, for instance. I'm amazed that my cousin mentioned it."

"What happened to your Jewish relatives during the war?" Nadja asked.

Irina said she didn't know. She was born after the war. "I'm Polish," she repeated. She'd attended the University of Lublin, then returned to Przemyśl to teach in the high school.

"The father of a friend of mine was born here," Nadja told her. "Berman, Schammestik—have you ever heard those names?"

Irina shook her head. "Maybe we can find them in the Jewish cemetery. We can go there tomorrow before you leave."

When they left the house the next morning, Bogdan was already waiting by the car. He was sullen and didn't return the two women's greeting. He crawled unwillingly into the back seat. Irina's house was in an old, rundown part of town with narrow streets and tall dark buildings with laundry drying on the balconies.

It was a small cemetery, surrounded by a crumbling stone wall. Amid a sea of high grass and wild bushes were the half-sunken stones, humps of rough concrete like the backs of flayed animals.

There was no writing on them; their naked pediments lacked any inscription. A few gravestones were made of black marble and, without exception, bore as the year of death 1942.

Nadja walked through the high grass, still wet with dew, taking pictures. Then she took the film out of her camera, got out the other exposed rolls in her camera bag, and gave them to Irina. "They'll be safe with you," she said. "I'll pick them up on my way back."

They wished each other good luck, and Irina wished Nadja a pleasant journey. Nadja glanced back toward the car in which Bogdan sat smoking. "I wish I could ditch him," she said. "He's a real millstone around my neck."

"Hang onto him," Irina advised her. "It's dangerous on the other side of the border. You always read about people getting waylaid by bandits." Irina turned down the offer of a lift home and had them drop her off at the edge of town. She kept waving to Nadja until the car disappeared at the end of the poplar-lined road.

———

Irina was the last person to see Nadja before she disappeared. The customs officers at the border recalled the car and the papers but not the woman's face or what she wore. They couldn't remember whether she'd said anything or asked a question.

On both sides of the border stretched the plain, the fallow land abloom with yellow flowers, the plowed fields brown, the rows of poplars moving past like caravans on the horizon.

Chapter 20

ONE HUMID NIGHT a week after Nadja's departure, Max had a nightmare. He saw her lying face up in a pool, clear water rippling over her wide open eyes. Her hair lay fanned out on the bottom as on a pillow. As he started awake from the dream, he knew for one unconscious moment that she was dead, but as he slowly returned to wakefulness that knowledge was extinguished and only the image remained.

Nevertheless, he lived through the next few days in a restless tension he couldn't explain to himself. Only when Nadja's father called up to tell him she was dead did Max know that he had been subconsciously awaiting this phone call, and while he still held the receiver numbly in his hand, the dream image rose up again.

Nadja had had an accident in the Ukraine, "A car accident, they say." He thought he detected skepticism in her father's voice.

Max went to visit him in the house he had first seen from the outside twenty years ago. He entered the living room where the presence of Nadja's stepmother, dead now for many years, was still palpable. The low-ceilinged room was overflowing with cheap knickknacks, all surfaces covered with fruit bowls, stuffed animals, and crocheted antimacassars, and amid all this kitsch sat a bald little old man whose almost aristocratic lack of pretension didn't comport at all with this environment in which he seemed to feel at home. He offered Max coffee and cookies as if he had slid easily into the role of a housewife.

"You were a friend of my daughter's?" he asked, gazing at him with an expression that didn't reveal how much he knew.

Max nodded.

To Max, there was something unreal about the way her father said *my daughter* and *were*. It was as if Max had never really been fully conscious that she was somebody's daughter, too, loved even if she didn't want to admit it. And that she *had been* but was now irretrievably gone. In this *were* the finality of Nadja's death leapt out at Max for the first time, a finality that would torture him for weeks until he thought he could no longer bear it.

"We'd known each other since 1974," Max said, and was himself astonished at how much time had passed, Nadja's entire adult life.

"Forgive me," her father began cautiously, "I don't mean to be indiscreet . . . Were you close to each other, I mean . . . ?" He was looking for the right words but couldn't find them, and fell silent.

Did I love her; did she love me? Max completed in thought the questions of the man sitting across from him. Now it didn't matter anymore, and for precisely that reason he could suddenly grasp with utter clarity that she had never stopped loving him and that she had shaped her entire life according to his expectations: her profession, her search for lasting fulfillment. He was left behind with an overwhelming feeling of failure, and his failure was irrevocable.

"You could call it a kind of love," said Max, "although we lost track of each other for a long time."

Gratitude shone in the old man's brown eyes and a warmth that Max hadn't expected. Then Nadja's father started fiddling with the crocheted ruffle of the tea cozy while surreptitiously wiping away tears.

Later he told Max that he didn't believe for a minute that his daughter had had a car accident. He'd repeated again and again, "No, that would never happen to my daughter." She was always on the go and never had anything happen to her. They found her by the side of the road in a cornfield. She must have been lying there for several days and they were only able to identify her from the address book they found in her pants pocket. Her cameras, passport, money, all that was gone. "That can't have been an accident," her father said.

"What did they find on her?" asked Max.

Her father got out the jeans they had given him, stained and crusted with blood. Max recognized the torn blouse and the worn-down shoes. She'd walked across the wet meadows in those shoes on the last day and put them in the sun to dry while she went barefoot in the house.

"What are you going to do?" he asked.

Nadja's father gave him an inquiring look.

"We should get to the bottom of this and find out the real cause of death, don't you think?"

"The autopsy says head trauma," said her father, lost in thought. "The Ukrainian police assume it was a traffic accident."

"Without witnesses, without a car, just a dead woman by the side of the road?" Max asked, shaking his head.

"What difference does it make now?" asked the old man simply. "Even if we could prove it was murder, it wouldn't change the fact that she's dead."

When they said good-bye, he took Max's hand in both of his. "You know," he said quietly, "we weren't very close. She never forgave me for my second marriage."

That same evening he called up again to ask if Max knew how Nadja wanted to be buried.

"A Jewish burial, of course," said Max.

But there were no documents and there wasn't enough time left to get someone in London to search her apartment for proof that she really had become a Jew. She had never mentioned which congregation she belonged to, and no one knew which rabbi could attest to her conversion.

And so Nadja was buried in the Catholic cemetery, without a priest, at Max's insistence. The members of the Jewish community came, Eran read the prayers for the dead, and Max said kaddish in the midst of crosses and graves that each looked like a tiny flower garden. And without a minyan.

They drove to Max's house, washed their hands, and ate what Malka had brought along. Many of them treated Max as though he were the widower. The oldest community members talked about Nadja, recalled the first time the thirteen-year-old had shown up at the prayer house, how singlemindedly she had continued to attend. They praised her loyalty during all the long years she'd been away, for almost every year she'd spent the High Holy Days with them. They regretted that Nadja hadn't found happiness.

Later, after they left, Max walked down the meadow behind his house to the river. A pale, fragile moon swam among white clouds in the long early-summer twilight. The meadow was wet with dew that moistened his ankles like cool water. He bent over and buried his hands in the grass. The cool breeze made him shiver. At the riverbank he turned and looked back up the hill toward his house, standing remote and foreign on its rise as if it had nothing to do with him. Suddenly his whole life seemed as impersonal and far away as this house. Nadja and Spitzer were dead. What was he still doing here?

The return climb, steeper than he expected, was taxing. Every time Max stopped to rest and catch his breath, the broad glass wall of the veranda mirrored the wide sky and the light remaining from the sunset. Anyone standing at the windows and waving in excitement would have remained invisible. But Nadja had always laughed and waved back, hadn't she? Had she really seen him or did she just want to make him happy and so waved on the off chance that he might be there?

Nadja's father sent him Irina's letter and the rolls of film Nadja had left with her. The letter reported Nadja's last evening and told about Bogdan, whom Irina described as a *slippery character*, and said that Nadja had had a premonition. She'd mentioned that she would rather have continued the trip without her passenger. Irina didn't think it had been an accident, either, but she seemed to share the fatalism of Nadja's father. She wrote that it was probably too late for an investigation now, anyway.

The photos showed squares with baroque town houses, their worn walls radiating a beautiful, faded charm. The verdigris on onion domes shimmered behind broad plane trees. It was a dream world that opened before him. There was something trancelike about it. Max thought he could sense Nadja's mood, her yearning, as he looked at the pictures—these lonely, straight country roads, lined with poplars and heading unerringly toward a point just below the horizon, and this melancholy green plain, without the slightest diversion for the eye, expressing nothing but emptiness: the emptiness of the sky pressing down upon it, the absence of human beings, yawning emptiness that evoked anxiety. These were pictures of unendurable loneliness. She must have taken the last photos at the cemetery in Przemyśl—these must be the graves of his relatives, these coarse, mutilated remains of the old cemetery. Only now did he remember reading somewhere that the gravestones from Jewish cemeteries in eastern Poland were used in the construction of supply roads for the Wehrmacht.

It was on this afternoon that Max decided to return to New York while he still had the strength to resist the paralysis and pain of his losses. The emptiness left behind by the deaths of Spitzer and Nadja would never be filled, not if he stayed here, at any rate. He had to escape this town and this house if he was to survive.

Once he had booked a flight, he was relieved. Now he could think about the chronicle again, too, which had been lying untouched on his desk for weeks. He'd continue to work on it in New York.

In these last weeks the scaffolding disappeared from the old synagogue. Its stucco was so fresh it still looked moist. It was a beautiful, classicist temple with long, narrow Romanesque windows and a broad cement forecourt bordered on one side by the decrepit community building.

At the opening ceremonies Max, as a guest of honor, sat in the first row between Frau Vaysburg and Malka's Daniel. It was a bright, austere room, its gallery supported by slender columns branching into graceful arches. The empty Torah ark was covered by an embroidered blue curtain, before which stood the speaker's lectern on a wide stage.

Thomas saw to it that Max was introduced to all the town dignitaries. There was standing room only in the temple and the entrance at the back was crowded with curiosity seekers, but the members of the community were all seated in the front row. Behind them guests were still coming in and there was the same muted hum as before a concert. Those present knew each other. They shook hands, waved to friends, took their seats.

A chamber orchestra played Mendelssohn and then everyone in town who had something to say stepped up to the lectern in order of importance. They quoted the words of famous dead Jews and called for dialogue and more tolerance toward everything foreign. A Catholic dignitary exclaimed emotionally that it was time to clear the way for a mighty expression of determination "in spite of what happened in the past." Then a school chorus sang *Shalom Aleichem*.

In this room, thought Max, his parents had stood beneath the marriage canopy and Spitzer had been called on to read the Torah for the first time, half a year before he fled the country. There would be concerts here, cultural events. Guided tours of the city would pause here, talk tactfully about its history, and discuss the peculiarities of Jewish religious architecture. And, as usual, the community would probably assemble on Friday evenings in the prayer room. It was more practical.

No one found it surprising that Max was leaving for an extended period of time, as if they had all been expecting this from the very first.

"Will you come back to see us on the High Holy Days?" asked Frau Vaysburg.

Max shook his head. "That's too soon. Maybe at Pesach."

"Okay then, see you at Pesach!" they called after him.

"The mayor's throwing a celebratory dinner," said Thomas. "We're invited."

"No," Max said, "I'd like to go home."

Thomas drove him to his house, and Max invited him in for a little while. Even in the heat of midday, a cool, almost imperceptible breeze blew up from the river and lazily stirred the leaves. The symmetrical bright green leaves of the wisteria were climbing the wooden trellis between the white pillars. It hadn't bloomed yet; that would take a couple of years. Gnats danced in the trembling light among the leaves.

"You're going to leave all this now, in the summertime?" Thomas asked. "Just when it's most beautiful?"

"I'll be back," said Max.

"And why are you taking off so suddenly?" Thomas wanted to know.

"Since Nadja's death I'm not quite sure what I'm actually doing here," Max said, more to himself.

"We always look for what we've lost in the wrong place," Thomas said at last.

Later, after he'd gone, Helene came by and told him excitedly about her plans. She was going to visit her cousin in Tel Aviv. She'd already booked the flight.

"Maybe you'll meet a young man in Tel Aviv and never come back," Max teased her.

She turned red. "I'll tell you all about it," she said, "when I get back."

"I'll be in New York by then, but you're welcome to visit me there anytime."

Helene promised she would do that for sure. She was in a fever of expectation and full of the hectic thirst for action young people feel when they've suffered the loss of a loved one, Max thought.

"I'll send you the chronicle as soon as it's finished," he told her as they parted.

"You've got to write everything down that you didn't tell me."

Facing her in the hall, he couldn't help searching her face for the elusive traces of Spitzer's features.

"I'll miss you the most," said Max.

Helene gave him a quick hug. He was astonished to feel how slender and firm her body was.

Without regret Max watched the town and its surrounding hills growing smaller beneath him, until the plane broke through the cloud cover. He had paid a long visit to the region and the town to which he was bound by early memories, and as he had intended, he'd at least experienced each season of the year in that place.

Now he was flying back to New York, where nothing unknown awaited him. His old friend Eva would pick him up. She would throw herself into his arms and exclaim, *Welcome home!* She'd never understood his love for Europe.

He would see the ocean again. He'd often yearned for its soothing vistas and the rhythmic sound of the surf. From Coney Island Beach he would search the horizon across the water as he had in childhood and know without longing: over there was his house, waiting for him. By tomorrow he would resume his walks through Central Park, in the evening, after it had cooled off.

He'd need to call up his business partner Mel first thing after his arrival and then a whole list of friends and acquaintances, until he got tired of talking. The proprietor of the delicatessen on the corner of Broadway would be certain to welcome him back effusively and ask where he'd been for so long, and the monosyllabic old Greek who looked after Max's building and did repairs would also show he was pleased in his own quiet way.

At Paola's, where he was a regular, he'd have no trouble getting a table, even if they were all booked up. He told himself he'd go somewhere new every day—to the theater, to Lincoln Center, to the Village—until there was nothing left for him to see anywhere in Manhattan. There, in New York, he was Max—just Max, not Herr Berman. He felt a wave of warmth rising within him and getting stronger the closer he got to New York.

Glossary

ALIYAH. Literally "ascension," emigration to Israel.

ALTE KÄMPFER. "Old fighters," the term for early members of the Nazi Party.

BESSAMIM. Spices, such as cinnamon and cloves, kept in a small casket and used in the ceremony ending Shabbat.

BIMAH. The lectern on which the Torah scrolls are placed to be read during the service.

CHAROSET. A mixture of fruit, wine, and nuts eaten at the Passover seder to symbolize mortar used by the Jewish slaves in Egypt.

DEUTSCHNATIONAL. "German nationalist," designation of an Austrian political movement founded in 1867 and advocating the unification of the German-speaking areas of the Habsburg Empire with Germany.

DOLLFUSS. Engelbert Dollfuss (1892–1934), Chancellor of Austria 1932–1934, dissolved parliament and established an authoritarian fascist regime.

GAU. See *Reichsgau* below.

GYMNASIUM. Secondary school leading to university study.

HEINE. Heinrich Heine (1797–1856), German Jew and one of the greatest German poets of the 19th century.

KIPFERL. Austrian croissant.

KOL NIDRE. Prayer that begins the evening service of Yom Kippur.

MATURA. Diploma earned by passing a set of examinations in the last year of the Austrian *Gymnasium*, admitting the student to university study.

MEZUZOT. Small parchment scrolls inscribed with Deuteronomy 6:4–9 and 11:13–21 and placed in a case affixed to the doorpost of Jewish houses.

MISCHLING. "Half-breed," the Nazi classification for people with some Jewish blood.

NSDAP. *Nationalsozialistische Deutsche Arbeiter Partei* (National Socialist German Workers' Party), the official name of the Nazi Party.

OBERGRUPPENFÜHRER. "Head Group Leader" in the SA.

REICHSFLUCHTSTEUER. Penalty fee charged to Jews for *Reichsflucht*— "fleeing" or leaving the Reich.

REICHSGAU. "Imperial province," an administrative unit of the National Socialist state that replaced the federated *Länder* of the Austrian Republic.

SA (STURMABTEILUNG). "Storm battalion" founded by Hitler in 1921 as an armed party militia, reduced in importance after the Nazis took power in 1933.

SIDDUR. Literally "order," prayer book.

STAFFELFÜHRER. Squadron leader.

STURMBANNFÜHRER. Stormtrooper captain in the SA.

THIRTY-SIX RIGHTEOUS. In rabbinic literature, the thirty-six righteous souls required to sustain the world.

VÖLKISCHER BEOBACHTER. *The Folkish Observer,* Nazi Party organ published in Munich.

WEINHEBER. Josef Weinheber (1892–1945), Austrian poet close to the Nazi movement.